BITTER PILL

BITTER PILL

FERN MICHAELS

WHEELER PUBLISHING
A part of Gale, a Cengage Company

**LIBRARY OF CONGRESS CIP DATA ON FILE.
CATALOGUING IN PUBLICATION FOR THIS BOOK
IS AVAILABLE FROM THE LIBRARY OF CONGRESS.**

ISBN-13: 978-1-4328-8522-9 (hardcover alk. paper)

Published in 2021 by arrangement with Zebra Books, an imprint of Kensington Publishing Corp.

Printed in Mexico
Print Number: 01   Print Year: 2021

BITTER PILL

PROLOGUE

London, present day

Charlotte Hansen peered closely into the magnifying mirror on her vanity. "Why do I keep having these fog-like moments?" she whispered to her reflection.

Looking down at the array of prescription bottles, she could not remember which pills she was supposed to take next. *These are supposed to help me, but I feel like I'm getting worse.* She had numbered the white caps of the green bottles to make it easier but had forgotten to replace the caps when she took the first three pills. She wrung her hands in dismay. *I simply cannot tell Maryann that I've messed up my routine again. For sure, she'll have me put under observation. And what would they observe? A sixtysomething woman losing her memory? Nothing too odd about that.* She heaved a big sigh and decided to skip the rest of her morning routine of taking twelve different pills. *What difference will one dose make?*

Unless her daughter, Maryann, was counting the pills. With that thought, Charlotte flushed what was left of her morning dose down the toilet. She splashed water on her face, took another deep look in the mirror, and decided she could fake it for the day if necessary.

Charlotte had thought a visit to London to see Maryann and her grandson Liam would raise her spirits, but instead, she seemed to be in a downward spiral. She would discuss the matter with Dr. Marcus at her next appointment. Checking her desk diary, she noted she was due to see him the next day. Charlotte didn't care for him very much, even though he was effusive and turned on the charm. But he had been recommended by her new personal physician in Aspen — who had insisted she have a doctor on hand, particularly in a foreign country. Apparently, Dr. Marcus and her new doctor, Dr. Harold Steinwood, who had taken over the practice of her longtime physician, Dr. Robert Leeland, had studied together in Switzerland; and when Charlotte had told Dr. Steinwood that she would be traveling to London, he had insisted that she get in touch with his classmate, Dr. Marcus. In time, she would reevaluate this "miracle doctor" and his "cure" for mental acuity and longevity, but for now she was content to get dressed and prepare for the rest of her day.

Sag Harbor

Dr. Raymond Corbett strolled around his two-hundred-square-foot walk-in closet, deciding which cashmere blazer he would wear to the party. It was finally going to be his big night in the Hamptons. After years of being overlooked by almost every yacht club and country club on the South Fork of Long Island, he had persuaded the Longboat Yacht Club to allow him to become a member. The membership came with a very high price tag. Apparently, one could buy one's way into the stodgy organization, which catered to old money and the nouveaux riches. One either had to own a yacht over eighty-three feet, be a power broker, or be some sort of celebrity. He was none of those. He was merely a physician who specialized in longevity wellness. Yes, he had been treating patients for almost a decade now, prescribing placebos and mind-altering drugs to women of a certain age — mostly rich widows, to be precise.

He took one of his Tom Ford designer blazers from the rack and frowned at the brass buttons. They needed to be polished. Now. He pressed his finger down on the house intercom. "Henry!" he bellowed. "Meet me in my dressing room. Now!"

A soft voice replied, "I will be there right away, sir."

Corbett tossed the Tom Ford blazer on the bed and then chose an Armani blazer to wear. He thumbed through his new collection of striped button-down shirts and picked a shirt from one of his favorite designers, Brioni. Recalling the $820 price tag, he snickered. Yes, he would almost look like a million bucks. Almost. The jacket, shirt, Gucci shoes, and Audemars Piguet Royal Oak Concept 44MM titanium watch totaled almost $160,000. He'd leave the pinkie ring home. No sense being ostentatious. He snickered to himself again. Tonight was the night he would reveal to the members of the yacht club that he would be displaying a painting at a private exhibit: one by Marc Chagall that was once thought to have been stolen and burned by the Nazis. He had made arrangements to acquire it at a private sale brokered by Christie's. Tonight he was having a party, basically in honor of himself, at the yacht club. Once he had possession of the Chagall, he would hire a private security company, which would cost a small fortune, to deliver the artwork and keep guard over it during the gala he would hold at the club, then take it to a special locker at the Museum of Modern Art. He had made arrangements for the museum to borrow the painting in the fall. He wanted to spend his summer being known in the Hamptons as a great art connoisseur.

Yes, his group of "longevity" doctors — and their new protocol to moderate the progress of aging — had brought him and his two partners the wealth to live an extravagant lifestyle, something he was enjoying immensely. He had a co-op in Manhattan and now this modest home in Sag Harbor.

Corbett knew that he and his partners would have to retire soon — before the world learned the truth. There were two old biddies who could ruin it all. Lorraine Thompson had died of an accidental overdose, and Marjorie Brewster had had an incident that sent her into convulsions, the treatment for which put her in a semi-conscious state. Even with the waivers and nondisclosure agreements their patients had agreed to, those incidents would eventually pop up on someone's radar. They had been lucky enough to fly under the radar for a good long while. These were simply a couple of mishaps. He, Marcus, and Steinwood had made a killing. He smirked. *No pun intended.*

But enough of that. He picked a silk ascot, which added an additional three hundred dollars to his already ridiculously expensive ensemble, and left for the party.

CHAPTER 1

Pinewood

Myra Rutledge repositioned herself on the antique settee on the terrace of her farmhouse. The letter she was holding in her lap was disturbing. Looking around at the luscious flowers overflowing their Italian terracotta pots, she inwardly smiled at their beauty, but that did not change the gloom that had descended on her.

"Good morning, love," Charles, her husband and partner, said, giving her a peck on the cheek. "Why so glum? It's a spectacular day!"

Myra picked up the letter and handed it to Charles. "It's from Charlotte."

"What seems to be the problem?"

"This letter. She sounds very depressed and a little disoriented," Myra answered.

Charles began to read. "My dear Myra, I am visiting Maryann in London. I thought it would be a good change of scenery for

13

me, but I'm feeling rather low. I've been somewhat forgetful lately and get a little 'foggy' at times. I am seeing a doctor here, Dr. Julian Marcus, who has me on a boatload of medications. He was recommended by my doctor in Aspen, Dr. Harold Steinwood, who took over Dr. Leeland's practice. I was wondering if I could come by for a visit on my way back to Aspen. You always cheered me on . . . even when my first book submission was turned down! Don't want to intrude, but I could really use a friend right now."

Charles stopped reading. "Well, old girl, there doesn't seem to be anything else to do except get her here as soon as possible."

"Oh, Charles, you are such a dear. I know all the people coming in and out can be disruptive at times, but things have been very quiet for a while, and there doesn't seem to be anything on the horizon to change that. I know you were relishing our having time alone, but I have a bad feeling about this thing with Charlotte. Back in the day, she was always the Pollyanna." Myra took his hand and brushed her lips along his fingertips.

"Keep that up, and we'll have to lock the doors!" Charles chortled. Then Myra playfully slapped his hand away.

"Please make the travel arrangements for her. I'll send her an e-mail telling her to expect a full itinerary by the end of the day." Myra was feeling more like herself — giving Charles orders, which he gladly acted upon.

"Will do, love. But do you suppose we should check on her availability first?"

"My instincts are telling me we need to do this pronto!" She gave him a pat on the bum. "Now go!"

Charles took a small bow. "At your service, my lady."

Charlotte's father had been the groundskeeper for Myra's family's farm when she and Charlotte were teenagers. She and her father had lived in one of the small cottages on the property, and Charlotte, Myra, and Annie would explore the vast farm and make up stories together. Charlotte had gone on to become an author of children's books. She had made a tidy sum of money, though it was nowhere near the size of Myra's fortune. Not to mention Annie's. The Countess Anna Ryland de Silva was thought by many to be the richest woman in the world.

Charlotte had had a few best sellers early in her career, and toy manufacturers had licensed some of the characters. She'd been able to put her daughter through a pricey prep school and an equally expensive college. She had also established a trust for her grandson's education, but this still left more than enough money for her to lead a very comfortable life. Her lifestyle was not really extravagant, but she could travel when and where she wanted and could play a round of golf whenever she felt like it in Aspen during the summer. She usually spent the winter months visiting friends in Florida, Arizona, Saint Thomas, and Barbados, and she made regular trips to the UK, where her daughter, Maryann, lived with her husband and Charlotte's grandson.

Several days after she had sent the letter, she received an e-mail from Charles, husband and confidant to her friend Myra.

Greetings from across the pond. Myra and I have arranged for you to join us at Pinewood. Please review the attached itinerary and let me know if it meets with your satisfaction.

Charlotte could almost hear the British accent in Charles's e-mail. And she wrote back:

Sounds divine! Hope I am not putting

anyone out?

Absolutely not! We are very excited to have you as our guest. Please let us know if there is anything else you need before you embark. Happy landings. See you in two days.

Charlotte reviewed the itinerary:

9:00 A.M. Private car pickup at 1223 Mulgrave Rd., Croydon 12:00 P.M. United Flight 919, first-class ticket from Heathrow to Dulles. Open return. Private car service to greet at airport and take to residence. Driver's name Edward. Cell: 703-555-1987

Charlotte smiled as she read the e-mail. "Leave it to Myra and Charles to take care of everything." She immediately felt a weight lift from her shoulders. . . . Or was it from her mind?

CHAPTER 2

Myra gushed on the phone to Annie. "Guess who's coming for a visit?"

"Knowing you, Myra, it could be the queen of England," Annie teased.

"Well, at least you have the country correct, smarty-pants. But it's Charlotte! She was visiting her daughter in London and is stopping here on her way back to Aspen."

Annie had first met Charlotte when they were young teenagers, when Charlotte's family had lived on Myra's parents' farm. The last time the three of them had been together was when they took a trip to Sedona, Arizona, to "sit on a few rocks." They still giggled over how sore their backsides were after climbing Bell Rock and perching on the Schnebly Hill Formation to experience the sunrise at the summer solstice. They would often debate about what hurt their bottoms more: the red rocks or sliding down the banister of Myra's farmhouse.

"It will be nice to see her again," Annie replied. "What brings her here? Besides to visit with her girlfriends?"

Myra fiddled with her pearl necklace, a habit she had developed many years ago, when she would be lost in thought after the death of her daughter, Barbara. "Hmmm . . . I —"

Annie immediately interrupted her. "I know that 'hmmm,' and I bet that right now you're clinging to those pearls."

"Oh, aren't you the clever one?" Myra shot back.

"Maybe it's because I know you so well. Spill. What's going on?" Annie could be a relentless interrogator when she wanted to get to the heart of the matter.

"I received a letter from her yesterday. She seemed . . . out of sorts, you could say."

"We *all* feel out of sorts from time to time. How out? And what kind of sorts?" Annie often said it was like pulling teeth to get Myra to talk about her feelings or something she wasn't sure she could share.

"She's having some . . . How did she put it? 'Foggy moments,' " Myra replied.

Annie kept prodding. "That's not unusual. What else is going on?"

"I'm not sure." The sound of Myra's voice

told Annie that she was worried.

"My dear friend, if I know you — and I am sure I do — you will get to the bottom of it sooner rather than later."

Myra chuckled. "You do know me, don't you?"

At that moment, Charles appeared with a tray of freshly baked scones and tea. "How about a little break?"

"Annie, I have to go. Charles is plying me with those luscious raspberry scones. Oh, I want to have a dinner party for Charlotte. Get as many girls as are available. I think having our group around will lift her spirits. You and Fergus will be here. Friday. Eight o'clock. Unless the two of you want to show up early. Fergus can help Charles in the kitchen, and you and I can sample the champagne. We wouldn't want anyone getting sick, now would we?" Myra giggled at her own words.

"That's an invitation I cannot refuse. Shall we come by at, say, six?"

"Six is perfect. If Charles needs Fergus here sooner, I'll let you know." After she got off the phone, Myra looked up at Charles, who nodded in agreement. He set down the tray of scones and poured his beloved her favorite tea.

"So, my dear. What exactly do you have in

mind?" Charles took the seat across from Myra. "I can almost see those wheels turning."

Myra reached for her pearls again. "I'm not quite sure. I think the dinner party and a few relaxing days here will cheer Charlotte up, raise her spirits, but I am definitely not happy about this large number of medications she referred to in her letter."

"What did she say exactly, when you called her?" Charles leaned in closer to read the expression on Myra's face.

"I'm not clear on it yet. The treatment hasn't been approved by the FDA, but she is enrolled in some sort of trial. It's like the Wild West of medicine. No rules to speak of."

"Yes, apparently, one signs a waiver in those cases," Charles chimed in.

"And, I'm willing to bet, all their money," Myra snapped back.

"Now, love, before you get your vigilante pants in a knot, let's see what else Charlotte has to say. Maybe she's just feeling a little blue."

"I do hope so, Charles. I really do. But something isn't sitting right with me."

Charles rolled his eyes. . . . He could feel a mission coming on.

CHAPTER 3

London

After three days of arguing with her daughter, Maryann, Charlotte snapped her suitcases closed and eyed the collection of medicine bottles on the vanity. She had secretly stopped taking them after mailing her letter to Myra. It had been almost a week. Everything had been happening so fast, but she felt much better. Maybe it was the anticipation of visiting her friends, or maybe it was the absence of "supplements" coursing through her body. Either way, she hadn't felt this lighthearted and alert in a long time.

She thought a moment. *How long has it been?* She could not recall. *Darn it, Charlotte. Get a grip,* she whispered to herself. *You're going on an adventure. Let's not think about any of it. At least not for now.* Feeling good was very welcome after all the months — yes, it had been months — of being in a

22

fog. Even though she wasn't sure how many months, she was certain it had been much too long. She also knew that she had to stop talking to herself. Or, at the very least, not get caught doing it! If she was caught, they would really put her in a loony bin.

There was a slight rap on her door. "Mother, I wish you would reconsider." When Maryann came into Charlotte's room, she was finally being gentle instead of the screeching banshee she had become when Charlotte told her she was cutting her visit short.

"What is going on? And what is Dr. Marcus going to say about your leaving so soon?" Those had been the talking, or shouting, points, day after day.

Finally, quoting Clark Gable as Rhett Butler, Charlotte had replied, "Frankly, my dear, I don't give a damn." Charlotte had said it with calm determination, her way of letting Maryann know that the conversation was over. That had been two days ago, and neither had spoken to the other until now.

Charlotte was hoping that she would not be leaving on bad terms with her daughter. "Maryann, I do so appreciate your hospitality and concern for me, but I cannot change my plans now. Myra and Charles, as well as Annie and Fergus, have made a lot of arrangements."

"But what about *my* arrangements?" Maryann was getting a little heated again, realizing that she was probably not going to convince her mother to stay. "And Dr. Marcus?"

Darn it. Maryann wished she hadn't mentioned the doctor. His name seemed to be the "Niagara Falls" catalyst — the old comic routine when some guy goes berserk anytime he hears the words *Niagara Falls.* Yes, the mere reference to him almost always set her mother off.

But why? And why so suddenly? Maryann backed off her scolding and gave her mother a hug. "Mom, you know I want what's best for you." She tried to choose her next words carefully. "I'm just concerned about your health. That's all."

"To be perfectly honest, I haven't felt this good in . . . , well, since I can't remember when." Charlotte had a lilt in her voice, which Maryann hadn't heard in a while.

"I'm so glad. Maybe these treatments are working!" Maryann gave her mother another hug, but Charlotte stiffened and looked toward the vanity, where her pill bottles were.

"What? What is it, Mom?" Maryann

24

stepped back and gave Charlotte a quizzical look.

Thinking about what she had been doing for the past several days — flushing her pills down the toilet — Charlotte decided to change the subject so as not to let on about her secret.

"You know how much I hate to fly."

"Well, it *is* first class. At least if anything happens, you'll go out in style!" Maryann thought she was being humorous, but it only made Charlotte shudder.

"That makes me feel so much better," Charlotte replied sardonically. She took a deep breath and reached for her daughter. "I know you mean well, my dear. But I'm getting antsy, and besides, I think Liam would rather be spending more time with his friends than with his grandmother."

"Don't be ridiculous! Liam loves you! He misses you all the time!" Maryann protested.

"I know, but he's almost eight years old. Little boys want to go out and play with their friends. Not take walks every day or play board games. Spelled b-o-r-e-d." That finally broke the tension, and both women laughed and hugged.

"You will call me when you arrive at Myra's?"

"Of course, darling. But it is six hours' difference. You may already be in bed."

"Just do it, please."

"I should be arriving at Myra's around five in the afternoon their time, so it will be about eleven o'clock here."

"That's fine. I'll sleep better knowing you're safe and sound."

"Safe, yes. Sound? To be determined." Both laughed at the double entendre. Maryann grabbed the bigger of the two suitcases and headed out the door. Charlotte scooped up the meds and threw them in her tote bag.

At first, Charlotte had been going to flush all the pills, but then she had decided she should bring them with her. She still wasn't sure if they were effective or not, but if her mood over the past few days was an indication of their usefulness, it was clear that she did not need them. Maybe she would ask Myra and Charles their opinion. Charles was not a doctor, nor was Myra, but between the two of them, they undoubtedly had connections to top medical professionals. Then she grimaced at her thoughts. Maybe it was too much to ask of her generous friends. She ultimately decided she would take each day as it came. That thought gave her a little peace of mind.

Minutes later, the lobby intercom buzzer

sounded. "Ride for Mrs. Hansen."

"She'll be right down," Maryann said to the disembodied voice that had come out of the box on the wall. She turned to her mother in earnest. "Please be sure to follow up with either Dr. Marcus or Dr. Steinwood."

Charlotte grunted. "We'll see, my dear. I'll decide after I get back to Aspen." She gave her daughter another big hug. "I'll be fine. I promise."

The Range Rover was humming softly as the driver helped her inside. He stored her luggage in the rear compartment and handed her the tote.

Charlotte peered into the bag and checked the medicine bottles, almost six thousand dollars worth of pills. She had no idea what kinds of medicines they were, but she was determined to find out. She zipped the tote with the drugs, sat back in the luxurious leather seat, and willed herself to relax. She then recalled her other favorite movie quote, this time Vivien Leigh as Scarlett O'Hara — *Tomorrow is another day.* She smiled. *Yes, I'm feeling much better today. Thank you very much.*

CHAPTER 4

Pinewood

That same afternoon, the day of Charlotte's arrival, Myra had Yoko bring armloads of flowers from her greenhouse to decorate every room in the farmhouse. It was still early spring, and Myra's gardens were not yet in full bloom. Only the potted plants on the terrace, which Yoko had helped her plant, provided an array of color to brighten the end of a long winter.

Hearing the commotion in the foyer, Charles wiped his hands on his apron and joined several of the sisters, who were carrying what seemed like hundreds of blooms.

"Coming through!" Yoko shouted as she carried an armload of peonies, with the dogs yapping at her feet. It was organized pandemonium.

Myra gasped at the sight of the colorful blooms. "Yoko! Where did you find peonies

28

this time of year? They are absolutely gorgeous!"

With Yoko's arms filled with the massive bouquet, one could not see her face, and it seemed as if the flowers spoke when she answered, "I know people!"

A rip-roaring laugh filled the room. Everyone in Myra and Annie's circle knew *someone*. And it was those "someones" who assisted the women when they were on a mission. But today it was about flowers, food, and friends.

Kathryn parted the flowers hiding Yoko's face. "Peekaboo!"

"Very funny," Yoko chided Kathryn. "How about lending one of those big hands of yours!"

Kathryn grabbed the flowers and set them down on the large table in the entry. "Myra, where do you want these?"

Charles looked at the dozens, no hundreds, of flowers. "Did you bring the entire greenhouse with you, Yoko?"

Yoko tilted her head in Myra's direction. "What do *you* think? Everything but lilies."

Charles nodded. Of course she did, and of course, no lilies. House rules. Lilies could be toxic for dogs and cats.

Myra surveyed the dozens of arrangements and began giving orders. "Tulips in

Charlotte's room. They were always her favorite — a sign of spring. Fuchsia peonies can stay here, white peonies and the cherry blossoms go in the dining room, orchids in the drawing room, and gardenias in the bathrooms. Blue irises in the master bedroom and sunflowers in the kitchen."

The women grabbed the vases in unison and made quick work of placing them according to Myra's instructions.

Maggie, whose insatiable appetite was the stuff of legends, was the first to ask, "What's for dinner, Charles?"

"Besides your cuticles?" Charles gave her an admonishing look.

Maggie held up both hands. "Look! I actually got a manicure!"

Everyone stopped in their tracks.

"You got a what?" Kathryn roared. "I've gotta see this." She grabbed Maggie's hands. "Well, I'll be darned. What gives?"

"I thought it might help me to stop biting them. But now I'm cracking my knuckles, just like you!" She nudged Kathryn with a playful elbow to the ribs.

More laughter and cackling ensued.

"We all have our little quirks, dear." Myra gestured with her hand on her pearls.

"Yes, but your quirk is elegant. Mine is,

well, juvenile. Or neurotic," Maggie interjected.

"Neurotic?" Kathryn teased. "You won't
get an argument out of me!"

Another round of giggles sounded until
the chime of the doorbell interrupted the
joviality.

Charles took charge of the door. "Must be
the liquor store. I ordered Aperol for our
aperitif cocktails."

"My new favorite!" Annie exclaimed. "Ap-
erol, prosecco, and a splash of seltzer.
Garnished with a slice from a juicy orange.
Refreshing!" She smacked her lips. "Yum!"

"Okay, everyone. Now that we have the
flowers sorted, let's get started on setting
the table. I know it's still early, but I think
all of you will want to freshen up before we
turn our attention to Charles and Annie's
latest favorite libation." Myra gestured to
the dining room.

"Where are Nikki and Alexis?" Kathryn
asked.

"Finishing up a trial. They should be here
momentarily," Myra replied, giving Charles
a sideways look that said, "Don't you say a
word." And in his usual fashion, Charles
gave a knowing nod.

With speed, accuracy, and movements
that seemed to mimic synchronized swim-

ming, the women began to set the table, each one knowing her assignment. They would create a glorious display fit for a queen.

Isabelle called into the kitchen, "The Tiffany or Waterford trumpet flutes?"

"I think the Waterford would be better for the aperitif. We like to layer the cocktail," Charles explained. "First, you add the Aperol to the glass, and then you pour the prosecco gently, so it floats on top of the Aperol, then just a little splash of seltzer. And, as Annie indicated, serve the whole thing with a slice of orange, and voilà!"

"A most beautiful and tasty delight," Annie observed.

"Perhaps Charles should introduce that ambrosia to us now. 'Get the party started,' as they say," Maggie said, tossing in her two cents.

"Perhaps we should wait," Myra said patiently. She knew the girls were getting excited about the dinner party. They had met Charlotte several years before, when she was signing at BookExpo in Washington, D.C. "We don't want to be snockered before Charlotte gets here."

"But she *knows* us!" Kathryn chuckled. "But I suppose you're correct. We still have a couple of hours and some chores before she gets here."

Nikki and Alexis made their entrance through the usual spot, the kitchen.

"What is that fantastic aroma?" Nikki quickly pecked her mother on the cheek and gave Charles a hug.

"Charles has been fussing with a new secret recipe." Myra was only half kidding. Charles was the equivalent of a Michelin-star restaurant chef. She didn't know how he had learned to create such fine cuisine, but she appreciated it, nonetheless. There were a number of things in Charles's background about which Myra knew very little, but she knew more about it than most. And she trusted him with her life, the life of her adopted daughter, Nikki, and those of the "sisters."

Fergus had been an "associate" of Charles when Charles was in MI6 and Fergus was a high-ranking official at Scotland Yard. She did not know all that much about Fergus's early career, but if Charles trusted him, and Annie adored him, well, that made him someone Myra could trust completely.

"Mmm . . ." Maggie took a big inhale. "If dinner is as good as this smells, well, I hope you have enough for everyone besides me!" The women giggled at the ongoing joke about Maggie's appetite.

At that moment, Isabelle called from the dining room, "Which dinnerware?"

"The Hermès Mosaique will go nicely with the Waterford," Myra answered. She was fidgeting with her pearls again.

Charles came up behind her and asked in a whisper, "What are you fussing about? The girls, Fergus, and I have everything under control."

She gave him an affectionate pat on his cheek. "I want to know what Nikki and Alexis found out about Dr. Wonderful." Myra was referring to Charlotte's Aspen physician, Dr. Steinwood.

"Speaking of which, Avery should have the intel on Dr. Marcus any minute now," Charles added. "I know you wanted to have some background before Charlotte arrives. Let me check the oven. Then I'll go downstairs and see if Avery has sent anything."

Avery Snowden had been involved in many counterintelligence operations back in the day, and the Sisterhood now considered him their full-time private investigator. His small army of professional operatives could find out almost anything about anyone and could track them in ways that would make Sherlock Holmes blush.

"Oh, Charles, you know the rules. You made this one yourself — no business during cooking or dining," Myra reminded him.

"Yes, dear girl. But I promise I won't do anything. I'll just check."

Nikki gave her mother a nod to indicate she needed to speak to her in private.

Myra lifted one finger, as if to say, *Give me a minute.*

There were no secrets among the women. If anyone had come across a situation that she thought needed to be addressed, she would bring it to the table, and the sisters would take a vote. If they agreed to deal with it, they would lay out a strategy for the mission, with each sister getting an assignment. At the moment, Myra, Annie, Nikki, Alexis, and Charles were in the preliminary stages of finding out what they could about the two doctors and their "longevity protocol." If Myra's instincts were correct, and they usually were, the group would be convening for a vote lickety-split.

But all of that would wait until dinner had been served, followed by dessert, tea, and coffee, and the twelve-foot walnut dining-room table was back to its pristine state, the dishes and pots and pans were gleaming, and not a crumb was in sight.

For now, the preparations for their arriving guest were proceeding apace.

Chapter 5

The girls stepped back to admire the gorgeous table they had arranged for the dinner party. Myra was correct. The beautiful Waterford crystal complemented the stunning Hermès china, both sitting upon the crisp white Pratesi tablecloth. The centerpiece of cherry-blossom branches and white peonies made a statement that could be described only as exquisite. Small votive candles were scattered throughout. The girls engaged in high fives and a lot of whooping. Even the dogs barked in approval.

Charles peeked around the corner and walked in holding a small tray of popovers in one hand. "You certainly outdid yourselves, girls! This deserves a treat." The dogs went wild at the word *treat.* Charles reached into his pocket with his free hand and produced a handful of doggie biscuits. His pockets were seldom without them.

Maggie snatched a popover before anyone

else did. "Oh my. This is heaven. Charles, I don't know how you do it." The girls elbowed their way to the silver platter on which rested the airy, fluffy pastries.

"We prefer to call it Yorkshire pudding, but you Yanks call them popovers. This is just a test recipe. The real deal will be served at dinner." Charles took a small bow as each sister stuffed a flaky morsel in her mouth.

Annie elbowed her way into the middle of the ongoing bedlam to snatch the last popover. "It's almost three o'clock, ladies. I think it's time we let Charles continue his artful preparations and we clean up our act."

As the women dispersed, Myra gave Nikki and Annie a signal to meet in the drawing room.

"Nikki, what were you able to find out about Dr. Marcus and Dr. Steinwood?" Myra held her breath.

"They both have medical degrees from Ross University School of Medicine."

"Ross University? Is that like Joe's School of Dentistry?" Annie could not resist making an attempt at humor. Myra gave her a sideways glance.

"It's in Barbados."

"Barbados?" Annie and Myra asked in unison.

"Yes, the beautiful island in the Caribbean." Nikki tapped her phone for more information. "It appears that they also have certificates from the University of Lausanne in Switzerland. The two of them and a third partner have a joint medical practice called Live-Life-Long in three cities — Aspen, where Dr. Steinwood practices, London, for Dr. Marcus, and New York, where a third partner, Dr. Raymond Corbett, is located. His practice is located in the Hamptons, on Long Island. Their specialty — they claim — is integrated medicine for maintaining one's youth."

"Sounds fishy to me." Annie was the first to comment.

"That was all I could find today without digging deeper. I want to confirm their backgrounds but will probably need Charles's or Snowden's help." Nikki glanced up at the two other women. "Uh-oh. I know that look."

Annie and Myra both crossed their arms and shrugged. "What look is that," Myra asked?

Nikki pointed a finger, first at Myra, then at Annie. "*That* one! And *that* one!"

"Before we get ahead of ourselves, let's file this information away. Charles is waiting for some intel, as well. And we do need to see how Charlotte is feeling and try to get whatever information we can from her without making her feel that she's undergoing an interrogation." Myra stroked her pearl necklace. "For now, let's have a wonderful dinner party and save this business for later. Rules, you know." She smiled as she waved her hand in the air, indicating the scrumptious aromas emanating from the kitchen.

Each departed to her own private quarters to prepare for the evening. Annie knew she had plenty of time to get Fergus out of the house so she could take a long, hot bath. Her biggest concern was which of her rhinestone cowboy boots to wear. Nikki would FaceTime Jack. It seemed like an eternity since she had last seen her husband's face. With both either working on a case or on a mission, there hardly seemed time for their relationship. But it was strong and steady, and each of them had the highest respect for the other. After the conflicts they had been through in the very beginning — when Nikki thought she and Jack were over — she knew their love and dedication would lead them in the right direction. Who was it that sang "Love Is a Battlefield"? she wondered. Ah yes, Pat Benatar. Nikki chuckled, remembering one of the fights they'd had. The argument had ended when

Nikki, who was totally frustrated, broke out singing the last line of that song, causing both her and Jack to have fits of laughter.

Myra went to the guest room to make certain everything was perfect for Charlotte's arrival. She could have had her friend stay in one of the guest cottages, but Myra wanted Charlotte under her and Charles's watchful eyes. Besides, the guest room was located on the other side of the library, where Charlotte would have total privacy yet be close at hand.

The suite rivaled that in any five-star hotel. It was five hundred square feet and had a king-size bed adorned with Raso Quagliotti thousand-thread-count sheets, a stone fireplace, a wet bar, a fifty-five-inch television, a love seat, and barrel chairs. The bathroom was complete with a sunken tub, a separate shower with four showerheads, a heated floor, heat lamps, a commode in a private area, and a double-sink vanity that stretched across one wall. Floor-to-ceiling windows along the bathtub overlooked a garden. Myra fussed with the tulips for a while, then wrote a short note:

My dear friend,
I hope your visit with us will soothe your soul and bring you joy. Stay as long as

you like. And you know I mean it!

Love,
Myra (and Charles and the dogs!)

She placed it against one of the vases and took a final sweeping look around the room. She was satisfied that this was a refuge for her friend.

The barking of the dogs signaled that Fergus had arrived. It was almost as if the dogs had a special yelp for every individual. Smart critters.

The English lilt in the background confirmed it was Fergus as he handed out treats to the dogs. "C'mon, girls, there's enough for all." He also knew to keep treats handy.

Myra often worried that the dogs would get fat on all the treats they got. Charles would argue that they had the run of the property and availed themselves of it regularly. "Enough cardio for all of us."

Myra went to the master suite and picked a casual pantsuit and light-colored blouse. After checking her makeup, she slipped on a pair of flats and headed to the kitchen.

"It does smell delectable." She gave Charles a peck on the cheek.

"You are looking quite fetching, my dear." Charles eyed his wife. Of course, whatever she wore or didn't wear, she never looked less than beautiful to him.

CHAPTER 6

Charlotte settled into the comfortable seat next to the window. A flight attendant approached her and asked, "May I get you something to drink?"

Charlotte thought for a moment, then said, "Yes, champagne please." She was feeling good. Writing to Myra was the best thing she could have done for herself; Myra always knew what to do and what to say.

Charlotte had come from humble beginnings. Her father had been the groundskeeper for Myra's family farm. During the Civil War, the farmhouse had been a way station for the Underground Railroad, and the tunnels beneath it had remained ever since. There had also been a few small outbuildings, which had served as sheds and feeding stations over the years.

She, Myra, and Annie would sit in one of the old sheds and tell each other stories. That was when Myra had first encouraged

Charlotte to start writing, which had led to her becoming a very successful author of children's books. She had married, had a daughter, divorced, and kept writing. All through that time, Myra had been building her own empire, Mary-Ruth Candy, which had made her one of the wealthiest women in the country. That was when Charles had entered the picture.

Charles had recently relocated from the UK, with a résumé to rival James Bond's, British accent included. However, if you saw the actual résumé, it would be redacted to the point that no information could be found on it. He had convinced Myra to hire him as head of security for her company, assuring her he could handle all her needs. At the time, little had Myra realized he really meant *all* of them.

Charlotte was going through each of the women in her head. There was Nikki, Myra's adopted daughter. Thank goodness for Nikki. After Myra's daughter, Barbara, was killed, Myra tumbled into a deep depression, until one day she seemed to have awoken from the pit of despair and had a new lease on life. Perhaps that was what Charlotte was feeling now: a new lease.

Then there was Annie. Anna Ryland de Silva. The countess. What a hoot she was.

Annie and Myra had been friends even before Charlotte met them, but they had always made her feel welcome. Annie was wealthy beyond anyone's imagination. Some said she was the richest woman in the world. Maybe she was. And she seemed to know everyone, as well. Quite the mover and shaker but unassuming. She and Myra both dressed the way you would expect a housewife from Queens or Staten Island to dress. Except for maybe those rhinestone boots that Annie affected.

Charlotte didn't know the rest of the girls well. She had met a few, but it was always in a large social or business setting. She knew about most of their backgrounds and the crazy accusations that they were a vigilante group. Charlotte could not comprehend that her dear friend would be doing something so controversial, although it did sound exciting.

The plane departed on time, and after two glasses of bubbly, Charlotte was given a blanket and pillow and dozed off for the duration of the flight.

The ding when the overhead lights came on startled her awake just in time to hear the captain say, "Ladies and gentlemen, we are making our final approach to Dulles Airport. Enjoy your stay and thank you for flying United."

Charlotte pulled out a compact mirror and lipstick and made sure she hadn't drooled during her long nap. With a quick fix, she wrapped her pashmina around her and was ready for the next leg of her journey. She pulled the paper from her tote bag. "Edward will meet you at baggage claim." *Edward. Edward. Edward,* she repeated silently. That was part of her "treatment" — to repeat words until they stuck.

As she reached the carousel, spinning with suitcases, backpacks, golf clubs, and an assortment of packages, she saw a gentleman with a sign: CHARLOTTE HANSEN. *That was easy,* she said to herself. She gave him a wave, and he quickly approached her, tipped his chauffeur's cap, and asked her to describe her luggage. Once he spotted the suitcases, he grabbed them and led her to the town car awaiting them.

"Myra and Charles are the epitome of grace and hospitality," she remarked to Edward.

"They are indeed."

After the thirty-minute ride from the airport, the large iron gates of the farm loomed before them. It was just as she remembered. The trees, the gardens, the landscaping. All so meticulous. She wondered if the old swing was still in the back. Knowing Myra, it probably was. Charlotte hoped so. She wouldn't mind sitting on it again and letting the air blow through her hair.

The sound of dogs barking their welcome made her smile as Myra flung the front door open. "Charlotte! So good to see you!" Big, big hugs, and kisses on both cheeks. Myra stepped back to take a good look at her friend. "My dear, I think you've come to the right place." Charlotte looked weary, but there was still a gleam in her eyes.

"Myra, I cannot thank you and Charles enough for rescuing me from God knows what."

"You just relax, and we'll sort it all out. Come. Follow me. We'll get you settled, and then we can have an aperitif."

"Sounds divine." Charlotte linked arms with Myra as Annie flew into the foyer.

"I have an arm, too," she announced, linking herself to the two other women, with Charles toting the luggage behind them.

"Leave it to Fergus to be invisible when it comes to heavy lifting," Charles teased Annie.

"I think he's minding the roast," Annie poked back.

"If that's how to describe what he's doing, then indeed. I fear that Fergus's only talent in the kitchen is stuffing his mouth," Charles reminded everyone.

"Charles, be kind. Fergus is the best cleanup man for your KP duty!" Myra chided him.

"I will leave you women to chat and unwind before Fergus has a chance to ruin my dinner." With that, Charles chuckled and left the three women to gab.

Myra and Annie helped Charlotte unpack as they caught each other up on superficial things. Myra was careful not to prod Charlotte too much. She wanted Charlotte to offer the information they needed freely and not feel that she was being grilled for it. If only to save her any embarrassment.

Myra gave Charlotte a big hug, and Annie wrapped her arms around both of them.

"Freshen up, dear. Charles will call us when we are about to start the festivities."

"I hope you didn't go to too much trouble. The tickets and the limo service were over the top."

Myra and Annie gave her a wry look. "You can't be serious," Annie hooted. "You're dealing with *us*, remember?"

Loud laughter filled the room.

"I cannot tell you how much better I feel right now." Tears started to well in Charlotte's eyes.

"And you just got here. Just wait until dinner! You will feel like you died and went to heaven," Annie said, smacking her lips.'

When Myra made her way back to the kitchen, she noticed a slightly grim expression on Charles's face. "What is it, dear?"

Charles cleared his throat. "We have some new information about the 'miracle doctors.' Avery sent it a short while ago. Fergus is downstairs, sorting it out."

"Charles, you know the rules," Myra admonished him.

"Yes, old girl, I do. My point is, we are going to have to think seriously about this situation, gather the intel from Nikki, then read Avery's report. There is definitely something amiss."

Myra took a deep breath. "At least she's here and out from under them."

"For now," Charles reminded her.

"Yes, for now, and she isn't leaving until we get to the bottom of this." Myra pecked him on the cheek and patted his fanny. "That roast smells divine." She knew how to change the subject, even if it was only on the surface she thought as she headed to the dining room.

In the meanwhile, Charlotte was making

her way from the other side of the farm-house toward the dining room. The aroma coming from the kitchen was calling to her. She realized that she hadn't eaten much in the past fifteen hours.

When she approached the dining room, she gasped at the beautiful table setting. In the middle of the table was a large vase with branches of cherry blossoms surrounded by white peonies. The arrangement had to be at least four feet high.

"This is breathtaking," she gasped. Glancing at the place settings, she could barely speak. "Myra! This is spectacular! You didn't tell me this was going to be a formal affair. Who on your A-list is coming?"

Myra put her arm around her friend. "*You* are my A-list. And, of course, the girls, Charles, and Fergus." Lady barked, as if to say, "What about us?" Myra reached down and rubbed the dog's ears. "You, too, of course!" Lady gave an approving woof.

Soon after that, Annie returned after her leisurely bath and started pouring the Aperol and prosecco. Within a few minutes, the rest of the guests arrived: Kathryn, Yoko, Isabelle, Nikki, Maggie, and Alexis. Annie greeted them at the dining room door with a tray of beautiful flutes filled with the colorful beverage.

There were hugs all around, each trying not to splash the other with her freshly mixed drink.

Shortly thereafter, Fergus appeared with a tray of hors d'oeuvres: miniature crab cakes, stuffed mushrooms, mini quiche. A plate of foie gras was nestled on the side table, next to a crystal bowl of caviar, with all the accompaniments. It was the opening act for one of Charles's masterpiece culinary performances.

Maggie dived into the first thing she could touch on the tray. "Easy, girl. There is a lot more to come." Charles gave her a disapproving look and handed her a linen cocktail napkin.

"Oh, Charles. You know how much I love food, especially *your* food," she said, going into defensive mode.

"Yes, dear, but do try to slow down. We have many courses, and many hours to indulge ourselves." Suddenly, Charles's British accent made him sound very formal.

Maggie elbowed him and faked an Italian accent. *"Capisce!"*

Everyone took their regular place at the table, with the guest of honor in the center.

They all bowed their heads, said grace, and gave thanks, after which Charles and Fergus began serving the meal. With each course, groans of delight filled the room.

Charlotte raised her glass to make a toast. "To the finest, most generous people I have ever met. Thank you so very much for this wonderful experience."

Everyone clinked everyone else's glass. Nikki, Charles, Myra, Alexis, and Annie gave each other the look that said, "You ain't seen nothing yet."

By eleven o'clock, the dishes had been cleared and dessert and brandy were being served in the drawing room. Charlotte could barely keep her eyes open, which meant she would soon be sound asleep. Myra, Nikki, Annie, Alexis, Fergus, and Charles were going to burn the midnight oil to uncover what they could about the likely not-so-good or good-for-nothing doctors.

Myra and Annie linked arms with Charlotte once again and walked her to her room.

"This was a wonderful evening." Charlotte affectionately squeezed their arms. "I cannot thank you enough."

"Sleep well, dear friend. If you need anything, just pick up the phone and press the intercom button." Myra kissed her friend on the cheek, and Annie followed suit.

Charlotte was weary yet felt satisfied. She

was looking forward to hours of slumber in the sumptuous bed.

CHAPTER 7

London

"What do you mean, she left town?" Dr. Julian Marcus shouted into the phone.

"My mother decided to go back to the States." Maryann was slightly embarrassed that her mother had not contacted the doctor personally.

"But the treatment! The protocol!" He sounded frantic. "This will not bode well for the scientific legitimacy of our findings if she does not complete the series of treatments!" He sounded as if he were close to foaming at the mouth.

"Dr. Marcus, I am very sorry, but there was nothing I could do to stop her from leaving." Maryann was starting to get her bearings. *Who the hell does he think he is, yelling at me like this?*

"You should have phoned me," he said, softening his voice. He knew that if he didn't get his hands on some cocaine soon, he was going to lose it entirely.

"I thought I could talk her out of leaving, but she insisted. She packed her bags and left yesterday." Maryann waited for the next barrage of criticism.

"Very well, then. I trust she will continue the protocol with Dr. Steinwood in Aspen?" He was hoping their latest cash cow would continue her treatment once she returned to the States.

"I suppose, but she is spending time with some friends in Virginia before she heads home."

Marcus erupted again. "Did she at least take her supplements with her? I warned you that patients can get disoriented. This is not good, Maryann. You gave me your assurance you would monitor her."

"Dr. Marcus, I appreciate your concern, but I can do nothing more than try to convince her to act in a certain way. I am neither her jailer nor her caregiver. My mother is a grown woman with her own mind. And given her list of accomplishments, it is clearly a very fine mind indeed."

"The very state of her mind is the issue!" He continued to rant. "I cannot be held responsible should something happen to her."

Maryann was growing frustrated but held

her ground. "I totally understand, Dr. Marcus. Will you contact Dr. Steinwood, or shall I?"

"That's all right. I'll handle this. Good day!" He slammed the phone down on his desk so hard that it scratched the leather inlaid surface. "Damn it," he shouted to no one. He picked the phone up and scrolled through his contacts, looking for the "delivery boy" — the one who would bring him his weekly supply of the intoxicating white powder.

After punching in the numbers, he sent a text: **Coffee. Three sugars.** That was code for an eighth of an ounce of cocaine, although he thought he should probably get more. It seemed he was running out of it faster lately. He sent a second text: **Coffee. Six sugars.** He hoped the idiot understood what he meant.

He drummed his fingers on his desk and looked at his Rolex. It was still too early to call Aspen. He started pacing. *What's taking that moron so long to get here?* Deep in thought as to how he was going to make up the twenty-five thousand dollars he had been counting on from Charlotte Hansen, he nearly jumped out of his Armani suit when his cell phone rang. *"What?"* he screamed into the receiver. "I thought I told you *never* to call me!"

"Sorry, Doc, but my man says you owe him over five K. He wants his money before he'll serve you any more 'coffee.' " The whiny voice on the other end was almost snickering.

"Tell him I'll have it to him this afternoon." Marcus was careful not to spook his connection.

"Uh . . . I don't think that's gonna work. Ya see . . . he's all fired up today, so I can't brew the blend without some cash." The cockney accent talking in drug code was infuriating Marcus, but he knew better than to challenge his supplier. He checked his wallet, then the office safe. Only two thousand.

"Okay, listen, I have almost half of that here now. What if you bring me one coffee with three sugars?" Marcus needed his fix, sooner rather than later.

"Dunno, mate. I'll have to check." The delivery boy ended the call abruptly.

Marcus continued to pace, his anxiety growing with each passing minute. He knew he had been going through about $250 a day with his habit, which at times seemed like chump change. But the more he sniffed the white powder, the more he wanted. Maybe it was time to step it up. Try something different. Again, the phone made him jump.

"Okay, Doc. Half now, but then you pay the other half by the end of the day, or the party is over." Ultimatum having been delivered, the call ended abruptly.

Marcus was starting to perspire. Yes, he needed to change up his game. He checked his watch again. *Time is moving much too slowly.*

CHAPTER 8

The war room

Confident that Charlotte was sound asleep, the kitchen was sparkling clean, and the other dinner guests had departed, Nikki, Alexis, Myra, Charles, Fergus, and Annie descended the moss-covered stone steps to the dungeon, where the war room was located. Entering the chamber, each saluted Lady Justice and they all sat down at the round table. This was where they would exchange information and plan their strategy for a mission.

Nikki started. "It appears, and I use that word lightly, that all three doctors graduated from Ross University School of Medicine in Barbados."

Annie let out a snicker, recalling her comment about "Joe's School of Dentistry." Myra shot her a look.

Alexis picked up the narrative. "It could be true that they attended Ross. However, their status at the University of Lausanne seems a bit sketchy. While copies of their admission applications could be found, there is no record of their having actually enrolled, much less graduated." She looked up at Charles, anticipating additional information from him.

"Avery concurs that there is no documentation about their actually undertaking studies in Switzerland, but, as we know, the Swiss are very tight lipped when it comes to sharing information." Charles continued, "The other odd thing is the existence of a big gap between graduating from Ross and applying to Lausanne. About ten years. We have not yet been able to fill in that blank. Nor can we establish that they ever enrolled, not to mention attended classes, at Lausanne."

"What about when they supposedly left Lausanne?" Myra queried.

"That seems to be a big piece of this puzzle, as well, but Avery and his people are digging deeper."

Back to Nikki, who let out a sigh. "And neither Alexis nor I could find any evidence that either of the two practicing in the US are licensed to practice in Colorado or New York or that Dr. Marcus is licensed to practice in England, much less London. All three may be guilty of practicing medicine without a license, even if they have medical degrees."

"How does *that* happen? A doctor who isn't licensed?" Annie was incredulous.

"Have you ever looked up any of your physicians' credentials?" Charles asked pointedly. "We look at the certificates on the walls, but do we actually question their qualifications further? Especially if they have taken over someone else's practice or been referred by a friend or family member."

They looked around the table and shrugged in unison.

"My point exactly." The tone of Charles's voice indicated how he felt. "What we have been able to ascertain is that these three men met at some point — most likely at Ross. We need to find out what they were doing during those missing ten years."

Myra interjected, "I think it's time we brought everyone into this and took a vote, although I know how I am going to vote already. We need to get to the bottom of this! God knows who else they are preying on." Each of those present raised a hand in agreement. "Excellent. Let's call a meeting for tomorrow afternoon. I'll arrange for a mini spa day for Charlotte, so she'll be out of the house while the meeting takes place."

Myra fingered her pearls, this time with less anxiety and more resolve.

Charles was the first one to stand. "All right, everyone, we shall reconvene tomorrow at noon. It will give us a 'lunch appointment' excuse."

Annie agreed to contact the available sisters, and it was understood that Charles would prepare lunch, with Fergus as his able assistant. Fergus didn't mind playing second fiddle to Charles in the kitchen. He claimed it helped him to relax. Once he had made a joke about "*relaxing* and *Annie* never being in the same sentence," for which he had got a pinch on the ass that turned black and blue.

The following morning, before Myra checked in on Charlotte, she and Charles debated whether Charles should prepare a traditional London fry-up or bangers and mash.

Myra groaned. "Dear, we're all going to gain ten pounds over the next two days."

"Myra, we cannot allow our guest to wake up to an Egg McMuffin, now, can we?"

Myra chuckled at Charles's jest. An Egg McMuffin in that house was never going to happen unless Charles prepared it himself.

In his own kitchen. With his own ingredients.

Myra suggested, "How about eggs, sausage, home fries, and toast? A little more American. You can wow her with your British bangers over the weekend."

"Only if you let me include back bacon," Charles pretended to protest.

"If you insist." Myra glanced at the large grandfather clock in the foyer. Seven o'clock. "If I do my math —"

Charles interrupted, intuitively knowing Myra was calculating the time in London and how much jet lag Charlotte would have endured. "It's noon, old girl."

She nodded. "Daylight saving time. I never understood why we had to change the clocks. Arizona doesn't do it."

"Because the day is long and hot enough," Fergus chimed in as he rounded the corner from the kitchen.

"Good morning, mate!" Charles clapped him on the back. "Ready to crack some eggs?"

Fergus laughed. "Why am I thinking it's going to end up more in line with cracking some heads?"

Charles gave him a wry grin and raised his eyebrows in agreement.

On the other side of the house, Charlotte

was beginning to stir as Myra peeked into her room, with two of the dogs trailing behind and wagging their tails in anticipation of pats on the head, hugs, and ear rubs.

The shades had been drawn, and the room was cool, with the slightest bit of light filtering through. Charlotte raised her head and stretched, which signaled the pups to vault onto the bed. "Well, good morning!" she gushed. "So nice to see you, too!" She reached for Lady and rubbed her on the head. "Myra, I need to get a dog."

Myra chuckled. "Excellent idea. But for now — if you're ready — Charles will have breakfast on the table in about thirty minutes."

Charlotte peeked across the room and looked in the large mirror on the opposite wall. "Oh dear Lord! I'm a mess! I can't leave the room like this!" She was half serious.

"Nonsense. I'll get you a headband while you put on some clothes. I made an appointment for you to get a massage, hair, manicure, and facial. I know how grueling those transatlantic flights are."

Charlotte checked the dial on the clock. "That's wonderful. But it's only seven fifteen. How did you manage it at this early hour?"

Myra made a tsk-tsk sound. "Darling, must you ask? Your appointment isn't until eleven. They will serve you a light lunch between the facial and the hair appointment."

Charlotte rubbed her eyes. "Seriously?"

"Would I kid you?" Myra said solemnly.

"You are too good to me!" Charlotte launched herself out of bed and gave Myra a big hug.

"My pleasure, my dear. You get yourself tidied up, and I'll bring you a headband. What color are you wearing?"

Charlotte looked around the room. "Gee, I have no idea."

"Did you bring a tracksuit? Something comfortable?"

"That's pretty much what I live in when I'm home." Charlotte's face brightened.

"Well, you should feel right at home here. So, what color are you wearing?" Myra asked again.

"Navy."

"Righto. I'll be back in a few." Myra turned and was surprised that neither of the dogs moved. "They hardly ever cheat on me." She laughed and snapped her fingers, and the dogs hoisted themselves off the bed and followed Myra to her suite to retrieve a headband for Charlotte.

Good, she thought to herself. *That will give us several hours for our meeting and any other business we need to conduct today.*

Chapter 9

London

Dr. Julian Marcus paced the floor of his office, perspiration streaming down his cheek. "Where the hell is that damn boy!" He was close to bellowing but caught himself. No need to alarm the nurse and receptionist. He checked his Rolex again. *Damn.* It had been an hour. *Where the hell is he?* The sound of the phone intercom made him jump so high, he almost wet his pants. More sweat ran down his face. He pulled out a crisp linen handkerchief from his pocket and patted his forehead.

With shaking hands, he took in a deep breath to steady his voice and pressed the intercom button. "Yes, Gloria?" he politely asked the receptionist.

"It's your coffee, sir." Gloria made a face at Dr. Marcus's nurse, who was standing next to her. She could never understand why the doctor did not drink the coffee in the office. It was a Nespresso, for heaven's sake. But he insisted on a special blend that one of the Turkish cafés served.

"Send him in," Marcus barked.

"Yes, sir." Gloria pushed the quiet buzzer that opened the plate-glass door that led to the private office and patient rooms. She pointed to the skinny twentysomething and jerked her thumb in the direction of the doctor's private office. "You know where to go."

Without any acknowledgment, the pimply-faced, grubby excuse of a youth whizzed past her.

"That guy gives me the creeps," Gloria snarled. "I wouldn't drink a cup of coffee that bloke brought me if you gave me a hundred quid."

The nurse nodded in agreement and shrugged, and the two of them went back to work.

Marcus tried to keep himself calm. He did not want to ruin the arrangement he had with Jerry's employer, Francis (Franny) O'Rourke. Franny didn't consider himself a drug dealer. He thought of himself more as a concierge. He "procured" special orders for the very rich and upwardly mobile pseudosocial elite: famous and not-so-famous musicians, artists, fashion designers, and models. He maintained a network of drug dealers. Whether it was weed, hashish, cocaine, heroin, fentanyl, opioids, or acid, Franny O'Rourke was your one-stop-shopping provider of mind-altering enhancements. He charged a "finder's fee" of 25 percent, but it was worth it to most of his clientele. Except Marcus. The fee was rather steep, and his habit was increasing.

Marcus handed over the envelope with the cash. "Why the pressure?" he coolly asked.

"No pressure, mate. Just doin' what I'm told." Jerry shuffled his feet.

"I believe you have something for me?" Marcus was not in the mood for games.

"Oh yeah, that. Franny says no dice until you pay up." The kid wiped his sniveling nose with his ragged sleeve.

Marcus thought his head was going to explode. "We had a deal, damn it."

"Maybe you and Franny did, but it seems like one of you queered the deal. Like I says, doin' my job." Jerry was squirmy, and it made Marcus uncomfortable. One never knew what a drug addict would do. And of all people, Marcus should know.

Trying to think quickly, Marcus suggested, "What if I get something better than cash?"

"What? Are you daft? Nothin' is better

than cash."

"Ask Franny if he'll take the dosh in diamonds." Marcus knew he could pinch one of his wife's diamond earrings without her ever knowing. Her collection would make Harry Winston blush.

"Eh, I dunno 'bout that, mate." Jerry continued to shuffle his feet. He wiggled as if he had ants-in-pants syndrome.

Marcus tossed his cell phone to Jerry. "Buzz him. Text him. Do whatever. And make it snappy. I don't want those nosy biddies out there wondering what's taking you so long to deliver a coffee."

"All right . . . all right. But I'm using my phone. I don't want him freakin' out from some odd phone number showing up on his mobile. Private, ye know."

"For cripes' sake. Get on with it, damn you." Marcus felt as if there were steam coming out of his ears.

Jerry punched in a few numbers. "Yeah, it's me. So I'm with the doc, and he wants to trade with diamonds." Jerry pulled the phone away from his ear because of the yelling on the other end.

" 'At's what he said. Diamonds." Jerry shrugged at Marcus and handed him the phone.

"What's this? Diamonds?" The voice from

70

the other end was cold but intrigued.

"Yes. I can get you the equivalent of what I owe you later this afternoon." Marcus puffed up his chest, feeling a win coming on. A moment later, he handed the phone back to Jerry.

"Franny? Yeah? Well, all right." Looking at Marcus, Jerry repeated what he had heard. "Five o'clock?"

Marcus nodded in agreement.

"Right you are." He hit END and turned to Marcus. "I'll be back at five." Then he slouched out the door.

Marcus checked his watch again. Norma would be at her club for at least another hour. Depending on when the ladies started drinking, it could be much longer. Pressing the intercom button, he said softly but firmly to Gloria, "I'll be back in an hour."

"But, sir, you have two patients waiting." She rolled her eyes at the nurse.

"Tell them I have an emergency. They can either wait or reschedule." He grabbed his Stetson, raincoat, and umbrella and moved quickly out the back entrance.

Gloria looked over at the two women sitting in the sparse waiting area. "I'm terribly sorry, but Dr. Marcus had an emergency. He'll be back in an hour, or you can reschedule."

The women looked at each other. One got up and left; the other stayed to wait. Both were supposed to be new patients. Patients for the Live-Life-Long trials. Even if Marcus knew he was possibly walking away from another pool of money, his fix was of the utmost importance. There would always be another dupe in search of a miracle rejuvenation.

CHAPTER 10

Pinewood

Myra arranged for Edward to drive Charlotte to the spa. He was to phone Myra when Charlotte was finished and heading back to the farm. Myra gave Charlotte a big hug. "Enjoy your respite, my dear. We'll have tea when you get back."

"You are truly spoiling me." Charlotte already had a glow about her.

As soon as the car passed through the iron gates that protected the property, Myra made a dash to Charlotte's room to check her medication bottles. She pulled out a dozen Ziploc bags, a marker, and a pad of Post-it notes from her pocket. She wrote the names of the medications, the dosage, and the frequency for each and took one pill from each bottle. Nikki and Alexis's law firm used a special lab when they needed to double-check toxicology reports for some of their criminal defense cases. The lab was very discreet and got paid well for its services.

Myra heard the dogs yapping as cars pulled into the driveway. Alexis, Nikki, and Maggie had arrived, followed by Yoko and Isabelle. Kathryn was scheduled to haul something or other to North Carolina and would catch up with them later.

Annie was in the kitchen, inspecting the lunch Charles had prepared: grilled salmon with wilted greens. Simple. Dinner would be a different story.

Hugs all around, lots of dog petting, and the women marched into the kitchen to fix their own plates. Sitting around the large wood-planked kitchen table, which overlooked the terrace, they spoke about some of the more interesting things happening in the world and their lives. Yoko was providing the plants for the landscaper working on the latest building complex Isabelle had designed; Isabelle was continuing to hone her hacking abilities, though she knew she would never be as good as Abner; Maggie was investigating the latest administration scandal while juggling the daily crush of political news; and Alexis and Nikki had just finished suing a fast-food chain for a pattern of discrimination against African Americans. With no big cases on their plate, it was a good time for them to catch up on paperwork. All in all, their lives were moving at an abnormally normal pace. But they knew all that was about to change.

After finishing up their lunch, the girls took their plates to the counter, scraped any leftovers into a bowl, and placed them in the dishwasher. They all had their own assignments, and the kitchen was spick and span in thirteen minutes.

They descended the dimly lit stone steps, entered the war room, and saluted Lady Justice.

Myra began the meeting. "As you know, Charlotte is visiting us for a stay of indeterminate length. Part of the reason, actually most of the reason, is that I received a very disturbing letter from her a little over a week ago. She had been feeling 'foggy,' as she put it, and lethargic, almost depressed. She was seeing a doctor in Aspen who runs a clinic called Live-Life-Long. A Dr. Harold Steinwood. Evidently, he and two other doctors run similar clinics, and when Charlotte told Steinwood she was going to London, he insisted she see one of his partners, Dr. Julian Marcus —"

"Live-Life-Long?" Maggie interrupted.

"Yes. You've heard of them?"

"About a year ago, a woman in Sagaponack, New York, who had been in their program, died of an overdose. Another woman outside Aspen went into convulsions and slipped into a coma, but no evidence connecting the treatment to the convulsions could be found. And as far as the overdose is concerned, they believe that the woman took it deliberately, that she committed suicide. Family said she had been despondent."

"Was there a suicide note?" Alexis asked.

"Yes. A scrawled note that said, 'I can't do it anymore.' They also found high levels of phenobarbital in her system. The odd thing was that she had no prescription for it, so they don't know where it came from. I looked into it briefly but couldn't come up with any evidence that would prove the clinic culpable," Maggie explained.

"Well, that's very interesting. And disconcerting. Nikki did a little research on the three doctors." Myra nodded toward Nikki.

Nikki said, "They all attended Ross University in Barbados."

Myra quickly shot a look at Annie, who was going to burst out laughing. She couldn't get past "Joe's School of Dentistry."

Alexis took over. "They also applied to attend Lausanne, in Switzerland, but that was ten years later. There doesn't seem to be any record of their graduating or even attending."

Annie broke in. "This is why we're here today. We want to get to the bottom of this 'miracle cure' they talk about on their website. They offer alternative solutions for aging, memory loss, and so on. They provide videos on living life well and long, which offer nothing more than commonsense advice. But they offer to customize a program for each individual. They don't post any of their fees, and each patient is told that she will get a plan designed for her particular needs. I say 'she' and 'her' because virtually all their patients are women, usually wealthy widows. I am sure they charge exorbitant fees, and their testimonials could very well be faked. You know how Amazon has 'verified purchase' after a review? Well, Live-Life-Long can claim to verify reviews as coming from someone who has utilized their services since they are the only providers of this program."

"Wow. Sounds like a real scam," Isabelle observed.

They all nodded in agreement.

"I took one pill from each of the bottles Charlotte brought with her." Myra produced the bags and the information she had copied. "I want to get these tested to find out exactly what each pill is. Nikki, can you get these to the lab you and Alexis use?"

"Absolutely."

"I know our practice is to take a vote, so I am asking, who is in favor of looking into this?"

Everyone voted in the affirmative.

"In her letter, Charlotte mentioned getting an injection every week, but she didn't say what it was or what it was for. The only other evidence we are missing is what they were injecting," Myra noted.

"If we can get her DNA, we can send it to the lab, as well. It's not as good as a blood test, but it might give us some clue," Alexis observed.

"I was going to suggest that she make an appointment with our physician since she has been feeling so poorly." Myra looked at Charles. "But I don't know if she would want to do that. I guess I can approach her when she gets back from the spa."

"And I will catch her DNA from her cup when we have tea this afternoon," Charles offered.

Annie pulled out a sheet of paper. "Okay, this is what we are going to need. First, more background on Live-Life-Long. Articles of incorporation, holdings, assets . . .

Nikki and Alexis. Second, dossiers on Marcus, Steinwood, and Corbett . . . Fergus and Charles. Third, a DNA sample . . . Charles. Fourth, lab tests of meds . . . Nikki and Alexis. Depending on what they find, we will decide what strategy to adopt. But first, we need to know what we are dealing with."

The group nodded in agreement.

"Okay, ladies. We will meet back here in three days, if not sooner," Myra said.

High fives all around. As the meeting broke up, each of the sisters saluted Lady Justice.

CHAPTER 11

Aspen

Dr. Harold Steinwood flipped through the latest Maserati brochure. It would be part of his growing collection of high-end sports cars. The Lamborghini Aventador model was still out of reach. Yes, $417,000 would be a big chunk, even if it was not as much as the two-million-dollar Bugatti some comedian had bought, decided New York City was a good place to go for a spin, and wound up rear-ended by someone driving a Honda. Why would anyone take a car like that onto the streets of New York City? Idiot. The repair work, the good doctor understood, was going to cost over two hundred thousand dollars.

Harold Steinwood had no desire to flaunt his vehicles, and for the present, he was satisfied with his assortment of cars: a Jaguar XJ, which was what he drove most of the time; a Porsche 911; a Lamborghini

Gallardo; a Bentley Flying Spur; an Aston Martin Rapide S; and soon, a new Maserati. None would ever leave their garage/showroom on his property just outside Aspen. Yes, this new one would be custom built. A Maserati GranTurismo MC, 454 horsepower. That would bring the value of his current collection to almost two million dollars. Not a bad hobby to have. If this year yielded as much profit as last, he would put the Ferrari 488 on his wish list, too.

When the phone rang, he looked at his watch. Who would be calling at seven in the morning?

"Yeah?" Steinwood answered.

"Marcus here. That Charlotte Hansen patient of yours got away from me."

"What do you mean, got away from you? How? Where?" Steinwood was confused.

"She left London. Went to visit some friends on her way home."

"So, what's the problem?"

"It's an extended stay with the friends. I have no idea when she is going to get back to Aspen, and she left without finishing her program. That's almost twenty-five thousand dollars down the drain," Marcus said.

Steinwood was still distracted by the glossy brochure of his soon-to-be new automobile. "Well, Julian, old boy, you are going to have to come up with a solution, or at least your contribution to the till." As far as Steinwood was concerned, Charlotte Hansen was Marcus's problem. Each of them had to pay a fee into the kitty, which was reinvested in the company and used for, among other things, slick office spaces, although Marcus's in London was far more modest than those of his American partners. Londoners were not as impressed with glam and glitter as were Americans.

"Yeah, I know that, but I'm a bit strapped at the moment." Marcus was starting to sweat again. He knew his partners would not tolerate being shorted any more than Franny O'Rourke had.

"What do you mean, strapped? You pulled in over a quarter mil during the past three months. And that was *your* share!" Steinwood was getting impatient with Marcus.

"Yeah, I know. It's my wife. She keeps spending money on all sorts of things." Marcus knew that was only half the problem. His little hobby of snorting cocaine was the other half.

"Well, just don't give her any," Steinwood admonished him.

"That's just it. She keeps the house accounts, and I just get the bills." Now Marcus was whining.

82

"So close the accounts."

"She'd kill me. It's her way of showing off to her friends. They go out to lunch several times a week and order bottles of Dom Pérignon!" More whining.

"Marcus, not to sound rude, but your wife is *your* problem, not mine. Rein her in. I've gotta go." Steinwood was about to hang up when he realized they had not settled the Charlotte Hansen issue. "Now what are we going to do to get Charlotte Hansen back into the program?"

"I was hoping you could help me out there, buddy."

"And how do you propose I do that?" Steinwood had a modicum more tolerance for Marcus's high-strung disposition than Corbett did.

"What if you call her daughter here in London and tell her you are going on vacation and that you want to be sure you see her before you leave?" Marcus was close to begging.

"How is that going to help?"

"I figure at least we'd have some idea when she is going to go to Aspen or return to London." There was desperation in Marcus's voice.

"I'm sure you want her to return to London so you can get your twenty-five grand, correct?" Steinwood had the feeling that he was being played.

"That would be just jolly, old sport."

Steinwood heaved a big sigh. "Okay, I'll call the daughter when I get to the office. I have her contact information there."

"Spectacular!" Marcus was feeling slightly optimistic. Just slightly.

After returning his gaze to his brochure, Steinwood gave his phone a sideways look and hit the END CALL button. He'd deal with the daughter in a little while. Meanwhile, he needed to choose an interior finish for the custom-made car he was ordering.

Back in London, Marcus hurried to his apartment to grab a pair of his wife's earrings from the safe in her dressing room. No, not a pair. Just one. This way she'd think she lost it somewhere. He pressed the buttons on his wife's jewelry safe. The whirring sound stopped as the locks moved into place. Marcus heaved the heavy door open and spotted the drawer where his wife kept her diamond stud earrings. She must have had a dozen pairs of all cuts and carats. She'd never notice one missing. Marcus took a step back and gave the bounty of jewelry a good hard look.

"There must be over a half million dollars' worth in here. Probably more," he muttered out loud. He gave a sigh of relief. "I could easily nick enough to pay the partners if that roving Hansen woman doesn't return." It didn't seem fair, though. She would be going back to Aspen, which meant that Steinwood would get the money that should be his. He hoped Steinwood could persuade Charlotte to return to London. Maybe through her daughter. Didn't parents always want to please their children?

He wrapped the diamond in a fresh handkerchief. The one in his pocket was sopping from having to mop his brow repeatedly. Then something struck him as odd. He had stopped sweating as soon as he opened the safe. He smirked. "Diamonds are not only a girl's best friend. They are at the top of my list right now." A sense of excitement came over him. In just a few hours, he would have what he had been craving all day and would settle his debt with that damned Franny O'Rourke to boot.

After Steinwood hung up the phone, he wondered what could have accounted for the panic in Marcus's voice. *Twenty-five grand is a lot of money to lay out if you don't have it coming in. Poor schmuck,* he thought to himself. *That wife of his is going to be the death of him.*

Steinwood and Corbett knew that the gravy train was going to come to an end soon. They had skated through the two mishaps: Lorraine Thompson's overdose and Marjorie Brewster's coma in Aspen. Three of Steinwood's patients had threatened to bring malpractice suits after spending hundreds of thousands of dollars each and being no better off than before the treatment began. He had politely reminded them of the waiver and nondisclosure agreement they had signed. Ironclad. As long as nobody died. But that was a problem. Because somebody had died. And someone from *Natural Way Magazine* was breathing down Corbett's neck for an interview. The one thing they did not need was publicity, since they were practicing medicine without a license, a fact that too much transparency might bring to light.

Live-Life-Long managed its reputation through false advertising and phony review websites and blogs. Yes. It was definitely time to convene a meeting with his partners and develop a strategy for exiting the healthcare profession unscathed. He snickered at the words *health care.* As applied to their work, an oxymoron at the very least.

86

CHAPTER 12

Pinewood

When Charlotte finished her spa visit, she felt like she was walking on air. She couldn't remember the last time she had felt so rejuvenated, including the time after getting her shots from Drs. Steinwood and Marcus. She was beginning to question her judgment. Maybe their longevity program wasn't right for her. She decided to discuss it with Myra. Myra was always so wise about things like this, and if necessary, Charles could provide information about the program and the doctors. Yes. She was going to talk about her "condition." Whatever the heck her "condition" was.

The sleek town car pulled through the gates at the entrance to the farm. Charlotte was almost giddy at the thought of spilling her guts to Myra. The driver opened the passenger door and helped her out of the backseat. She reached over for the beautiful package wrapped in white linen, adorned by an equally beautiful orchid. It was a box of Myra's favorite white chocolate. Charlotte was so pleased that the spa was only a few doors from the chocolatier. Even though candy was the source of Myra's fortune, the little shop was owned by a French couple who made the most divine white chocolate. For years, Myra had tried to get her kitchen crew to replicate the taste, all to no avail. Charles had once whispered in her ear, "My dear, sometimes a little mystery can be exciting." Charles would occasionally use that phrase, which always made Myra blush with delight. Charlotte knew Myra would protest, but Charlotte was determined to show her appreciation for all the attention and care she was being shown.

Edward, the driver, tipped his hat and walked Charlotte to the front door. Rarely did anyone come through the main entrance. The sisters always used the kitchen. As the door swung open, Charlotte was greeted by all five dogs yapping in anticipation of pats and snuggles. "Oh my goodness!" Charlotte said gleefully. "I don't have enough arms!" She handed the box to Charles as he tried to round up the pups. Charlotte squatted and sat on the floor, then let the dogs climb all over her. She cackled with glee.

Charles was very pleased to see Myra's friend in such a good mood. She seemed almost euphoric.

"I thought I heard laughter and yapping," Myra said, entering the foyer with a huge grin on her face. She, too, was thrilled to see Charlotte in such a joyful mood. *Maybe this is the time to start prying for information,* she thought. *Well, not right now, but soon. Perhaps during tea.* Myra smiled to herself. *Charles will serve a nice glass of sherry, which should put Charlotte into a state of complete relaxation. Not that she could get any more relaxed without passing out.*

Addressing the pooches, Myra announced, "Okay, girls. Let Charlotte get her bearings so we can have tea." As if the dogs understood English, they all rolled over, vaulted up, and sat in a straight line.

Charlotte was dumbfounded. "How in the . . . ?"

"It's the 'Okay, girls' command," Charles interjected. "They also know they will get a t-r-e-a-t." Though Charles had spelled it out, the dogs knew exactly what he meant, and tails were wagging as if to the beat of a drum. "And they can spell."

Everyone roared with laughter, causing the dogs to yip and yap some more.

"Come," Myra said, helping Charlotte up off the floor. "Do you want to change your clothes, or are you comfortable?"

"If I were more comfortable, I would be a muddle of mush!" Charlotte said happily. She linked arms with Myra as she was led to the small atrium adjacent to the kitchen. "Oh, this is lovely. I don't remember seeing it last night." Charlotte took in the expansive view of the outdoor garden area. With its floor-to-ceiling glass walls, the atrium seemed to float through to the terrace.

Myra placed her hand on Charlotte's arm. "There was a lot going on here last night. And you were a bit jet lagged."

"Is it new?"

"You know how much I love my gardens. Well, one winter, Charles and Fergus surprised me by building this space. It brings the outdoors in, and I can have my tea out here all year long," Myra explained.

Charles continued with the explanation, leaving out the part about the sisters being on the lam. "Myra had been under a lot of pressure and had been away. I wanted to create a space for her to unwind. Yoko provides the interior landscaping as well as the exterior."

"It's a little slice of heaven," Charlotte remarked, in awe.

"Come and sit." Myra gestured to the table, loaded with a bounty of scones, fruit, finger sandwiches, and small cakes. Charles pulled out a chair for Charlotte and one for Myra and they both sat down.

"I could get used to this." Charlotte beamed.

Charles took Myra's hand and gave it a quick peck. "I will leave you lovely women to chat. I have some items I need to work on. Not the least of which is dinner."

Charlotte let out a pleasant groan. "Dinner? After all this?" She swept her hand across the bounty of their high tea.

"This is just to hold you over." Myra chuckled. "Charles, what is on the menu?"

As Charles was exiting, he replied over his shoulder, "Oven-roasted branzino with a rice pilaf and asparagus. We'll start with a Bibb lettuce salad with toasted almonds in a raspberry vinaigrette dressing." Charles ticked off the details as if he were the maître d' at a five-star restaurant.

"No head, please?" Charlotte was almost begging, knowing branzino was often served whole.

Myra patted her hand. "Not to worry. Charles fillets it for us. No head. No bones."

Charlotte relaxed back in her chair. "Will the girls be joining us?"

"Just Annie and Fergus. Nikki has some work to catch up on and wants to do some FaceTime with Jack, who is out of town just now. There are certain technologies I'm not crazy about, but that one seems to be something they enjoy when they're apart. It keeps them 'connected,' as Nikki would say. An electronic tether." Both women giggled. "The rest of the girls are all working on various projects." Myra was not about to reveal the true nature of those projects.

Charles returned briefly and poured each of the women a glass of sherry and served it on a silver tray, bowed, and left them alone to chat.

"So, dear, how are you feeling?" Myra said, changing the subject.

"Honestly, I haven't felt this good in quite a while. This clear. This calm. Must be the way you're spoiling me." Charlotte almost started to blush.

"I'm very happy to hear this. But you know, I insist on spoiling you." Myra gave Charlotte another reassuring pat. "So, tell me, who is that Dr. Marcus you were seeing in London? What was he treating you for?" Enough time had passed, and Myra had to start digging for more information.

"It's almost embarrassing to talk about." Charlotte sighed.

"Don't be silly. We're friends. You can tell me anything," Myra reassured her again.

Charlotte took a deep breath. "About a year ago, I was feeling, I guess you could say depressed. Not suicidal or anything like that. I was just lethargic and apathetic. Then I started to have problems remembering things. You know, can't find the keys. Why did I just go into the kitchen? My mind was wandering, I suppose, but it was starting to bother me a lot. All those things combined led me to think that I should see a doctor.

"My personal physician was retiring and had sold his practice to a Dr. Harold Steinwood. But Dr. Steinwood, it seemed, was a geriatrician and changed the practice to focus on aging. It's called Live-Life-Long. I thought, 'Well, that sounds like it's exactly what I need,' so I went to see him. He did the normal tests, EKG, blood work, urine, the whole nine yards. He said he and two other doctors, one in New York and one in London, had a joint practice specializing in longevity. The only problem is that the fees are not covered by Medicare or any other insurance. Apparently, it's too experimental to be covered. So if you agree to be enrolled in the program, you have to sign a release or waiver before you can be admitted. And an NDA."

Myra frowned. "No insurance? A release? A nondisclosure agreement?"

"Yes. He said it's done all the time because it takes so long before certain protocols are approved by the FDA. They have great reviews. Anyway, as I mentioned briefly in my letter, he set up a program for me in which I get a shot every week and take several different pills throughout the day." Charlotte paused to take a sip of her tea as she eyed the glass of sherry.

"What kind of shot? And what kind of pills?" Myra knew she would have the answer to one of those questions in a day or so, but she didn't want Charlotte to know she had been spying on her.

"Some kind of vitamin shot, and the pills are natural remedies for brain function, lungs, kidneys, and circulation. He gave me a personalized brochure with the information and instructions."

"Do you have it with you?" Myra asked.

"No. It's back in Aspen. The thing is, when I get the shot, I feel good for about two to three days. The pills don't seem to be doing much for my cognitive abilities, though. In fact, sometimes I think things get worse between shots."

"And how long have you been in this program?"

Charlotte thought a moment. "About four months. They say it takes about six months for the results to kick in."

Myra was pleased at the direction the conversation was going. She gestured to the sherry, hoping it would loosen Charlotte up even more. The need for information was urgent.

"What does he charge, if you don't mind my asking?" Myra was gentle with her prodding.

"It's been running about twenty-five thousand dollars a month." Suddenly, Charlotte looked a little sheepish, anticipating Myra's reaction.

Myra somehow managed to remain calm, but her blood was boiling. "That's a lot of money, dear. Especially if you're not feeling better. What is the time frame for this protocol? Months? Indefinitely?"

"I'm supposed to get a blood workup after six months, which is why he insisted I see Dr. Marcus in London. Not to lose the benefits of the treatment and invalidate the results, as he said."

"And then what?" Myra was still holding her temper. She wanted to strangle Steinwood, Marcus, and the other dirtbag partner. But their time would come. And very soon if the sisters had anything to do with it.

"I guess they'll make an evaluation and decide what, if anything, I need to do. But to be perfectly honest, I feel better now than I did while I was taking those pills. I haven't had a shot, either." Charlotte had a perplexed look on her face.

Seizing the moment, Myra offered the suggestion she had been waiting for an opportunity to make. "You stopped the pills? How about this? I'll make an appointment with my doctor and have him do a full workup. I trust him completely."

"Oh, I don't know, Myra. Isn't that a bit extreme?"

"Considering you have spent over one hundred thousand dollars and are not feeling better, I think it only stands to reason that you get another physician to consider your condition and give you a second opinion. And now you tell me you've been feeling better after you stopped? I won't hear another word of protest. I am going to call him right now. You sit tight and enjoy the scones. Charles made them while you were out. I'll be right back." Myra leaped from her chair and made a controlled dash into the kitchen and down the stairs to the war room.

After saluting Lady Justice, Myra came up behind Charles to see what he was looking at on his monitor.

Charles growled at what he was reading. It was news from Avery Snowden. On the other hand, Myra was jubilant because she had convinced Charlotte to see a doctor.

Both started to talk at the same time and then laughed at each other's excitement and agitation.

"You go first, dear." Charles smiled at her.

Myra took in a deep breath. "I got a good deal of information from Charlotte. She has been seeing Steinwood for four months, to the tune of twenty-five thousand a month!"

Charles snickered. "Yes, according to Avery, that seems to be the going rate for this 'sustaining your youth program.' " Charles accentuated the term with air quotes. "That is one of their taglines, by the way."

"Well, Charlotte has agreed to see Dr. Falcon for a complete blood workup. I am going to make the appointment right now, before she changes her mind." Myra was almost out of breath.

"Excellent. Snowden is still trying to fill in the ten-year gap between medical school and what seems to be a bogus application to the school in Switzerland." Charles hit a few buttons so the information would come up on all the monitors hanging on the wall.

"This is all very suspicious indeed." Myra shot him a look. "Have you heard from the others yet?"

"I think we'll be able to move up our meeting to tomorrow. If you can get Charlotte her appointment with the doctor, that will give us some time to review everyone's information."

"I'm on it." Myra winked, pulled out her phone, and punched in the private number of her physician. "Gerald? How are you? I'm fine. No, not an emergency exactly, but I have a friend who needs a physical exam and a complete blood workup." Myra explained to Dr. Gerald Falcon everything Charlotte had conveyed. "Would tomorrow be possible?" Myra nodded at Charles. "Nine? Perfect. How long do you think she will be?" Myra listened and gave Charles the thumbs-up. "Two hours. Excellent. Yes, I will tell her not to eat anything. You will? That would be wonderful. Thank you so very much." A high five, another salute to Lady Justice, and Myra was taking the steps two at a time.

Slowing down as she approached Charlotte, she spoke evenly. "Okay, my dear. We are in luck. Dr. Falcon can see you tomorrow at nine o'clock. You're going to have to fast, but Dr. Falcon's nurse will get you a sandwich afterward. They have a lovely garden, and you can have your lunch while you're waiting for the test results to become available."

"Oh, Myra, I don't want to put you out. I am sure you have plenty of other things to do besides carting me around."

"Don't be silly. I'll have Edward take you and bring you back. Dr. Falcon said to plan on staying for about two hours. There. Easy." Myra gave her a reassuring smile.

Charlotte stood and hugged Myra. "What would I do without you?"

After spending time chatting about Liam, Myra suggested that Charlotte take a nap. Dinner wouldn't be served for another three hours, and the massage was finally having its effect on Charlotte.

"Wonderful idea. I didn't want to be rude, but a nap sounds divine." The women rose from the table, and Myra walked Charlotte back to her room, followed by all five dogs. Myra pulled the drapes closed and turned down the temperature. She wanted Charlotte to have a long, restful, uninterrupted sleep while she phoned the sisters and made plans for the following day's meeting.

Satisfied that her friend had settled in,

Myra quickly moved through the house and down the steps. First, she phoned Annie. "Wait until you hear what I have to tell you!"

CHAPTER 13

The next morning Myra, Charles, and Charlotte were sitting at the long kitchen table. "Edward should be pulling up shortly," Charles announced. The girls would be arriving very soon, and neither Myra nor Charles wanted Charlotte to know there was something stirring, what with people coming and going at all times of the day. At least not until it became necessary.

Edward appeared at the front door of the farmhouse just as Annie and Fergus pulled the golf cart around to the kitchen door. It was often their mode of transportation between Annie's and Myra's. There were always at least two golf carts available to anyone at either of the homes. It was easier than pulling the cars around. And it was private. No one could see them moving about the vast properties. The same was true at Nikki and Jack's. They also kept golf carts on the premises. Sometimes there was a real "need for speed." However, it seemed like the "need for speed" always applied to whatever Annie was doing. She could take a curve on two wheels, much to Myra's chagrin. And riding in a car she was driving on the highway was invariably a white-knuckle adventure.

Edward whisked Charlotte away just minutes before the sisters arrived. After entering the house from the kitchen, they greeted one another with hugs and kisses, doled out dog snuggles, and distributed dog treats. Then the sisters marched down the stone steps to the war room, where they would direct the effort to uncover the doctors' schemes and would plan a mission to bring the unscrupulous practices of Live-Life-Long to an end and punish their perpetrators. And it would not be much longer if the sisters had anything to say or do about it.

After saluting Lady Justice as they entered, the seven women, Charles, and Fergus took their seats.

Myra began with the information she had gotten from Charlotte as Annie nodded at the hard truth. The women gulped at the amount of money. "Yes, over a hundred thousand dollars." Myra shook her head in dismay. "I wonder how many other people have gone through this." For the moment, that was a rhetorical question. They would find out soon. Whatever it took.

Charles conveyed the information he had received from Avery Snowden. "To recap, three doctors. Each has a practice in a different city. They've been doing this for almost four years. All graduated from Ross University Medical School. Ten years later, they each applied to Lausanne, but there is no record of their actually attending, let alone graduating. Their whereabouts during those missing ten years was something of a mystery, but Snowden was finally able to get a few details. It seems our medical professionals worked for a couple of pharmaceutical companies in Mexico. Interesting fact, twenty of the top twenty-five Big Pharma companies are in Mexico, so with their medical background, it was easy for them to get jobs and blend in. They each worked for Merck, Pfizer, and GSK. What their duties were is still unknown, but I suspect this is when they came up with the idea of Live-Life-Long. They applied to Lausanne when they were in Mexico. They flew to Switzerland for interviews, were accepted, but never attended."

Fergus jumped in. "Evidently, they found

a different way to make a lot of money with little risk. It appears they pinched some stationery from Lausanne and were able to forge diplomas. It was an intricate idea that took them a couple of years to engineer." He could see the sisters' faces grimace in disgust.

"Let's go over the time line again. They graduated from Ross, spent ten years in Mexico, applied to school in Switzerland but didn't go. They formed this medical group, Live-Life-Long, and spread out. Steinwood went to Aspen, Corbett to New York, and Marcus to London. We're still looking into where they bank. Their website is very slick. It features a virtual tour of the facilities and montages of older adults frolicking on the beach, riding bicycles, hiking. All very, very robust. And everyone is smiling or laughing. They did a spectacular job with their marketing," Maggie said.

Annie, who, as the owner of the *Post,* was Maggie's employer, gave an instruction to Maggie. "Maggie, I think you need to investigate that alleged suicide. I say 'alleged' because something stinks. The scribbled note said, 'I can't do it anymore.' Maybe she wasn't referring to her life. Maybe she was referring to the program. See if you can meet with the family. Tell them you're doing a story about depression in people over fifty. Let's use the word *silvers*. I don't like *elderly* or *seniors*."

"Actually, there is an alarming suicide trend among seniors. Er, I mean silvers," Maggie indicated. "Especially white men over eighty-five. What is even more fascinating is that they have the highest rate of suicide of any other demographic." "Wows" and gasps filled the room. "I will use that as a part of my angle for the story, adding that we are looking to see if there is a similar trend developing in women."

Annie continued, "We'll have to figure out a ruse to get information from the Brewster family about the one who went into a coma after having convulsions."

"When was that?" Alexis asked.

"A couple of months ago."

"Do we have the name of the hospital where she was admitted?" Alexis asked.

"We're working on that," Charles said as he made a few notes.

"Ideas?" Myra addressed her inquiry to the entire group.

Alexis spoke up. "What if Isabelle and I go there and tell them that Countess Anna Ryland de Silva is considering donating a wing? We ask for a tour of the facility, and Isabelle can hack into the system and pull up Brewster's files."

Annie jumped in immediately. "I do not think it's a good idea to use my name. I wouldn't want to go in there with a possible promise and not deliver. It is a hospital, after all. I don't think the hospital can bear any of the blame, unless, of course, they were negligent in some way. We'll have to find out where she was when she started having convulsions. Was she home or already in the hospital?"

"Either way, we're going to have to get her hospital records. We'll have to think of a different pretext. What about saying we're from the Olympic ski team, and we're on a junket, visiting hospitals that deal with a lot of skiing accidents?" Isabelle suggested.

"That could work. We'd have to spring it on them, so they don't have a lot of time to prepare and check into whether you're legitimate or not. Do you think that's possible?" Myra asked.

In unison, the group yelled out, "Anything is possible!" Hoots and fist bumps filled the air. The atmosphere was electric. The pieces were coming together.

Annie started to make a list.

1. Maggie — go to Sagaponack to interview Thompson family.

2. Alexis and Isabelle — go to Aspen to dig up Brewster hospital info.
3. Isabelle, I need you to get a schematic of the London offices. Can you do that before you go to Aspen?

"Shouldn't be a problem. I have a friend in London who was in several of my architectural design classes. We keep in touch. I'll reach out to him. The other offices should be rather easy. All plans have to be filed with the local building departments. It just might take a few days to cut through any red tape."

"I know people in the New York City Department of Public Works. If you have any trouble, let me know." Annie had some sort of connection with almost every top official in every major metropolitan area in the country. Probably in the free world. "If necessary, I can go to New York for a visit with the mayor."

"Well, I think you need a travel companion." Myra said that with a stone face. But then she and Annie burst into laughter.

Charles and Fergus gave each other the "Uh-oh, here we go" look.

Annie continued. "Okay. Number four. Myra and Annie go to New York. We still need a lot more background information about these three men. What do they do in their spare time? Where do they go on vacation? Family? Friends?" Annie looked at Fergus.

"On it. I'll have Snowden put some of his people on each of them. They can tail them for a few days. Check their comings, goings, and who they meet with."

"Okay. We're getting somewhere. As soon as Fergus and Charles get us their habits and haunts, we'll go to the respective cities." Annie was bringing the day's meeting to an end.

"What about London?" Nikki asked. "Yoko and I could go."

"Avery is having Eileen, one of his operatives, run it down. How soon do you think we'll have the intel we need to move this further?" Myra asked. "I don't want to disrupt Charlotte's rest and recovery here."

Charles reviewed his notes. "Probably a few days. Perhaps plan your trip in about a week from now. These men can't do that much damage in that short a time. Besides, we need to get the drug analysis back from Nikki's lab as well as the results of Charlotte's blood work. We can't go off half-cocked." He gave Myra an assuring smile. Looking at Yoko and Nikki, he added, "And if you girls need a chaperone, I would be happy to accompany you."

"Charles, do you think that's prudent? You know you would be risking incarceration or worse if you are discovered on British soil." Myra clutched her pearls.

"I'm sure Alexis can suit me up to look like their grandfather." Charles smirked.

"Let's rethink this. Perhaps Annie and I should go to London, and Nikki and Yoko to New York." Myra did not like the idea of Charles treading on unwelcoming soil.

"How about this?" Charles wanted Myra to stop fretting. "We wait for the intel from Avery, then decide who goes where depending on what info we get."

"Charles is right. Like any of our other missions, this must be executed properly," Annie said. Everyone giggled at the word *executed*. "No pun intended, people," she reminded them.

"All right. We do our homework and sit tight until our next meeting. Let's say three days from now. If we get the information beforehand, we can meet sooner," Charles said, bringing the session to a close.

Yes, there was an electrical charge in the air. The sisters were going to bring justice to the innocent people who had given their trust and large sums of money to these despicable creatures.

CHAPTER 14

New York City

Raymond Corbett paced the floor of his Manhattan apartment. He was on the phone with Steinwood. "So, you're telling me that you think Marcus is having a meltdown of some kind?" Corbett wasn't terribly concerned. Marcus had always been a little too high strung and low-brow for his taste. But he did have a good head for chemistry.

Steinwood explained the impending Charlotte Hansen debacle and how desperate Marcus had sounded.

"He never should have married that trollop of a gold digger." Corbett was picking out cuff links for his lunch with a possible investor. He was already thinking ahead about what he would do once Live-Life-Long had gone out of business. Corbett was of the opinion that the burgeoning industry of CBD oil was a good place to start. He could convert their "cooker" into a grow house.

The "cooker" was an abandoned warehouse in a remote area in Michigan, close to the Canadian border. It was where the doctors made the synthetic phenobarbital and Adderall they "prescribed" to their patients. They had hired several locals who either were ex-felons or were subject to arrest for some crime or other. All of them were happy to be getting paid cash under the table. And lots of it.

The bottles looked exactly like something from a pharmacy, but they were green instead of brown. The color had been chosen to give the illusion that the contents were natural. The labeling was a bunch of gibberish listing several herbs and roots. Unless someone tested the pills, no one would be the wiser. No one had questioned them. Ever. Even the workers weren't exactly sure what was going into the bottles. As long as they got their seven hundred dollars a week in nice crisp hundred-dollar bills, they were happy to fill the green bottles. That kind of money, plus whatever some of them were getting from the government, went a very long way in that remote and economically distressed section of the state.

"Raymond? Are you listening?" Steinwood barked.

"Yes, of course. So what do you propose to do about it?" Corbett refocused on their conversation. His mind had been wandering from CBD oil to his upcoming lunch at San Pietro.

"I told Marcus I'd talk to the daughter. Maybe she can convince her mother to go back to London. Marcus sounded quite desperate about the money. I told him to take away the wife's credit cards, but I think she has a finger up his nose."

"Huh. Maybe that's not the only thing that's up his nose. Remember, he had a bit of a problem when we were, *ahem,* between careers." Corbett continued to dress, deciding which to wear from an array of ties.

"He's been clean for several years. I can't imagine him going back to snorting coke. It almost killed him," Steinwood remarked.

"Indeed. He does have access to our inventory, but then he would have to pay or replace the goods, and at our list price. He's a big boy. I'm sure he'll figure out his finances. Look, I have to jump. Lunch at San Pietro. Good luck with the daughter. Ciao!" Corbett ended the call, fixed his tie, and donned the matching jacket to his wool-and-silk Canali suit.

Taking one last look in the mirror, he smirked. "Screw all of them," he said to his reflection. He would figure out a way to take control of the cooker. He could probably buy out Marcus's share if Steinwood was right about Marcus's finances, and Steinwood would also take the money. But at the moment he needed to create a strategy to exit Live-Life-Long.

By branching out into related areas, Corbett had parlayed his cut of the business into a very tidy sum of money — the possession of which he had gotten quite used to. It bought him the best tables in the most elite restaurants in New York. Not so much in the Hamptons. There was a level of snobbery from the old-money crowd that seemingly permeated the soil, which used to grow potatoes, and the waters, which had once employed many fishermen. *Who the hell do they think they are?* He would seethe when he did not receive an invitation to someone's private party. It wasn't enough that he paid handsomely to attend various fund-raisers — sometimes in excess of three thousand dollars per person! It infuriated him that he was never on the short list of invitees to the estates of Sagaponack and Water Mill. But this year it was going to be different. He would make one big lasting impression on those boorish old-money snobs, who had finally given him a membership in one of the yacht clubs.

Corbett made his way to the elevator bank and punched DOWN. Before exiting the lobby, he nodded at the doorman, who smoothly opened the door for him. Corbett strutted down Madison Avenue toward his destination, taking time to peer at a leather briefcase in the window of Bottega Veneta. Price tag — thirty-two hundred dollars. He didn't really need one but thought perhaps he should go to his lunch meeting with it. Would make him look business savvy. He glanced at his watch. He had chosen the Raymond Weil Maestro for today. Simple. Elegant. Not over the top. If he stopped in the boutique, he would be late for lunch. Not a good idea. His future was waiting. So were the truffles.

It was almost five o'clock in London, and Marcus was jittery. He kept checking his pocket to make sure the diamond earring was still there. He was feeling desperate. Desperate in a lot of ways. In just the past few months, he had gone through tens of thousands of dollars feeding his cocaine habit. He justified his actions by remembering that his wife went through more money than that on lunches, handbags, shoes, and expensive champagne. Like his partners, he knew that Live-Life-Long was unlikely to be around much longer. How ironic. He and his partners would have to split up, and he had no idea what would come next. Steinwood had family money to fall back on, and Corbett, well, he was just a dick and would finagle something. Corbett also seemed to have made a lot of money over the past few years, beyond what he had earned from the partnership. Leave it to him to grow his cut of the profits into a fortune.

Where is that damn boy? By the time the buzzer finally rang, Marcus was thinking he might crawl out of his own skin. He was drenched in sweat. Again. He reached into his desk for another dry handkerchief. Last one. He had to remind himself to bring more tomorrow.

Marcus gave Jerry a friendly pat on the back. "How was your day?"

Jerry shot him a strange look. "Since when do you give a toss about my day?"

"Aw, c'mon, Jerry. We've known each other a long time. And you had to drag yer arse here twice today." Marcus was being unusually casual with his delivery boy.

"Whatever. Got the gem?"

"Absolutely!" Marcus beamed as he

handed the diamond over to him. "Got my coffee?"

"Here ya go." Jerry dropped the coke packages on the desk. Marcus practically jumped on top of the cocaine, brushing Jerry aside. "Easy, old man. You don't want to be breaking the furniture." Jerry turned and headed out the door.

Marcus shoved his pinkie into one of the bags and pulled out a decent-sized wad under his fingernail. He sounded like a Hoover as he snorted his first hit. More beads of sweat appeared on his forehead. And his hands were still shaking. This was not good. He reiterated to himself that maybe it was time to change it up. Or perhaps change it down. Yes, maybe something to slow him down instead of speeding him up. But what? He didn't fancy shooting himself up with heroin. But maybe he could snort it. He'd give that some thought. For now, he would try to pace himself over the next couple of days. He had no choice. He had only a couple of days' worth of powder, and he couldn't pinch another diamond just yet. He was hanging his hope on Steinwood convincing that stupid woman Charlotte Hansen to return to London and continue her program.

CHAPTER 15

New York City

Avery Snowden had been in counterintelligence for decades. He had met Charles and Fergus several years ago, when MI6 was tracking suspected terrorists in London, assisted by Scotland Yard. It had been a bit tense among the men in the beginning — each trying to be top dog. But after a few clandestine meetings, they had developed the trust of a band of brothers. They'd been able to uncover a plot to strike several soft targets. Thanks to their intel, the raid they devised had gone off without a hitch and resulted in the arrest of half a dozen terrorists. The official record showed the suspects had been convicted and sentenced during a trial that was off-limits to the press and public. They had been transported to an "unknown location" and had never been heard from again. Justice could be sweet.

Avery had got his orders from Charles and

117

had put two of his best shadows on Dr. Corbett and Dr. Marcus. He would handle Dr. Steinwood personally. Eileen was a supersleuth and could plant a bug in the most highly guarded offices and homes. With occasional help from Alexis, master of disguise, Eileen could be anything from a Pakistani cabdriver to a school librarian. She would handle Marcus in London.

Sasha, another longtime operative of Avery's, would handle Corbett. She knew the streets of New York better than most cops in the NYPD. Getting out to Long Island was a piece of cake. She would employ the services of Wings Air, an outfit whose helicopter pilot she knew, intimately. He never questioned Sasha about her work. It was his understanding that she was a photographer for a very high-end private detective agency, the identity of whose clients was confidential. Which, for the most part, had the virtue of being true. Of course, Sasha never mentioned the parts of her activity that would be considered illegal.

Avery would take Steinwood on himself. He tapped out the information and instructions he had on the three men, or "subjects." Each operative would tail her subject for a week and would report to Avery every day. Avery would send their reports, as well as his own, to Charles, who would then share them with the sisters.

Day one was upon them. Dressed like a bike messenger, Sasha waited on the pristine sidewalk in front of Corbett's apartment building. It was one of the very few sidewalks in the city that was clear of all debris, especially dog poop. There were CLEAN UP AFTER YOUR DOG signs everywhere. Most New Yorkers referred to the statute requiring people to clean up after their pooches as the pooper scooper law. She could never understand why someone would want to walk six or seven dogs at a time — which was not uncommon in the posh neighborhood Corbett lived in. *Who in their right mind would want to carry that much dog poop on a hot summer day?* It was a question she had once asked her friend Carlos, who had been walking dogs for years.

"You get paid by the walk. If there are dogs who get along, I walk as many of them as I can. I can clear six or seven hundred dollars a day," he'd told her.

She'd shrugged. People in this part of town spared no expense on anything, and dog walkers were in high demand. Still, carrying bags of poop was not her idea of a good way to make a living. She also thought that having dogs in New York City wasn't fair to the dogs. They needed a yard. A place to run. Not to walk on sidewalks along busy streets, with cars honking, sirens blasting. People were selfish. Sasha was glad her interaction with most of them was from a safe distance.

She pulled her phone out one more time to get a good look at the man she was going to track. Five feet ten inches, medium build, neatly cut brownish hair, impeccable suit, Brooks Brothers trench coat. It looked like rain. She quickly spotted the well-dressed man leaving his apartment building and waited to see if he was going to hail a cab or get in a private car. Neither. He started walking south on Madison Avenue. She'd let him get a block ahead before she began pedaling the bike. His pace began to slow as he neared the Bottega Veneta boutique. He stopped and glanced in the window, then back at his watch, and moved on. Sasha could only imagine the thousands of dollars' worth of merchandise sitting on display. She knew she was going to draw attention to herself if she kept riding her bike like she needed training wheels, so she opted to get off the bike and walk it partway down the street.

Corbett stopped and peeked at the window of the restaurant. He did not do it to see if his lunch date was waiting but to get one more good look at himself. Satisfied with his appearance, he swung the heavy door open and entered. Sasha anticipated that this was going to be a long lunch.

Gerardo, the owner of San Pietro, greeted Corbett in a manner that puffed up his already inflated ego. "*Buongiorno,* Dr. Corbett! So nice to see you! Your guest is already waiting. Follow me." Manolo, the maître d', gave Corbett a modest nod and bow. Yes, Corbett loved the attention. It was going to bode well for his financial prospects.

Gerardo motioned to the table as the guest half stood to shake Corbett's hand.

"I see Gerardo has taken care of the wine. I called ahead to have him choose something I thought would be to your liking."

"It's quite nice." The man twirled the red Sangiovese liquid in the balloon glass. "You seem to be very popular here."

"I try to come here once a week when I'm not out on the island." People in the know understood that "the island" embedded in the phrase "on the island" was Long Island, not Fire Island or Coney Island. Exactly where on the island was usually noted in the next sentence. "In Sag Harbor." God forbid someone thought he lived in Hempstead, where the school system was rife with complaints about misappropriations and where the charges of police corruption had resulted in the chief of police being fired. Of course, his own business was as corrupt as anything that happened in Hempstead. But his corruption swindled only the rich and took private money, not the taxes everyone had to pay. Nor was any violence involved.

"Been out there for a golf outing a few times." The man's name was Leffert, as in one of the biggest tobacco families in the country. Because the market for cigarettes was in decline, tobacco companies were investigating new sources of revenue. The CBD business was a natural for them. "Lovely restaurant, too, by the way." Leffert glanced around the room and recognized the CEO of TD Ameritrade and the CFO of Home Depot. A gathering of the rich and powerful.

Gerardo returned with a glass for Corbett and poured from the $275 bottle of wine. "One of my favorites." Corbett lifted the glass and inspected its contents, swirled it in his mouth, and gave Gerardo a thumbs-up.

Trying to break the ice, Corbett engaged in some informal conversation. Sports mostly. Safe subject, for the most part. Manolo approached the table and began to recite the specials for the day, beginning with appetizers, then moving on to entrées. There had to be a dozen specials, all of which Manolo could articulate from memory. And if you missed any of the scrumptious dishes, he would go over the list again, this time in reverse order. That performance in itself was worth the money it cost to dine there. You could tell this was Manolo's passion. Corbett wondered what his own passion was, besides having prestige and money. After Manolo completed his presentation, he handed them menus, bowed, and returned to his station near the entrance.

"What do you recommend?" Leffert asked, displaying his Southern drawl.

"I usually start with the burrata with prosciutto and figs, then the fettuccine with shaved truffles." It was noted as "market price" on the menu, which meant very expensive.

Leffert perused the menu and motioned for Manolo to return to the table. "Can you fix me a veal chop? Rare?"

Manolo nodded and turned to Corbett.

"I'll have my usual."

Then, turning back to Leffert, Manolo said, "Signore, would you care to start with an appetizer?"

"Caesar salad, please."

"Grazie mille." Once again, Manolo gave a short bow and moved away from the table.

Corbett wondered if he should start the conversation, but Leffert was already there. He lowered his voice and leaned in slightly. "Tell me about this property you have in mind for a grow house."

Corbett almost choked on his expensive Brunello wine. He had not been expecting that question at the beginning of the conversation.

"Ah, yes. As I mentioned in our previous discussion, I became aware of Leffert Industries expanding into the CBD business. I have a very large piece of property in Michigan, not far from the border with Canada. The building is over thirty-six thousand square feet and could easily be converted into a grow house."

"The government isn't making it easy as far as legalization, and we're investing in real estate where growing marijuana is legal," Leffert said matter-of-factly.

"Of course. Very smart move. I am not necessarily looking to sell the property but perhaps to partner with a company looking for the same benefits." Corbett knew he could get a half million for the land and building, but he was looking for something more long range. Something that would keep bringing in the cash.

"I see." Leffert paused. "What kind of partnership did you have in mind?"

"Lease option? Percentage of profits? What exactly are *you* looking for?" Corbett was trying not to be cocky or anxious.

"Can you get me a survey of the property? I'd like to see the location and the schematic for the building."

Corbett thought for a moment. He did not want to reveal the exact location of the cooker. Not just yet. "I can certainly do that." He knew he could stall for a while, but for how long?

Outside the restaurant, Sasha was getting antsy. The men had been in there for two hours. She spotted her reflection coming off the door as the men finally exited the restaurant. She quickly shifted her fanny pack, which held a high-tech camera, in the direction of the men. A few snaps, followed by a backup using her phone. She should have enough images to identify the man with whom Corbett had had lunch. Sasha immediately sent the photos to Avery, jumped on her bike, and began following Corbett again.

This time he stopped and entered Bottega

Veneta. He felt he had earned it. His plan was beginning to take shape.

Within fifteen minutes, Corbett was seen leaving the boutique with a large shopping bag and heading toward his apartment building. Sasha spoke into her recording device. "Subject is returning to apartment after two-hour lunch at San Pietro with person yet to be identified. Photos sent at fourteen hundred hours." Sasha pedaled her way between the cars and settled outside the luxury apartment building, waiting for Corbett's next move.

An hour later, he exited the building, dressed in a pair of khaki slacks, a button-down shirt, and a gray cashmere blazer, carrying his new Bottega Veneta duffel bag. He had opted for the four-thousand-dollar bag instead of the briefcase when he had returned to the store. It was much more practical, he had told himself, and a lot more noticeable. He hailed a cab, and Sasha pedaled toward it, dodging other cyclists, cabs, Ubers, and buses. The taxi made a right turn down Lexington Avenue and pulled over at Fifty-Ninth Street. Corbett got out and got in line for the Hampton Jitney. A young, well-dressed collegiate-looking kid walked up to him. They shook hands and exchanged cordial greetings and eventually swapped manila envelopes. The young man smiled and nodded and waved as he walked away. Corbett put the manila envelope he had been given in his new bag. He found the smell of the Italian leather intoxicating.

Sasha thought it likely that what she had just witnessed was a drug deal, so she took a quick photo of the young man and hit the speed-dial number for her helicopter pilot pal. "Jason? Hey. You busy? Want to give me a lift to East Hampton?"

It would take Corbett almost three hours on the Jitney. The chopper would take thirty minutes. That would give her plenty of time to grab her gear and meet up with Jason. Once they landed, she would rent a car, wait at the Jitney's first stop in Southampton, and follow the luxury bus until Corbett got off.

Just as Avery Snowden landed in Aspen, his phone buzzed. Sasha had sent photos and some info. Avery immediately recognized the mystery man in the photos. It was Carlton Leffert, CEO and part owner of Leffert Industries. *That's odd,* Avery thought to himself. *Why would someone like Leffert be having a very expensive lunch with Corbett? I guess we'll find out.*

Avery unfolded himself from the small passenger plane that had brought him from Denver to Aspen. He really hated bouncing around in those things. It was like being on an amusement-park ride but without the fun. Happy to be on solid ground, he headed to the car-rental kiosk and punched in the membership number he had under the alias of Harry Walters. A set of keys and a contract were delivered by the machine. He picked them up and walked to the rental car. After he was behind the wheel, Avery pulled out a road atlas to get directions. He did not want to put anything into the car's GPS, so he had to rely on good old-fashioned cartography. But that was something all of them were used to doing: keeping the use of technology to a minimum when not in control or in a secure environment.

He found directions to his motel and registered under another assumed name, Walter Harrison. He was beat and hungry. He called Uber Eats and asked them to suggest a place where he could order a BLT and fries. After a long hot shower, he would pull out the maps and plan for the next morning, when he would begin tailing Dr. Harold Steinwood.

Eileen was already in Europe, so she

would arrive in London that same evening. Within the next twenty-four hours, they would have a good idea about the doctors' routines.

CHAPTER 16

Pinewood

Nikki burst through the kitchen door, waving a folder. "This is unbelievable!" The dogs were yapping in response to her brisk entrance. She stopped for a moment and gave each of them the required hug, rub, and scratch.

Myra hurried from the atrium. "What is it? Is everything all right?"

"Where is Charlotte?" Nikki was almost breathless.

"She's at Dr. Falcon's. She's getting a full workup."

"How long has she been off those meds?" Nikki asked as she tossed the folder on the kitchen table.

"Almost two weeks. Why?"

"Some of it is a cytochrome P450 inducer. Also known as phenobarbital — but this is some kind of synthetic version. Other pills were Adderall. And Adderall is in the same

130

class as cocaine and methamphetamine!" You could see the loathing in Nikki's eyes.

"What?" Myra was horrified. She looked as if she was going to start shaking at any moment. Charles came up behind her and put his hand on her shoulder.

"Let me take a look at those lab results." Charles calmly opened the file and began reading. "Turmeric. Ginkgo biloba. CoQ10. Nothing out of the ordinary there. But yes, the phenobarbital seems to have been in half the vials. All different milligrams. And the Adderall is in three of them." He continued to study the results.

Myra clutched her pearls. "Those bastards! They were doping them up!"

"They were indeed. The phenobarbital is probably what was making Charlotte foggy. Then they would introduce the Adderall every other day to give her a feeling of euphoria," Charles noted. "They put her on a pharmacological roller coaster."

Nikki chimed in, "That's what they must have been doing while working in Mexico. Coming up with a concoction they could package and sell."

Myra was on the verge of fury. "To think poor Charlotte was taking all that medication. It could have killed her!"

"That's exactly what I think happened to

Lorraine Thompson," Annie, who had joined them in mid-conversation, surmised. "She probably got confused about her dosage and took too many of the phenobarbital pills at once. We need to get Maggie on this immediately." Annie immediately sent a text to see how soon Maggie would arrive.

Coming through the door now, Maggie pinged back.

Soon after, the rest of the sisters arrived, and they all made a beeline to the war room.

They took their seats as Charles began. "We have the findings from the drug analysis. To say they were poisoning their patients would be an understatement. They carefully plotted the dosing to keep the patients off balance." Charles went through the list of drugs, dosages, and frequency, explaining each drug's purpose and the dangers and side effects. Everyone roared in disgust, and shouts of revulsion filled the room.

"Looks like that story about Lorraine Thompson and Marjorie Brewster just might have legs, after all!" Maggie shouted. "Annie, I'll get on both of them stat!"

"Good. Start with the Thompson alleged suicide. Charles received some intel on Corbett, and Sasha is tailing him now. Apparently, he is heading to Sag Harbor. Within the next twenty-four to forty-eight hours, we should have a good idea as to his routine, associates, and acquaintances. That should give you time to get in touch with the Thompson family and get out there," Annie said to Maggie.

Maggie took copious notes, then opened her laptop and pulled up the folder with the file containing what she had already written on the story. "Good thing I save everything," she said with glee.

"You're not kidding," Annie teased her.

"I'm *not* a hoarder," Maggie whined. "It's research!"

"Uh, I don't think those *People* magazines you have piled on your chairs in the office count as research," Annie kept chiding her.

"It's pop culture," Maggie halfheartedly protested.

"Culture, indeed." Charles smirked. "Surely you jest."

The sisters hooted with laughter. Maggie was always an easy target as the brunt of a joke.

Then the room quieted, and the group began to focus again.

CHAPTER 17

London

Eileen woke up at her usual 5:30 A.M., glad she had been only three hours away from London the night before. No jet lag or time-zone change. She grabbed a jogging suit, donned a fanny pack similar to Sasha's, then put her hair in a ponytail and pulled it through the opening in the back of her New York Yankees baseball cap. Aviator sunglasses hung from a Croakies strap around her neck. She snapped her fake Apple watch on her wrist. It looked like every one of them, but hers was different. It was a direct line of communication to Avery. She could call, record, and snap a small photo if necessary at the touch of a button.

She had memorized Julian Marcus's home address and his face from the company's website. He lived in the Plimsoll Building, so she headed in the direction of King's Cross, the newest up-and-coming area of

London. They had even gotten their own postcode — N1C. It was a bustling neighborhood, so it would be easy enough for her to blend in.

Eileen propped a leg on the curb and pretended to adjust her running shoes. She glanced at her watch and saw that it was seven o'clock. She wondered what time Marcus got up and left the building and how long she would have to remain in that pose before she looked like one of those street artists or mimes. *Maybe if I put a tin cup by my feet, I'll collect a few donations.* She giggled at the thought.

The main entrance door opened, and several men wearing raincoats and carrying umbrellas came out. She glanced in their direction. *No. Not yet.* She was changing her pose to stretch her hamstrings when the door opened again. There he was. Shorter than she had expected, with a roundish face, pink cheeks, and thinning brownish hair. He looked a little rumpled. Almost as if he had not gotten a good night's sleep. *Yes,* she thought, *Photoshop can make anyone look good.* She was surprised that for someone in the "ageless beauty/longevity" business, he would leave the house looking like he had slept in his clothes. Maybe he would shower somewhere in the office.

She maintained a distance of half a block between them. At one point he stopped at a coffee bar and ordered tea, bought a newspaper, and then he continued his short walk to the office. She wondered if she should go back to the apartment building and check on the wife but quickly dismissed the thought. As of now, Marcus was the target. She would wait for further instructions as to whether Mrs. Marcus was also a person of interest.

Once Marcus entered the office, Eileen strolled over to a café and ordered a double espresso. She feigned a Brooklyn accent. "Gimme a double espresso with a shot o' milk."

The barista politely asked, "Do you prefer a cappuccino?"

"Nah. Just the double and a shot. Thanks." Eileen enjoyed using different dialects. This way, if anyone should inquire about her, they would have the accent wrong. Not that it ever happened, but it was always best to use extreme caution on a stakeout.

She observed two women in their sixties entering the opulent office of Live-Life-Long and clicked her second watch to mark the time the ladies began their appointment. An hour later, they exited with very posh-looking shopping bags. In order to glimpse what was inside the bags, Eileen would have to fake a stumble in front of them. Being careful not to knock them over, with skill and agility, Eileen took a pratfall in front of them, landing on her ass. Both women gulped in shock and then dropped their bags to help her.

"Are you all right, love?" cooed the taller of the two.

"Should we call a medic?" the other added.

"No, no. I'm aw right." Eileen answered, as if she had just gotten off the N train from Coney Island. "This is so embarrassin'. I'm soo sorry." She brushed herself off but continued to sit on the sidewalk so she could get a good peek in the bags. As the women reached down to help her up off the ground, she noticed beautifully packaged boxes with nothing written on them. Time for small talk.

"I feel ridiculous. Such a klutz. I hope I didn't cause you to break anything." She peered into the bags.

"Oh, not at all. Just some special vitamins to keep us young!" The taller woman giggled with delight.

The shorter of the two gave the taller one a sideways embarrassed look.

"Oh, don't mind her. I keep telling Gladys

that if the opportunity is there to feel more youthful, then why not?" said the taller woman.

Gladys chimed in. "Yeah, but it's very expensive, and I'm not feeling any different, Lydia."

"Gladys and Lydia. I'm Dorothy. Guess I ain't in Kansas anymore. Not like I ever been." Eileen cackled, trying to keep the conversation going.

"Good heavens, no, you are not. Are you sure you're all right? Can we get you some tea? Water?" Lydia offered.

"Tea? Like, seriously?" Eileen kept up the accent.

"Of course, dear. There is a place right across the square. Come along. We don't want our American cousin to think we're inhospitable." Lydia was obviously the kinder of the two.

Gladys interjected, "We don't have a lot of time, love, but we don't want to leave you until we know you're perfectly all right."

"Oh, I don't wanna put you out. I already took up too much of your time. And I'm really okay," Eileen/Dorothy replied.

"We have about thirty minutes before we need to catch the Tube. Come along." Lydia took Eileen by the elbow and guided her to the tea shop.

"This is really nice of you guys. I mean, you ladies."

"First time in London?" Gladys asked.

"Yep. Can't cha tell?" Eileen took a seat between the two women, hoping she could steer the conversation back to vitamins. "I couldn't help notice the beautiful boxes. Are you saying those are vitamins?" She was trying to sound curious, but in a hokey way. "I never seen vitamins in boxes like that! Must be pretty special." She sat back, pretending it was more of a rhetorical statement.

"They are indeed. So where are you staying?" Gladys quickly changed the subject.

"At a friend's flat in Covent Garden." Another lie, but it was part of the job.

"Lovely. How long will you be here?" Lydia asked.

"Only for another three days." More lies. Well, maybe not. She really didn't know how long she was going to be there. She looked across the courtyard and noticed a skinny, disheveled twentysomething man enter the doctor's building. She couldn't bolt, so she repositioned her fanny pack on the table to take a photo of the very out-of-place mangy-looking guy. He looked as if he hadn't washed his hair in a week. What would someone who looked like that be doing at a place like the doctor's?

Lydia had said something, but Eileen had been distracted. "Sorry. I thought I saw someone I knew. Wouldn't that be a hoot? Imagine running into someone all the way across the ocean. How crazy is that? But it wasn't him. Sorry. What were you sayin'?"

"I said it's too bad you won't be around for the cinema opening," Lydia repeated.

"Oh yeah. Well, I'm just happy I was able to get away for a couple o' days. I think I've taken up way too much of your time. You have been so, *so* nice. And, again, I am so, *so* sorry about falling on my butt in front of you." Eileen reached into her pocket to pull out a few euros. "Will this cover it? Or are you not doing euros anymore? Hard to keep track."

Both women chuckled at the all-too-familiar issue of Brexit. "Please. It's our treat. After all, you fell on your bum in our country. The least we can do is give you tea," Lydia said.

"You guys are so nice. Thank you again." Eileen shook their hands and moved quickly toward the doctor's office, bobbing and weaving among the people on the street in order not to be seen by the two women she had left sitting in the tea shop.

A few minutes later, the scraggly dude left the office. Another quandary — Follow him or stick with the doc? She took a photo of him and then she looked at her watch. It was only ten o'clock. Avery was in Aspen, where it was seven hours earlier. It would be 3:00 A.M. there. He could still be awake, considering he had changed time zones twice, which meant his body clock was still on 1:00 A.M. She took the chance and pressed the button on her fake Apple-watch phone.

"You okay?" Avery was wide awake and surprised to hear from Eileen at that hour.

"Yes. I'm fine. Two things. There is a guy who went into the office who looks extremely out of place. Should I tail him or stay in front of Marcus's? I took a photo from a distance. The telephoto lens captured a good shot of him. Sending it over to you now."

"Good. Stay on Marcus for now. Isabelle should have the blueprints for both his apartment and his office shortly. Probably late afternoon your time."

"Will do. What about the wife?"

"See if there's a pattern in Marcus's day-to-day life for the next two days. Then you can tail the wife."

"The other thing is I literally bumped into two women coming out of the office with very posh-looking shopping bags."

"You bumped into them?" Avery sounded surprised.

"Well, not exactly bumped into them. I pretended to trip and fell on my ass in front of them. I was trying to get a look inside the bags."

"And?"

"And not much. The bags contained beautifully packaged boxes. I said I hoped I didn't break anything, and they told me they were vitamins. Sorry I couldn't get more info out of them, except one of the women didn't seem very happy with the results so far. They took me to get a cup of tea. That's when I spotted the scraggly guy."

"You are good." Avery smiled.

"Thanks, boss. I'll be in touch."

"Be safe," Avery said before he ended the call. He forwarded the photo of the mysterious guy to Charles.

Marcus was trying not to have a hissy fit. That creep Jerry had shown up unannounced with a message from Franny. "Cash upon receipt. Or a few baubles. No more credit."

"But why?" Marcus whined.

"Dunno. Big guy wants it that way. Says he ain't no bank."

"But he gets a twenty-five percent commission!" Marcus knew he might as well be talking to the wall.

"What of it? If you want somethin', yer gonna have to pay as you go." Jerry turned on his filthy sneakers and walked out.

Marcus realized that he needed to come up with a plan. One thing he knew for sure: stopping the cocaine wouldn't be a part of it.

CHAPTER 18

Pinewood

Charles poached some eggs to finish preparing a breakfast of Canadian bacon, wilted spinach, and the aforementioned eggs, all sitting on an English muffin. "Here you go, dear." He placed the dish in front of Myra while she continued to jot down some notes. "I can see the wheels turning. What is on your mind, love?"

"I think it's time we let Charlotte know we're investigating the situation. It's going to become more difficult to have our meetings without her noticing. Don't you agree?" Myra asked.

"Absolutely. She should have full knowledge of what those bastards were doing to her. Dr. Falcon said her lab work should be in by noon, so let's wait and give her all the information at once," Charles suggested.

"Do you think it might be a bit much for her to absorb?" Myra stopped her writing and looked up at her husband.

"Not if we are methodical about it. And I can say with absolute certainty, you, my dear, are very methodical." With that, Charles bent to give Myra a peck on the side of her mouth.

"Indeed, I am." Myra sat taller in her chair. "I think perhaps we should tell her together with Annie and Fergus. It could be overwhelming to have all the sisters sitting at a table, staring at her. She might be embarrassed."

"Excellent suggestion. I'll ring up Fergus and Annie and have them come by for lunch." Charles pulled out his phone and punched in the speed-dial number he had for their friends.

"Meanwhile, I'll bring Charlotte a tray and tell her we're going to take a walk after she has breakfast." Myra was formulating a plan to ease her friend into learning about the machinations of the Sisterhood.

Isabelle was the first to call Charles that morning. "Spoke to Sebastian, my friend in London who studied architecture. He's sending over the blueprints for Dr. Marcus's place. Should have them around one o'clock. I have Steinwood's already. I'm going to send them over now so you can forward them to Avery."

"Splendid. Avery sent some intel on him from Eileen. I'll share it with the group when everyone arrives later. By the way, Myra and I think we should bring Charlotte in on this. It's going to become increasingly difficult for us to operate without her knowing about what we're doing. And we most assuredly do not want to send her packing. She is still in a fragile state."

"I think you and Myra are right. Did you ask the others?"

"Not yet. We were just discussing it before you phoned. We're thinking we'll do it at lunch with Fergus and Annie. We don't want to do it in front of everyone, just in case it would embarrass Charlotte."

"Good idea. What time are we convening today?" Isabelle asked.

"Let me check with the others and get back to you."

"Roger that." Isabelle ended the call.

Charles called Annie to ask her to contact the sisters to see who would be available later that day. He also explained that he and Myra wanted to inform Charlotte of what they had discovered, and he asked Annie to bring Fergus over for lunch so they would be there when everything was explained to Charlotte.

Annie agreed, ended the one call, picked

up the phone again, and began reaching out to the sisters. Within a few minutes, Annie sent Charles a text: **All in. Four o'clock. Dinner at six, please.** ☺

Myra returned to the kitchen with a tray of empty plates. "Our girl has a very good appetite. She said she hasn't eaten this well in months."

"It's those pills they were giving her. Nausea is another side effect." Charles grimaced at the thought of Charlotte being poisoned by those creeps.

"Well, that part is over for Charlotte. But we need to stop these men from doing it to others. And I would love to get some of Charlotte's money back." Myra was contemplating how that would happen, but they still needed to gather more intel.

"Oh, I am sure you and the sisters will come up with a very fine plan."

"What plan?" Charlotte asked, startling both of them as she entered the kitchen.

Myra took a deep inhale and fiddled with her pearls. "Charlotte, dear, please sit down."

"Myra? What's wrong? Is everything all right?" Charlotte grabbed the back of one of the kitchen chairs to steady herself.

"Well, yes and no." Myra looked to Charles for assistance.

Charles took Charlotte's arm and assisted her into a chair. He patted her hand. "Now, now. Don't fret. Everything is all right —"

"At least for the moment," Myra interrupted.

Charlotte had a worried look on her face. "Please tell me. What is going on?"

Myra pulled her chair around and gently turned Charlotte's shoulders so they could sit face-to-face, knee to knee. Myra began, "First, I want to apologize."

"Apologize for what?" Charlotte burst out, causing Lady to yelp, which started a short howling session among the dogs.

"Please, it's okay." Myra took Charlotte's hands in hers, again glancing up at Charles.

"Charlotte," Charles began again, "we have been doing a little research on your Drs. Marcus and Steinwood. Concerning the vitamins and medications they've been prescribing."

"But how?" Charlotte implored.

"That's what I wanted to apologize for," Myra continued. "You know we love you very much, and when we received your letter, we were very concerned."

"Oh yes. You have been wonderful hosts." Charlotte sighed.

Myra was beginning to vacillate between feeling guilty for invading her friend's privacy and being energized by the idea of fixing the situation. "Charlotte, I breached your trust." There. It was finally out.

"What on earth are you talking about?" Charlotte was almost pleading.

"When you were at the spa, I went into your room and took samples of your drugs, vitamins, or whatever it was that Dr. Marcus was calling them." And there was the rest of it.

Charlotte was taken aback, but not in a disturbed way. "My goodness. Myra, why didn't you just ask me?"

"Because that was before you told me what was going on, and I know this is going to sound totally ridiculous, but I didn't want to pry! Well, at least not to your face!" Myra and Charlotte howled with laughter at the contradiction. Then the dogs joined in. It was a cacophony of yaps and laughs.

The room vibrated from the barking of the dogs responding to the arrival of Fergus and Annie.

"What have we here?" Fergus reached into his pockets to reward each dog with a treat. Mostly to quiet them down. "What is so hilariously funny?"

"Care to share?" Annie asked, chuckling.

Myra inhaled slightly. "I was trying to explain to Charlotte that I stole some of her meds because I didn't want to pry" — she paused — "to her face!"

Hysterics broke out again.

"That is a bit ironic, wouldn't you say?" Fergus added his opinion.

"Yes." Myra caught her breath. "We were going to wait for you to get here, but Charlotte overheard me and Charles talking about plans and asked us what it was about. And here we are."

"How far into the explanation have you gotten?" Annie inquired.

"That was it. You walked in just as I was about to explain." Myra gestured for everyone to sit down. "Let's continue."

"Charlotte, while the humorous aspect of this has come to light, there is a much more serious issue at hand." Charles needed to steer the conversation to the nuts and bolts of the scheme the doctors had concocted. "We had the pills tested, and what we discovered is very disturbing."

Charlotte began to go pale. "What . . . What do you mean?"

"Some of them were relatively harmless herbs, but every other bottle in the sequence contained low dosages of a drug that works like phenobarbital. It's a narcotic. Probably why you were getting foggy, as you said. The next day you would take a low dose of

Adderall, which is in the same class of drugs as cocaine."

Charlotte started to tremble. Myra grabbed a cashmere throw from the atrium and wrapped it around her friend. "There. There. It's all going to be all right. You are perfectly fine now."

Tears started streaming down Charlotte's face. "They could have killed me," she whispered. "No wonder I was feeling highs and lows. They told me that it takes several months for our bodies to adjust and things would be level after six months. That's when they're supposed to reevaluate you." She put her hands to her face. "I've been such a fool!"

Myra hugged Charlotte. "You were not being a fool. You went to a doctor whom you thought you could trust. And then, when you were feeling a bit off, you reached out to us. That was a very wise move. And let me remind you, you stopped taking those pills when you were not feeling right. So, you are far from a fool."

Everyone murmured in agreement. Annie stooped down to wrap her arms around Charlotte and Myra.

Fergus interjected, "While we are on the subject, can you bring the pill bottles down here? I want to see if there are any legal markings on them."

Wiping the tears, Charlotte nodded and looked up. "So what do we do now?"

In unison, Annie and Myra exclaimed, "We thought you'd never ask!"

High fives and hoots, then the dogs. Yes, there were some big surprises coming for a trio of good-for-nothing scoundrels. The game was afoot.

CHAPTER 19

Aspen

Avery Snowden peered out the motel window. The mountains were spectacular, topped with the last of the winter snow and beautiful aspen trees. He wasn't much of a snow or winter guy, but he could certainly appreciate the natural beauty of the area. He checked the digital clock on his laptop. It was 6:00 A.M. He sent the photo Eileen had taken of the mysterious guy to Charles to see if he had a police record. Charles had many ways to get that sort of information. The photo was a clean shot of the kid's face. Yes, Eileen was very good at her job.

The laptop pinged, indicating that a big file was being downloaded. It was the blueprints of Steinwood's house and office. The buildings were only five minutes apart by car. He had rented a car and an SUV and would switch between the two. He didn't want one vehicle to be seen too many times in the same place. The night before, he had parked the first rental a block from the motel. He had then taken a cab to another rental agency and had used the same alias, Walter Harrison, to rent the SUV that he had used to register at the motel. The first car had been rented to Harry Walters. It was his own way of keeping track of what names he was using, at what time, and at what place. So far it had worked for him.

After the file downloaded, Avery, aka Harry, aka Walter, took a good long look at the office, which was close to the Baldwin Gallery. Surprisingly, there was not much security. The reception area was front and center as you entered the office. A small waterfall was the backdrop for the reception desk. There was a hallway on each side, with glass doors leading toward the back, where there were two rooms for patient consultations. A large private office was in the far corner and had what appeared to be a very large vault — a Scripps Safe TRXP Series pharmacy safe.

That's a lot of steel, Avery thought to himself. *I wonder what big secrets they're keeping in there. I'm sure Charles and the sisters will find out.*

Next, he looked at the prints for the house

on Crystal Lake Road. He let out a low whistle. There was a detached garage that was almost as big as the six-thousand-square-foot house. Another mystery to be solved. But first, he had to visit the office of Live-Life-Long and plant a bug in the reception area. This way he could hear when they were closing, so he could break in and plant bugs in the big office and the patients' rooms.

Avery unwrapped the muffin he had brought in the night before. He glanced at the small dresser, which held a pathetic-looking pot with something that resembled coffee and packages of synthetic milk. *Sometimes these surveillances come with no perks.* He smirked at his private sense of humor. Aspen was a small town compared to others. It was a resort, and the locals knew who was or was not a tourist. In Avery Snowden's line of work, it was imperative to maintain a low profile, which was more difficult than usual when he was operating in a small community. Blending in or being invisible was the only way to approach it.

By eight o'clock, after he had taken a shower, Avery was picking at the crumbs from the muffin he had devoured and was on his way to the Live-Life-Long office. He would go in and pretend that he was a bit lost. And could they give him directions to the Baldwin Gallery? He would then surreptitiously stick a very small microphone transmitter, one the size of a watch battery, either under the receptionist's desk or on a plant or something that was on the counter. It would depend on whatever opportunity presented itself. Once it was installed, he would listen until the office closed for the evening, then would reenter through the back door to plant the rest of the surveillance devices. He was surprised that there was virtually no security system in place. But maybe all they were concerned about was what was in that vault. That would be the challenge. Circumventing what little office security the place had would be a walk in the park.

He drove the SUV two blocks away from the Baldwin Gallery. He walked to the office from there. This way he really seemed lost. The outside of Live-Life-Long was minimalistic. Just a white, frosted-glass front door with a logo etched into it. The minute you entered, you were greeted by aromatherapy of lavender, vanilla, and cedar. He suspected they were pumping oxygen into the room, as well — the way they did at casinos to keep you alert and awake until you lost all your money. There was soft New

Age music playing in the background. Two very attractive women — who appeared to be around fifty — sat behind a white counter that held two purple orchid plants. *Perfect.*

He slapped on a charming smile and approached them. "Good morning. I am sorry to bother you, but I seem to be a bit turned around. I was looking for the Baldwin Gallery, and it appears I'm walking around in circles. Would you mind setting me in the right direction?"

Both looked like they had come out of a mold. Something akin to *The Stepford Wives,* but older. Great marketing strategy. Sassy and sexy at sixty.

One of the women stood and leaned across the counter. "No trouble at all. When you go out the door, make a right. Go down to the stop sign and make a left. Go two more blocks, and it's on the right. You can't miss it!"

"Obviously I did!" Avery gave the biggest charming smile he could muster as he secretly placed the listening device on the back of one of the orchid plants. He laughed to himself. *A plant for a plant. Funny.* "Thank you very much. Enjoy your day." He turned and walked out.

After placing an earbud in his ear, he was pleased to hear them chatting about him.

"Nice-looking man. I wonder how long he's going to be in town." He smiled and continued to walk back to the SUV. He passed a recreational marijuana shop and wondered how the doctor felt about that kind of competition. *Or is it?* He shrugged. Next thing on his agenda was to look at the house and that massive garage.

Avery drove around town to familiarize himself with the streets and devise a plan to get back into the office sometime that evening. He doubted there were any street gangs or kids hanging out. It was a very pristine, high, as in very high-end community, and was listed as one of the top twenty richest zip codes in the country. No riffraff here. After scoping out the neighborhood, he headed to Crystal Lake Road, a very short distance away. As he was approaching the house, a Jaguar XJ came soaring out of the driveway, almost side-swiping his SUV. "Jerk." Then he realized that the reckless driver was Dr. Steinwood himself. He slowed down and surveyed the front of the house. No other cars were in sight, either on the road or in the driveway. It was going to be difficult to be inconspicuous. The idea of a utility truck came to mind. No one would question it.

He quickly phoned Charles. "Hey, old

boy. I need some assistance in acquiring a utility truck. Power company. Cable. Something like that. It's rather sparse here, and a stakeout might be challenging, unless I had a reason to be parked on the street."

"I'll ring Kathryn. She seems to know every highway, truck, and driver across the country. I'll ring you back." Charles immediately called Kathryn.

"What's up?" Kathryn bellowed into the phone. Her voice was as big as she was tall.

"We need to get Avery a utility vehicle pronto."

"He's in Aspen, correct?"

"Yes."

"I'm on it. An hour. Two, tops," she replied in her husky voice.

"Thank you." Charles immediately called Avery. "An hour. Maybe two."

"Roger that." Avery was still deciding if he should park the SUV down the road and try to get a glimpse of the property from behind.

He drove a little farther and found a small area on the side of the road where he could stop and be off the main drag. He sat for a few minutes to get a sense of the traffic flow. There was none. He got out of the car and walked through the woods that surrounded the five-million-dollar property. There didn't seem to be any activity near the house. He wondered if Steinwood had the same flimsy security at the house as he had at the office. He pulled out a pair of small binoculars and started scanning the trees. And then he looked for fencing. Nothing he could see yet. He turned his attention to the roofline of the house. On each corner was a camera. He could count five from his vantage point. But they were all pointing toward the garage. *Odd.* Must be something going on in there. Once he got back to his motel, he'd go over the blueprints again and see if the security system was listed. He would also be eavesdropping on the conversations taking place in the reception area at the office to determine when the coast was clear for a break-in.

By the time he got back to his room, Charles had called with information about a utility truck. "Kathryn said she is going to have to fly to Denver and pick up the rig herself. She'll meet you in Aspen around midnight. This way, you can get the truck outside the house before he leaves in the morning."

Avery Snowden checked his watch. He had no idea what time the Live-Life-Long office closed for the day. There had been no indication anywhere. They probably conformed their schedule to their patients'. After all, the patients were the ones paying the exorbitant fees, and God knows what else.

His ears perked up when he heard a man's voice getting louder in the background.

"That about does it for today, ladies. Enjoy your evening."

From what Avery could glean, the doctor was leaving the office, and the women were preparing to do the same. The woo-woo music stopped, and he could hear them rustling and chatting about what they were going to do for the evening. One was meeting her boyfriend to go dancing, and the other was meeting her sister for a movie. Nothing suspicious about either of their plans.

He would wait another hour or so before he returned. That would still give him several hours before he had to meet up with Kathryn. The plan was to park on different streets and meet at a Starbucks, where they would exchange keys and directions to their vehicles. Kathryn would take one rental back to Denver. That would still leave Avery with a rental and a utility truck.

He reviewed the office blueprints again. No security cameras in the front. Just one at the rear door, facing in one direction.

There was also an alarm system that could be dismantled by a three-year-old with access to the Internet. *Cripes. You can learn to do almost anything from YouTube.* Avery shook his head. *What a world.* He laughed again at himself. *Indeed.*

After donning a black running suit, black cap, black gloves, and black sneakers, Avery slipped out of the motel and walked down the street to the first of the two rentals. He double-checked his gear. He had magnets for the alarm system and four bugging devices. He parked the car a few blocks away, began a slight jog in the direction of the office, and made a turn onto the street behind it. Behind the buildings, there was a small walkway running parallel to the street. It was where the trash bins and electric and gas meters were located. It would qualify as an alley, but they would never call it an alley in this town. No, it was considered public works access. *Whatever.*

Avery made sure he approached the rear of the office from the side at which the security camera did not point. After looking in both directions for other pedestrians and cameras, he neared the door. Within seconds, he had picked the lock and disengaged the alarm sensor. He listened carefully for any sounds of company. All quiet. He would plant the bugs in each patient suite, and the office in the back that housed the impressive vault. Safecracking wasn't necessarily his forte, but he knew enough people who made a very lucrative living doing so, if he needed to call in an expert.

Avery opened several file cabinets in search of information, but the files were coded in colors and numbers. No names, just what appeared to be dates of office visits. *Odd.* Maybe it was all on a hard drive. He booted up the desk computer, but it was password protected, and there wasn't enough time to try to gain access. The critical move was to get the place bugged so the sisters could carry out the next stages of their plan.

After checking that all the recording devices and the strategically placed cameras were operating properly, he e-mailed photos of the safe directly to Charles. Taking one last look around, he was satisfied. Avery reset the alarm sensor, locked the door, and carefully moved down the alley. He looked at his watch again — 8:00 P.M. He had an hour before he had to meet up with Kathryn.

He returned to the motel to change into something more "outdoors country" appropriate, in place of the ninja look. Or was it the bank-robber look? Either way, he didn't want to stand out among all the flannel shirts and Timberland boots.

Avery entered the Starbucks and gave the room the once-over. It looked like an L.L.Bean convention. He would blend in just fine. Kathryn entered a few minutes later, looking like her usual self. Jeans, hiking boots, denim shirt. *Perfect.* She nodded at him and walked to the counter and ordered a double cappuccino and a hot chocolate from the barista. After paying for the beverages, she sauntered over to his table and placed the hot chocolate in front of Avery.

"Wasn't sure if you were in need of caffeine or an antioxidant," Kathryn's husky voice boomed across the table.

"Thanks! I'll take the chocolate. It has a lot of benefits. Improves blood flow, lowers blood pressure, and may reduce my chances for heart disease." Avery gave her a wry grin.

"Had I known all that, I would have gotten two. For me." Kathryn smiled, which was something she didn't do all that easily. She had been through hell and back. If it were not for Myra and the other sisters, she couldn't imagine where she would be now. One could say she was happy, but the scar on her heart from losing the love of her life would never go away. *Content* would probably be a better word.

Both placed their keys in the middle of the table, finished their drinks, picked up the other's key ring, and gave directions to their vehicles. Kathryn would spend the night at a different motel and would head back to Denver in the morning. Avery would park the utility truck a block from his motel and would retrieve it at the crack of dawn.

CHAPTER 20

Pinewood

The landline in the kitchen was ringing. Very few people knew that number. Charles glimpsed at the caller ID and saw that the call was from the UK. At first he was hesitant to answer, but then it occurred to him that it might be Maryann calling for Charlotte.

"Yes?" he asked in a very deep baritone voice.

"Hello, Charles? It's Maryann. How are you?"

"Very well, Maryann. Is everything all right?"

"Uh, yes." She hesitated. Charles noticed. "Is my mom available?"

"Yes, she's in the atrium with Myra. Hold on a moment." Charles brought the hand-held device into the room where the others sat. "Charlotte, it's Maryann. Don't worry. She said everything is fine." He handed the phone to her.

"Maryann, sweetie, all okay?" Charlotte wanted to hear it for herself.

"Well, yes, Mom." Another hesitation.

"Good. I'm surprised to hear from you."

"Okay, Mom, please hear me out." Maryann couldn't dance around the issue any longer. "Dr. Steinwood called me from Aspen. He said he was concerned that you were missing appointments and that this lapse could have detrimental effects."

"Oh?" Charlotte was being coy as she motioned for Myra and Charles to listen in as she put the phone in speakerphone mode. "I don't know, dear. I'm feeling quite fantastic right now. Maybe the program has already worked, and I don't need to continue." She looked up at her friends, who both gave her a thumbs-up.

"Mother, would you at least consider it? Sleep on it, as they say. Please?" Maryann was begging.

Myra grabbed a pen and paper and wrote, "Tell her yes."

Charlotte looked stunned and shrugged her shoulders, as if to say, "Why?" But Myra was mouthing, "Yes."

"Oh, okay, honey. I will sleep on it. Happy now?" Charlotte was finally playing along.

"Yes, Mother. I know everyone will feel

better when you get back on track."

Charlotte took a finger and started swirling it around her temple, as in the "crazy" pantomime. "I'll give you a call in a day or so. Give my love to Liam and Allan. Bye, dear."

She couldn't wait to get off the phone. Turning to Myra and Charles, she said, "Now will one of you explain why I should consider going back to either one of those lowlifes?"

Myra took Charlotte by the hand and explained what was happening. The sisters were going to put an end to this charade.

"I really don't understand, Myra. What do you mean, put an end to it?" Charlotte was very confused and looked up at Annie, Charles, and Fergus for an explanation.

Myra started. "Remember when Barbara was killed? The driver got off because he had diplomatic immunity."

"Yes, it was horrible!" Charlotte exclaimed.

"Then you will recall how depressed I was? Nothing could snap me out of it until I was inspired to help other women who had been wronged and had got no justice."

Charlotte gasped. "You mean those stories about you are true?" Her eyes were as big as saucers.

"Yes and no," Annie answered. "Let's just say we help people, and we want to help you and the two other families that have been stricken with heartache by those doctors. You know about them, correct? The alleged suicide and the coma?"

"I heard rumors, yes." Charlotte was getting pale.

"We have some ideas, but we will require some assistance," Myra said.

"But how can *I* help?" Charlotte was becoming dizzy with confusion.

"Annie and I can be referrals. You bring us to see Dr. Marcus. That will get us inside legitimately," Myra suggested.

"Legitimately?" Charlotte seemed dubious.

"As Annie mentioned earlier, we help people. We have a large network that aids and assists in a variety of tasks. Fergus and I are the key contacts and disseminate information to the sisters in order to allow them to carry out their plan," Charles explained.

"Or 'mission,' as we call it," Annie added.

"Wow." Charlotte spoke in a whisper. "So what is the plan? Or mission?"

"We are in the process of gathering information about the three doctors. Once we know their strengths and weaknesses, particularly their weaknesses, we hatch a plan. Each sister brings her own personal area of expertise to bear." Myra was matter of fact.

Another "Wow" emerged from Charlotte's mouth.

"Indeed." Charles put his arm around Myra, who put her arm around Annie, who put her arm around Fergus. "We are part of a team. You have already met the others."

"You mean . . . the girls?" Wide-eyed saucers appeared again.

Everyone broke into laughter. "The sisters!" they said in unison.

Charlotte felt a level of excitement. Visiting Myra and Charles had been an excellent idea. "So, when do we start?" she asked, jubilation ringing in her voice.

"The sisters will be here in a couple of hours. We'll have a meeting. And then we'll have dinner, my special recipe of chicken cacciatore." Charles was a man of many talents.

By four o'clock, everyone had arrived except Kathryn. She was on her way back from Aspen and Denver.

Myra escorted Charlotte down the dark steps as the other women followed. Myra explained that they always salute Lady Justice upon entering and exiting. Charlotte was very nervous and made a weak attempt at complying.

Myra chuckled. "You'll get used to it."

Charlotte gazed around the impressive room. It looked like something you would see in a James Bond movie or in *Star Wars*. She wasn't sure which. "Myra, I almost feel as if I don't deserve the attention."

"Don't be silly. We've known each other since we were teens. And we have always trusted each other." Myra pulled out a chair for Charlotte.

"Ditto for me," Annie said and cackled.

The women pumped their fists in the air. "We're all in!"

CHAPTER 21

Sag Harbor

Sasha sat in a small sedan in the Hampton Jitney parking lot. Corbett did not get off, so she followed the bus to the next town. And then the next. And several more. He finally stepped off at the last stop, in Sag Harbor. He must have called ahead, because a taxi was waiting for him at the curb. Pulling down the brim of her baseball cap, she tailed the taxi from about a hundred yards. Traffic was very light, with just a few cars passing in the other direction. No one was behind her.

The taxi pulled into a driveway, but she could not see the house from the street, just the hint of a blue Mercedes through the hedges. Every property had privet hedges to block the view of the house. She would have to return on foot and hope there was no security fence. She looked around. *Nope. Just the privet.*

172

It was still early in the evening, and she wondered if anyone was in the house or if he was going to go out again. She would just have to wait and see. *But where?* She noticed a FOR SALE sign a few houses back. Maybe that house was vacant. She would check it out. After pulling her cell from her pocket, she called the number on the sign but got a recording. Sasha decided to take a chance and pull into the driveway of the house, pretending she was interested in possibly buying it. Even though her small rental car would make someone question whether or not she could afford such a large house and in that neighborhood, she decided if she were to encounter someone, she would say she was scouting out property for her employer. Yes, Sasha was quick on her feet. Avery Snowden knew how to hire the best.

She turned her car around and proceeded to the privet-shielded house. There was nothing in the driveway and no visible activity in the house. Just a lockbox on the front door for the multiple listing. *Perfect.* She would park the car there after dark. She hit the button on her fake Apple watch to check in with Avery.

"Target arrived. I'll send more info after I scope out any security issues," Sasha said to her wrist. "It's pretty sparse out here as far as human activity is concerned. Difficult to stay inconspicuous."

"I'm dealing with the same situation but got a utility truck. I'm parking it on the side of the road."

"Excellent solution. I am going on foot in an hour or so. Will probably be on my bike tomorrow. I'll check back with you later."

"Roger that." Avery ended the call.

Sasha waited in the driveway for another hour. Still no one on the premises. It was early in the season, so the summer crowds were not around yet. Confident that she was alone, Sasha slipped behind the car and changed into what she referred to as her "sleuthing suit." Same as Avery's: black, except she wore leggings. After checking to see that all her equipment was blinking green, she shut the flap of her gear bag and carefully made her way back to Corbett's property. She could tell that the neighbor to his right was not home. Probably just a vacation home for someone in the city. The place was dead, which provided a very good opportunity for Sasha to walk much of the perimeter along the privet hedges. She pulled out her night-vision glasses and placed an earbud in one ear to pick up any frequencies that would indicate security cameras, invisible fencing, or alarm trips.

She heard a slight hum, which let her know that though there was a security system in the house, it was not engaged at the moment. Sasha figured he would set the alarm when he went to bed or went out. She waited. No dogs. No other cars. Just Corbett.

Sasha moved to a position from which she could see the entire kitchen, which opened to a great room. She had a clear shot of what appeared to be the main living area. Corbett's blazer was draped over the wing chair where the duffel bag sat. He was still wearing the same trousers and shirt. She surveyed him as he went over to the wet bar and fixed himself a cocktail. He then reached into the duffel bag and pulled out what appeared to be a large catalog. Focusing her binoculars, Sasha could read the cover: *Christie's Auction and Private Sales. Summer Offerings.* She took a photo and e-mailed it directly to Avery with a note: Shopping list? Avery forwarded it to Charles, who was compiling all the intel.

Sasha watched Corbett for a few more minutes, while he sat and thumbed through the catalog, taking sips of his cocktail every few minutes. The expression on his face was ecstatic. Must be something very special. Usually, men had that look on their face

175

only when they were about to have sex or had just had sex. Some kind of jubilation. She wondered what could turn a man on in an auction catalog. *Never mind.* She didn't want to go there. She made her way around the rest of the privet, taking photos of the entrances. She knew they would be designated on the blueprints, which were waiting to be downloaded onto her computer, but an actual visual was always best.

Sag Harbor was once a whaling village. Over the past century, it had become a haven for wealthy industrialists during the summer months. This old fishing community was now filled with high-end boutiques, the same ones that could be found on Fifth Avenue and Rodeo Drive. Unless you were a megastar with a net worth over twenty million dollars, you had a small historic cottage on less than an acre of land. If you wanted to remodel it, you were limited when it came to what you could do on the outside, and it could cost hundreds of thousands to renovate. A lot of that 1880s wood could get rotten over the decades. Centuries. If you wanted to say you lived in the Hamptons, you had to pay the price and play by the rules, and these little towns had lots of them.

Surrounding the quaint hamlet were acres

of estates and cottages alive with tulip trees, the tallest hardwood on the East Coast. This made it easy for Sasha to find ample locations from which to peer into the second floor of the house. She followed Corbett's movements as he turned on the light in the hallway, then the ones in the master bedroom suite. Not any sign of a feminine influence. Maybe he was too much of a narcissist to have a girlfriend, even as wealthy as he was.

Sasha snapped a few more photos. The small balcony off the bedroom could provide easy access, so she took several shots at different angles. No security cameras. She guessed that since it was over 140 miles from New York City, and not necessarily an easy trip on a two-lane highway, they didn't get a lot of lowlifes showing up in Sag Harbor. Made sense. It was a long haul, so someone had to be motivated enough to make that trip. Sasha thought for a moment. *Except for several murders, all of which were about sex or money or both. Another type of white-collar crime. Domestic violence.* She immediately gave thanks for people like Myra and the sisters. At least some women would get justice.

After observing Corbett for another hour, she saw him go into the bathroom and

177

return wearing a robe and slippers. Was that some sort of a family crest on the toe? Seriously? Who was he trying to kid? They didn't know a whole lot about the trio of scumbags they were dealing with, but they were learning new info every day. And one thing they did know was that there were no aristocrats in Corbett's family tree.

It looked like he was in for the evening. Sasha took a good look around. No one in sight. She climbed down from the tree, returned to her car, and headed back to her motel. She needed to check on the blueprints of the office. That would be tomorrow's target.

CHAPTER 22

London

Marcus was beginning to sweat again. Steinwood was right. He needed to rein in Norma's extravagance. But how? She would beat him to a pulp if he even uttered the word *budget.* He paced some more; then it hit him. *Her diamonds!* He would slowly replace them with fakes. One, maybe two at a time. *Brilliant.* He laughed at the pun. He phoned Norma to see what was on her agenda. She always had one. Another laugh. Yes, indeed. He was energized by his new plan.

"Hello, dear. Tell me, what are your plans for today?" Marcus hoped she wouldn't be suspicious. He rarely showed any interest in anything she did. He only paid for it.

"Hello, darling. I'm lunching with Victoria and Blake. We're going to the Square." She could not have been more blasé as Marcus was adding up the tab in his head. "Why do you ask, darling?"

If she were any more apathetic, she *would be the one in a coma,* Marcus thought. *Not a bad idea, either. Nah. Too messy. Already dodged one of those.*

"I thought I might meet some chaps at the pub. Throw some darts. You know, typical stuff." He was making it up as he went along, although he would actually stop at the pub after he made the trip to a jeweler's. He planned to go to the other side of town, just in case Norma had a better nose for diamonds than she did for perfume.

Why on God's earth does the most expensive perfume smell like Pine-Sol on vomit? Marcus wondered. Norma probably didn't care what it smelled like. She cared only that she could tell everyone the price tag. *Cripes, she is a lot like Corbett.* He was stunned at the thought. *Wow. Some psychoanalyst would have a field day with that one.*

"Julian? Julian? I asked what time you thought you'll be home." Norma snapped him out of his fantasy of choking her.

"Sorry, love. I thought I heard someone calling my name. Dunno. Depends on whether or not I'm winning, I suppose." Marcus faked a chuckle.

"All right, dear. Then I won't rush back. The girls and I might take in a flick. Ta."

180

Norma ended the call without saying anything else.

It was late morning. Norma and her friends usually met around one. He had some time to see a patient. Finally. He couldn't blow off the same person two days in a row. He needed the money, and he never wanted anyone to be able to post bad reviews, even though they paid a lot of money to a cyber company to ensure that none saw the light of day.

Eileen would use the same tactic as Avery had in Aspen. She would go into the office, pretend she was lost, and plant a bug. She could study the blueprints while listening in once she got back to her room.

After tucking all her hair under the cap, she pushed open the white, frosted-glass door. The room was filled with the aroma of lavender and vanilla, and New Age music played in the background. Exactly the way Avery had described the office in Aspen. Two women in their midfifties sat behind a white counter that held two orchid plants. Both women wore white lab coats. The one wearing big black-framed glasses spoke first.

"Hello, love. Welcome to Live-Life-Long. How can we help you?" She had a lovely London accent.

181

"I feel sooo foolish." This time Eileen feigned a Southern accent. "I got off the subway. Ah believe y'all call it a toob?" She let the word linger. "Well, anyhoo, I was supposed to meet a friend at a café somewhere around these here parts, and I got myself all turned around!"

"There are several, dear. Do you have a name?" the second woman asked.

"Let me check. I know I put it in my bag. Hang on!" Eileen faked fumbling in her bag and let a few things fall onto the counter. As she was placing the items back in her purse, she surreptitiously slapped a listening device on one of the orchid pots. "Oh lordy, here it is." She pulled out a crumpled piece of paper that had once been a receipt and pretended to read it. "Café Druid."

The women smiled politely and gave her directions.

"Thank you, ladies, so very much. Y'all have yourselves a nice day." Eileen turned to leave and to look for another spot from which to observe the office until Marcus left the building.

He left much earlier than she had expected. Within a few minutes of her exit, he was already out the door. He was heading toward his flat. Eileen kept an eye on him as she quickly walked over to a souvenir vendor and bought a different cap. She ripped off the tags and threw them and her previous cap in a trash bin.

As she continued to follow him, it became even clearer that he was heading home. Maybe for lunch? She spoke into her sleeve to record his movements. They neared the entrance to his building, and Eileen slowed her pace as she watched him enter. She would find a place to wait.

Marcus entered his apartment, anticipating that Norma had already left. He was correct.

He walked into the large closet that contained the safe and punched the numbers. As an additional feature, the safe accepted only his or Norma's fingerprints when the numbers were punched in. He peered into the velvet drawers and had not the slightest bit of remorse when he removed a gold bangle bracelet with five carats total weight in diamonds. If he recalled, it had been appraised at fifteen thousand dollars. That would do him for a bit, provided he could talk Franny into trading that way. He'd even offer Franny a good discount.

He pocketed the bracelet and moved some of the others around. The tennis bracelet would also fetch a good sum. Probably ten thousand dollars. He was so gleeful he almost had an erection. He couldn't remember the last time that had happened. Yeah. Certainly not since he had married that gold digger. Men were idiots. He should be getting *something* out of this. But then he consoled himself with the cleverness of his new plan. He surveyed the area. Everything was in place.

Eileen watched as Marcus left the building and walked toward the Underground. She quickly followed and got into step with him. There were several people walking at the same pace, so it was not obvious that she was following him, not that he took any precautions to prevent being followed. When she had the opportunity, she pretended to rub her eye and spoke into the sleeve of her shirt, ticking off details of Marcus's movements. He entered the Underground station and it appeared that he was heading toward the other side of the city. She slipped into the same subway car and kept an eye on him. After about twenty minutes, Marcus exited the train. Eileen followed.

When he got out to the street, Marcus headed to a very fine jewelry exchange. Eileen couldn't risk getting too close, so she tried to pretend she was admiring some of the items in the store window. She could see Marcus speaking to a gentleman at the back of the store. Eileen snapped a photo of the gentleman with her wristwatch and sent it off to Avery with the name of the shop. In a very short time Marcus started heading toward the door and once he was back outside Eileen quickly turned away, and she watched him through the reflection in the window. He was heading back toward the Underground. Again, she kept a safe distance and continued to follow Marcus until he returned to his office. He had the biggest shit-eating grin on his face. Eileen was sure to capture that particular "Kodak moment."

Marcus felt as if he were walking on air. The jeweler had swallowed the story about replicating the bracelet: the wife wanted to be able to wear it anywhere without worrying about losing it. The jeweler said it would take two days. The cost was three hundred pounds. He would ask Franny if he wanted the whole piece or just the diamonds. Another stroke of genius — he would offer the rest of the piece free. That should satisfy Franny O'Rourke.

His next challenge was getting through the week with the small supply of cocaine he had on hand. He could chop up some of the pills they had locked away in the vault, but he knew he would have to pay top dollar to replace them. Maybe he could curb his urges a tad.

CHAPTER 23

Pinewood

Charles brought the group up to speed with the information that had been coming in. "As you know, Avery is in Aspen, Sasha's in New York, and Eileen's in London. As you can see from all the blueprints Isabelle procured, the three offices have almost the exact same floor plan. Eileen planted a bug in the reception area to find out when the office would be clear for her to plant a few more, and Avery has already bugged the office in Aspen. Today he's going to stake out the mysterious garage on Steinwood's property.

"Eileen spotted a rather grungy-looking bloke leaving the office in London and took a photo. We ran it through the channels, and it turns out this person is a two-bit criminal named Jerry Hardy. Breaking and entering, shoplifting, and purse snatching. Also, several arrests for drug possession, to

187

wit, pot and cocaine. It appears he has some connection with a drug concierge named Franny O'Rourke."

Charlotte tentatively raised her hand. "May I ask what a drug concierge is?"

The women began to giggle.

Myra placed her hand on Charlotte's. "Don't mind them. They can be a little jaded."

"Jaded? Us?" The sisters cackled with glee.

Charles cleared his throat and continued, "A drug concierge is someone who procures special orders for rock stars, wealthy men, models, designers. It's one-stop shopping. They can get their hands on almost anything . . . heroin, cocaine, acid, marijuana, roofies — also known as Rohypnol, the date-rape drug — fentanyl, which is a synthetic opioid, crystal meth. It's quite a menu. They also get a handsome commission, since money is no object to their clientele."

"What kind of business would this punk have with Marcus?" Isabelle asked.

"Now, that is a very good question. Around lunchtime, Eileen followed Marcus from his office to his apartment building. He was inside for just a few minutes. She then followed him across town, where he went into a jewelry store. She couldn't tell if he bought anything, but he came out with a wild look on his face. As she put it, 'He looked like the Cheshire cat.' He then went straight back to his office. She will be planting some bugs in Marcus's office later. Sasha will be working on Corbett, who is out in Sag Harbor. Sasha spotted Corbett reading a Christie's auction house catalog. According to her report, he had an expression of elation on his face while he was reading it. We need to find out what has enthralled both of these men so much."

Annie chimed in. "I can call Victor at Christie's, and Myra and I can pay him a visit when we go to New York."

"You are going to have a very busy schedule," Fergus observed.

"Yes, you are, because according to the blueprints, each office has a vault — a Scripps Safe TRXP Series pharmacy vault. We may need your safecracking expertise at all three locations. Those vaults are not easy to break into." Charles looked directly at Annie, who eagerly rubbed her hands together.

Charlotte gasped at the revelation that her old friend, perhaps the richest woman in the world, was an accomplished safecracker. The girls all chuckled at her reaction.

Myra said, "Three critical things we must

focus on. First, Maggie needs to talk to the Thompson family and see what we can learn about the circumstances of her death. Second, Isabelle and Alexis have to find out about Marjorie Brewster's condition. Finally, as a group, we need to decide how these poor excuses for human beings are going to pay for their sins."

"We need to find their Achilles' heels." Nikki tapped her pen on the table. "But I don't think it will be in those vaults."

"You are correct, but we do need to know what they're hiding," Charles replied.

"Myra also makes a good point. It's a twofold operation. Which do we pursue first? Or do you think we can gather what we need simultaneously?" Nikki asked.

"We should have more intel from Avery and his crew by tomorrow. Once we know what we are dealing with, we can assign everyone her duties," Fergus added.

"What about the snatch?" Yoko asked. "How will we coordinate three at once? We can't do that in stages, because the others will find out and probably flee."

"Good point." Myra touched her pearls. "I've been thinking."

In unison, the group chorused a teasing "Uh-oh" and broke into fits of laughter.

Myra shook her head and smiled. "As I

was saying. We know that emotional pain can be much more excruciating than physical pain. With the exception of children or pets, we need to find what would cause these men to suffer mentally."

"And I was hoping for another scorching." Alexis reminded them of their last mission, with a woman who had a penchant for very expensive shoes and abused her adopted son. She would have a very difficult time squeezing her feet into four-thousand-dollar Manolo Blahniks now.

"Ew. I remember how badly that smelled. Let's not do that again, please," Yoko added her opinion. "Can't we just send them off somewhere with Pearl?" Pearl Barnes was their "relocation" connection. She ran a secret underground railroad for abused women and children and occasionally freelanced for the Sisterhood. Except the people the Sisterhood provided were not sent to a safe house, but more like to the most unsafe place people would want to find themselves.

"As soon as we know a little more about these men, we'll be able to plan their grand finales, that is, the one before God gets His hands on them," Myra added.

Annie made a list:

1. Maggie on the Thompson story.

2. More intel from Avery's group.
3. Isabelle and Alexis go to Aspen to get Brewster medical records.
4. Myra and Annie head to New York to see Victor at Christie's. Depending on what is discovered, either stay or fly to London with Charlotte.

"Do we have any idea how much longer Avery's team will be?" Annie asked.

Fergus checked the monitor screens for any updates. "Looks like tomorrow. Day after, the latest."

"I'll call my pilot and let him know we'll be flying in a few days." Annie added that to the list.

Maggie slumped in her chair. "You guys get to have all the fun in Annie's private jet. I'm sure I'll be sitting in front of some spoiled brat in economy class who likes to kick the seat."

"Stop moaning. Instead of taking the shuttle, take the Acela to New York City from Union Station." Annie stuck out her tongue.

"If you insist." Maggie went to bite her nails but was stopped short by their unusually pristine condition and giggled.

"Hmmm . . . This really is a good deterrent."

Annie turned to her. "What do you have on the Thompson case?"

Maggie checked her laptop. " 'Lorraine Thompson, widow and mother, passed away at home of an apparent suicide. Family members said she had been very emotionally unstable as of late but were shocked that she had been despairing enough to have committed suicide. Her eldest daughter, Genevieve Ringwood, said her mother had been a bit manic but not necessarily depressed. "We would have done something about it if we had only known.' "The article goes on to offer the usual bromides. 'If you or anyone you know shows signs of depression, call the hotline.'

"I spoke to Mrs. Ringwood, who was very reluctant to talk to me on the phone, so I offered to interview her in person. She sounded a little . . . I dunno. Secretive? Like she was hiding something."

"If anyone can get her to talk, it's certainly you!" Annie chortled.

"I'm meeting with her day after tomorrow. She lives in Huntington, Long Island, so I'll take a car from Penn Station. I asked her if she had any paperwork on Live-Life-Long, which seemed to spook her a bit. She stammered but said she would look through her mother's papers and see what she could find. I thought that was very accommodating of her."

"Very," Myra said thoughtfully. "Perhaps she, too, has her suspicions but was afraid to voice them. Good job, Maggie. I'm sure once she meets you, she'll spill her guts."

"That's what I'm hoping for." Maggie took a little bow.

Charles and Myra could hear the dogs making a yapping sound, signaling it was getting close to dinnertime.

"I think we have plenty to work with now." Annie looked around the room. Everyone nodded in agreement.

"Let's eat!" On that note, Maggie, with the voracious appetite, brought the meeting to an end, and each of the sisters gave a fist bump and hooted their slogan, "Whatever it takes!"

"Which includes feeding Maggie." Charles gave the erstwhile newspaperwoman a wink.

The group saluted Lady Justice, climbed up the steps, and entered the delicious-smelling kitchen. Charles clapped his hands once and directed, "Fall to it!" That was the signal for everyone to perform their dinner duties, as well as for the dogs to line up for their evening meal. In less than thirteen minutes, the table was set, the dogs were fed, and the scrumptious casserole and side dishes were placed on the table.

They took a moment to say grace, and Charlotte added, "Dear Lord, bless these wonderful friends. I am so fortunate to have them in my life."

A resounding "Amen!" filled the room. Lady and her pups echoed the sentiment with their version of prayer — little yowling and a yap.

Once the table was cleared and the kitchen sparkling clean, the women headed back to the war room to see what other information might have come in.

CHAPTER 24

Aspen

Avery Snowden put on a pair of overalls, a flannel shirt, and a hard hat. He could easily pass for a lineman. He jumped into the cab of the utility truck and headed toward Crystal Lake Road. When he came upon the estate, he parked the truck along the side of the road and put out an orange cone and a MEN WORKING sign. He hoisted the bucket to the level of the tree line to get a good view of the property. From where he sat, he could see the front and side entries of the house, as well as the four overhead garage doors. It was eight in the morning. Should be some action soon.

Within the half hour, Steinwood exited through the side door and pushed a few buttons next to the garage doors. The closest door to Avery slid smoothly up the tracks. He couldn't get a good look inside, but what he saw was impressive. A glint of two very high-end sports cars from the reflection of the morning sun. Avery suspected there could be more. He definitely needed to get into that garage.

Steinwood pulled out the Jaguar and roared out of the driveway, just as he had done the day before. Avery quickly got out his small camera with the telephoto lens and snapped a photo of the cars before the garage door closed. He then sent the photo off to Charles who he hoped would be able to identify the cars. Avery waited several minutes before he brought the bucket down, then jumped out and walked up the driveway as if he belonged there. Cable service, if anyone asked. Getting past the cameras could be a problem. The layout of the garage did not seem out of the ordinary. It was the size of the garage that was striking. There were three doors on one side and three on the opposite side. The driveway wrapped around the building. He suspected there would be cameras on the other side, as well. He decided to move the truck to get a different vantage point. Maybe he would be able to see the other side of the garage.

Avery hopped back into the truck and moved it several yards and placed the orange cone and the sign behind it. This time he raised the bucket above the tree line and could make out a camera on the nearest corner. It was going to be a bit tricky, but he had been through worse. He simply needed to find out where the equipment that recorded the camera shots was kept.

Once he got back to his motel, he would check the electrical schematics again. It was possible he could jam the frequency. At least for a short time.

Eileen signaled to Avery that she was able to return to the London Live-Life-Long office. She was astonished that the lock on the rear door was incredibly easy to pick. But as Avery had discovered in Aspen, there was little information in the files. But there was a large vault in the closet of the corner office that begged to be opened. That exercise would have to wait until she got the all clear. Often, the sisters preferred to do the reveal themselves. It could get dicey. She did as Avery told her and planted a microcamera in the room that housed the vault. As she was planting a bug and camera in the rear office, she couldn't help but notice what appeared to be white residue on the leather-topped desk. She snapped a photo and made her way out of the building.

Next would be Dr. Marcus's flat. That should be easy enough. The Plimsoll Builld-ing had a rooftop conservatory where an event was held several times a week. She would dress appropriately for what would most likely be a fund-raiser. Her challenge would be finding an outfit that would work double duty. Chic enough for cocktails yet flexible enough for snooping. This was London. Almost anything would be fine. Probably the funkier the better. She thought of Emma Peel, the superspy from *The Avengers*. Maybe not quite a catsuit, but something definitely pleather.

Avery returned the utility truck to the same parking lot he had left it in before, walked to the rental, and headed back to his motel. He had a lot of work ahead of him. First was to listen to the recordings from the of-fice. Who came and who went and what was said. Second, he had to figure out how to disarm the cameras that faced the mysteri-ous garage.

He flipped open one of his laptops and opened the audio files from the office. He had been able to plant a camera the size of a pinhead on the inside door of the closet that housed the vault. The hope was to be able to see what was inside the vault when it was opened.

Avery listened. "Good morning, Mrs. Kaplan." The receptionist's voice came across the recording loud and clear. "How are we feeling today?" *Why do medical people always use the word* we? *Shouldn't they know how* they're *feeling?* Avery had little patience with people these days.

"I'm feeling a bit sluggish, to be honest," Mrs. Kaplan confessed.

"Well, Dr. Steinwood will have you fixed up in a jiffy. He'll be right with you. Please take a seat," the woman instructed. Avery could hear clicking. Probably her typing something into a computer.

A few minutes later, "The doctor will see you now." A soft buzz could be heard, presumably opening the glass doors that led to the patient examination rooms.

Avery switched to the hallway microphone. "Good morning, Elizabeth. Feeling a bit peaked? Let's see how we can make that better. Please, step inside."

A quick switch to the microphone planted in the patient suite. Dr. Steinwood continued, "Tell me. How long have you felt this way?"

Mrs. Kaplan's voice was just as clear as his. "A couple of days. I seem to have good days and bad ones. One day I'm fit as a fiddle, and the next, I'm just a wet noodle."

"As I explained, it takes our bodies time to adjust to the synapses and integration of the protocol." Steinwood was using some doctor babble on her. "Let's check your blood pressure." Steinwood buzzed for the nurse. "Sylvia, could you please come in here and check Mrs. Kaplan's blood pressure?"

"Certainly, Doctor," was the response.

"I'll get your supplements while Sylvia takes your pressure." Steinwood could be heard leaving the room as the nurse entered.

Avery followed the sound of Steinwood moving down the hallway and into the rear office. He heard the clicking sound of a door and switched to the camera, hoping Steinwood would open the vault, and he could get a look inside. *Genius!* Now, if Steinwood would only move just a few inches to the right, he would have a clear shot into the vault. *Bingo!* Hundreds of color-coded boxes filled the vault. Steinwood pulled a small portable table next to him and placed nine different boxes on it. As Steinwood opened each box, Avery could see eight green bottles with a numbered code. They looked like medications. The ninth box contained vials. Steinwood pulled one out. Next to the vault were shelves with beautifully decorated boxes. Steinwood placed the eight bottles in one of these boxes and then placed the box in a beautiful matching shopping bag. He put the vial in his pocket and reached for a syringe that was kept in a basket. After carefully locking the vault, he turned quickly. Avery was taken aback at how close Steinwood's face came to the camera. Then the screen went dark as Steinwood turned off the light.

Avery went back to the audio files. Steinwood reentered the room in which Mrs. Kaplan waited. "Here you go, my dear." Avery could hear the rustling of paper. Must be the shopping bag. "Now let's roll up our sleeve for our booster shot." *Again, with the first-person plural?* Avery shook his head. *What a con job.*

"Oh, Dr. Steinwood. I do appreciate what you are trying to do for me. I hope I start to see some results soon. At least get off this roller-coaster ride." Mrs. Kaplan almost sounded apologetic that she wasn't responding to the treatment faster.

"Now, now. Don't you fret. It takes time. We'll see you next week?" he asked kindly.

"Of course!" Mrs. Kaplan brightened. "Thank you so much. Have a lovely day." More paper rustling, and Avery switched to the reception-area audio file.

In a matter-of-fact voice, the receptionist said, "That will be eight thousand dollars, Mrs. Kaplan."

Avery almost fell off his chair. Those must be very special pills.

He fast-forwarded the recordings to see if there was anything else he could summarize for Charles. According to the timer on the recording devices, it was just around noon when Steinwood entered the reception area.

"Ladies, that will be all for today. Not to worry. You'll get your full pay. I'm going to a car show in Las Vegas this afternoon. I'll be back in two days."

Avery sent a report to Charles, along with the video footage.

Vault holds what looks like different meds in green bottles. Also vials. All unknown substances. Color coded and numbered. Saw one patient today. Leaving for a car show in Vegas for the next two days. O&O (over and out).

Avery was pleased with what he had discovered. Looked like a pill mill, but where were they coming from? That would probably be a riddle for Charles and the sisters to unravel. Meanwhile, he would scope out the house and the garage. *Car show.* Now it was starting to come together. Just how many and how expensive? would be the next questions.

CHAPTER 25

Pinewood

Returning to the war room, all the women saluted Lady Justice, Charlotte included.

Charles checked to see if any additional information had come in. "Splendid. More intel." Charles beamed. "Avery got a look inside the vault. Hundreds of boxes, all of which contained green bottles." He turned the monitor so everyone could see.

"That's just what mine look like!" Charlotte flinched in horror as Myra took her hand.

"And from the lab results, we have a pretty good idea what's in all those bottles," Nikki added. "Now the question that needs to be answered is, Where are the drugs coming from? Since these doctors are not licensed to practice where they have set up shop, these drugs could not have been obtained from pharmaceutical companies. That means they must be bootlegged."

"Indeed," Charles noted. "Avery also reported that he got a glimpse of what's in Steinwood's garage. He took a quick photo as Steinwood was leaving in his Jaguar. In the photo, you can see the partial hood of a Porsche nine-eleven and the Lamborghini insignia on another car. And Steinwood is heading to Las Vegas for a car show."

Nikki checked her laptop to see if any more information had come in about the doctors' holdings or the company itself. "Woo-hoo! Got some background info," Nikki interjected. "The company is a limited partnership."

"Please excuse my naïveté, but can you explain what that means? I'm just a children's book author." Charlotte giggled nervously.

"There are two classes of partnerships — general and limited. In a limited partnership, the partners' assets are protected, in that their liability cannot exceed what they initially invested. The business itself does not pay income tax. Each partner has to file an individual tax return. However, the partnership itself must be registered with the state in which it conducts business. That brings me to this next bit of information. The Live-Life-Long paperwork states that it is a consulting business. There is no mention of alternative medicine. That keeps them off the FDA's radar," Nikki explained.

"Very clever men," Myra said thoughtfully. "Do we know what each of the men invested?"

"Not yet. We're working on banking records now."

"Banking records? You can do that?" Charlotte was astonished.

"Let's just say we have ways to get the information we need," Nikki said.

"Goodness gracious. Sure sounds like it!" Charlotte was feeling giddy.

"From what Alexis and I could discover from their college records, Dr. Marcus was the better student at Ross. He excelled in chemistry. Dr. Corbett barely passed his courses, but he took online courses in business and marketing. Steinwood comes from old money, so we suspect he had the seed money for the operation," Nikki said.

Annie jumped in. "Excellent. Let's put these pieces together. The men met in medical school. Only one of them was a great student. Steinwood was a trust-fund baby, so he didn't care all that much. Corbett was a wannabe socialite. He probably came up with the scheme, especially after seeing how the rich vacation in Barbados. And how many of them are dowagers looking for the fountain of youth? Marcus was a whiz but needed more experience in pharmacology. And where are most of the drugs produced? Mexico."

Alexis continued what Nikki had started. "We contacted several obvious places of employment, under the guise of checking references. Corbett worked in the marketing department, Marcus in the labs, and Steinwood . . . Well, he had the worst record of all of them, getting fired from three different jobs at three different pharmaceutical companies. I guess he decided to hang out in Cabo San Lucas rather than work."

"This was a meticulous plan," Charles said pointedly. "And long range."

"Let's not forget the most important parts, devious and callous," Myra added, her blood boiling.

The sisters murmured in agreement.

Charles continued sharing the most current information Avery's group had gathered. "Eileen is attending an event tonight —"

"An event?" Myra interrupted with disdain. "We need her to do her job!"

"Easy, old girl." Charles put a hand on his wife's trembling shoulder. "The event is at the Plimsoll Building, which is where Dr. Marcus lives. There's a rooftop conservatory on the thirteenth floor. His flat is on the tenth. Eileen will gain access to the building and will make her way to his place."

Myra took in a deep breath. "But how will she know if the apartment is empty?"

"Ring the doorbell, dear."

Hoots of laughter filled the room.

"Oh, Charles, I wish you wouldn't patronize me." Myra gave him a stern look. "But I suppose I'm very sensitive about this entire matter because it's Charlotte." She smiled at her friend.

"I don't mean to be so much trouble!" Charlotte was teetering on the edge of tears.

"There, there. You are *not* trouble. I'm much more comfortable with details. That's all." Myra took another deep breath and managed to calm herself.

"Eileen has had a good look at the floor plan of Marcus's apartment. She'll know where to plant bugs and cameras. And she's quick. Most likely, she'll plant a listening device next to the entry door. She has the office wired, so she'll know when Marcus leaves. She is a crackerjack at her job," Annie pointed out, trying to defuse any additional anxiety.

"You're right." Myra reached for her pearls. "So, when are we leaving for New York?" She grinned at Annie.

"As soon as I hear from Victor."

"Fine." Myra turned to Charlotte. "I don't want to pressure you, dear. Do you think you're up for this escapade?"

"I've got my running shoes on," Charlotte said with gusto. "And it's not because I'm running away!"

The women thrust their fists into the air. "Whatever it takes!" Their slogan, their chant.

Annie's phone chimed. It was a text from Victor. **Lunch? Day after tomorrow?**

She turned to Myra and Charlotte. "Ladies, pack your bags. We're going to New York for lunch."

Responding to Victor, she punched in: **Absolutely! Per Se? The salon? One o'clock. I'll make the rez.**

Seconds later, Victor responded. **Splendid!**

Annie quickly punched in the number of her personal concierge with instructions for train tickets on the Acela, lunch at Per Se, and a suite with adjoining rooms at the Ritz-Carlton. "Okay! We're ready to roll. Maggie, you'll meet up with us at the hotel after your interview with Mrs. Ringwood. We'll have dinner and discuss our next move. By then, we'll have more background on the Thompson situation and what is so intriguing in the Christie's catalog."

"I'll pack the usual components you'll need to communicate with us. I'm assuming Fergus and I will be holding down the fort here," Charles offered with a wide grin.

"Darling, you are so right!" Myra beamed. Now the wheels were turning in the direction they needed to go.

CHAPTER 26

Sag Harbor

Sasha put her Brompton M6L folding bike into ride position. She loved its compactness and light weight. No more than twenty-four inches when folded and only twenty-six pounds. It could fit into most trunks and the backseat of any car, as well as in a helicopter. She was glad she had thought of it when she hitched a ride with Jason. Traffic was rather light on the East End of Long Island, and it would become pretty obvious if a car was trailing someone. But someone on a bicycle wouldn't be noticed.

Pedaling out to Corbett's place, she checked the odometer. It was five miles from her motel to his house and another five miles to his office in the village. *Easy peasy.* She rolled past the driveway and stopped to take a swig from her water bottle. She spotted the blue Mercedes. So, he hadn't left yet. Or maybe he had taken a cab? She hopped back on the bike, rode a few hundred yards down the road, and stopped again. This time she pretended to tie her shoe. After turning the bike around, she was heading toward Corbett's house again when a blue Mercedes passed her on the other side of the road. It was Corbett. She stopped, waited a few minutes, and then started toward his house again. There were no signs of movement outside. She stashed the bike in the hedge and carefully made her way to the back door, peeking into the windows. No movement inside, either.

After looking around for any other signs of life, she pulled herself up onto the second-story deck. She checked the sliding patio door. Unlocked. *This is going to be almost too easy,* she thought, until she heard the crunching of gravel in the driveway. She listened carefully as she leaned into the building, trying to conceal herself from view. She heard women's voices chattering in a foreign language. It was Russian. She could make out a few words that indicated they were there to clean the house. She had to think fast. She couldn't climb down without them seeing her. If she stayed in a fixed position, she might be able to avoid their attention. But for how long? After listening for a few more minutes, she realized that there were only two of them. Their voices trailed off as they entered the house. She could hear only mumbling from her vantage point on the deck.

Sasha checked her immediate surroundings. On the deck there were two chaise lounge chairs and a box, which probably contained the cushions for the chairs. With the agility of a cat, Sasha moved to the box and looked inside. As suspected, cushions. If she could maneuver the cushions to the chairs, she could stow away in the box until the cleaning crew left. Listening carefully for sounds from inside the house, she could tell that the women were in the kitchen below. The blare of a radio startled her. She held her breath. The music continued to play as the women kept yakking. She had to move quickly. One cushion. Then the other. Each set on top of a chair.

Sasha folded herself into the box and left the lid slightly cracked so she could breathe. She waited. Almost three hours went by. Her legs were getting numb. Then she heard doors slam and a car start up, followed by the same gravelly sound she had heard earlier. Five minutes more, then she should be free.

Peering out from the box, Sasha did a 180-degree scan of the backyard to make sure it was safe to come out. Once she steadied herself, she climbed out of the box and made a beeline to the patio door. Locked! One of the housekeepers must have done it. It was easy pickin's but would add another minute or so to her job, and she didn't know how soon Corbett would return. She still had to get into the office. Time was running out. Myra wanted answers. She and Annie would be in the city in less than two days.

Sasha picked the lock, slid the patio door open, slipped into the master bedroom, and placed one listening device between the bed and the sitting area and another in the enormous closet. She checked it for a safe. None. Then she placed bugs in the upstairs hallway and one in the guest bedroom. After swiftly making her way down the stairs, she placed two devices in the great room; one in the kitchen, near the snack bar; one in the utility room; and a third in the rear entranceway. She then made her way to the den. Sparse. One wall of bookshelves with drawers at the bottom but not many books; a solid piece of wood that served as a desktop, a Tycoon Executive chair, and two side chairs. Sasha went behind the desk and placed a bug near the phone. Landlines were still necessary in some places.

She pulled out one of the drawers at the bottom of the bookcase and grinned. There was a top-open security drawer safe embedded in the wood cabinet. It had a keypad lock. Most people didn't think about wiping their fingerprints off. Sasha pulled out a little dusting kit and lightly brushed the keypad. Four numbers lit up: six, four, seven, and nine. Now she had to figure out the sequence. She checked his stats. His birthday! June 4, 1979. *Ta-da!* Mortgage papers for the house, his will, and a deed to a piece of land in Michigan. She snapped photos of the documents, sent them off, then carefully replaced the papers in the same order she had found them. She slid the drawer shut and headed to the rear door. After looking outside to check for any other visitors, she closed the door behind her and made her way back to her bicycle.

It was time to check on the doctor's office. There was more traffic than there had been earlier as she pedaled her way to the village. Among the upscale shops and cafés was a building with a pristine white, frosted-glass door and the same logo that was displayed at the other offices of Live-Life-Long.

Sasha parked her bicycle at one of the racks across the street from the office. She would pull the same "I'm lost" ruse her colleagues had used. It was the easiest way to plant a listening device. No one ever expected it. When she entered, she noticed the same style, aroma, and sounds the other two had reported. But here, there was only one person sitting behind the counter. *Must be a slow day,* she thought.

When Sasha pulled off her cap, the hair of her blond wig framed her face. "Hello. I'm sorry to bother you, but could you point me in the direction of the Whaling Museum? I seem to be a little lost."

"Of course, dear. When you leave the building, stay to your left. At the end of the block, make a left on Main Street. It's just a ways down." The woman hardly looked up as she spoke. Sasha wondered how many times the woman had been asked that question. Sasha surreptitiously placed the listening device on the back of the orchid plant, expressed her gratitude, and trotted out.

Checking for sound, Sasha plugged in her earbud. Yep. She could hear the woman rustling about. The phone buzzed. "Yes, Dr. Corbett. Today? No, we have no other patients on the calendar for today. Was there someone you wanted to see? Someone you wanted me to contact?" She listened a moment. "Okay. Fine. Thank you. I'll lock up after you leave."

From what Avery had shared, it seemed as if these men didn't put in a whole lot of hours, except maybe Dr. Marcus. Still, Marcus didn't appear to have any more patients than his partners. But, then again, the doctors had been surveilled for less than two days.

Sasha looked around for a café and tried to spot where Corbett had parked his car. It must be in the back. Sasha was waiting for the receptionist to leave, but then it occurred to her that she might be parked in the back, too, so she listened very carefully for the sound of nothing. Once she felt it was safe to make a move, she would ride her bike to the corner, stash it, then make her way to the back entrance on foot.

Satisfied the office was empty, Sasha carefully walked to the back door while checking for security cameras on poles, rooftops, trees. Not too bad. She scurried behind a few trees until she was directly across from the door. She needed to walk at an angle to avoid one on the corner of the building next door. She fired up her pack and checked for an alarm system. Yes, but not engaged. She wondered if the receptionist was still there. She had already had one close encounter that day. She'd gladly skip more of them if possible. That box was tight.

She picked the lock, disengaged the alarm system, and proceeded to place the listening devices in the same places Eileen and Avery had. And the security camera in the closet.

She was in and out in less than eight minutes. Having the blueprints always gave one a leg up.

After the ten-mile ride back to her motel, Sasha tossed the wig into her bag, peeled off her clothes — boy, did she need a shower — and decided to try the little roadhouse on the other side of town. Maybe some honky-tonk music would be nice. She had had two very busy, productive days. What she really needed was a massage, a facial, and another massage.

CHAPTER 27

The war room

Charles could hardly keep his stiff-upper-lip demeanor as he reported back to the women. "Sasha has completed planting the surveillance devices. Three offices and two residences are now covered. By this evening, we should have Dr. Marcus's flat covered. As far as Dr. Steinwood's going to Vegas, do you think we should have Avery tail him there?"

"I think Avery should find out what is in that garage and the house. With Steinwood away, that should give Avery better opportunities to drill down to what brand of underwear he wears," Annie said smugly. The women snickered at the remark. "We know why he's going to Vegas. We need to know what he's doing in Aspen."

"Righto," Charles replied.

"Bummer," Alexis teased. "I was itching for a few slot machines."

"Not this time." Myra smiled. "I think we've found Steinwood's passion, so to speak. Expensive cars. We need Avery to find out how many he has."

"Roger that." Charles sent off a message to Avery.

"After meeting with Victor, we should have a good idea of what Dr. Corbett's hobby is, and after a day or so of surveilling Marcus, we should have his. That's when the game gets serious," Annie reminded them.

"I have some pretty good contacts with car dealers. Had to haul a few trailers in my day," said Kathryn, who had finally arrived at Pinewood. "I can take on that part once I get back from the Michigan trip. That should take only three days."

"Perfect." Myra beamed.

"This is all so complicated," Charlotte observed, awestruck by the complexity of how the sisters went about a mission. Then she giggled. "You should start your own private investigating company!"

The sisters hooted.

"We have much more in our toolbox to offer than surveillance. That's why we have Avery and his team," Nikki reminded her.

"Well, I'm just along for the ride," Charlotte said gleefully.

221

"I was hoping you'd be Annie's and Myra's chaperone," Charles joked.

"Chaperone?" Myra pretended to be offended. "When have we ever . . . never mind." She remembered, as did everyone else, and they started muttering.

"That will leave me and Charles here for the time being," Fergus noted. "Nikki is on standby. Isabelle and Alexis are off to Aspen, Maggie is going to Long Island, Kathryn and Yoko are headed to Michigan, and the two troublemakers are off to New York City and parts unknown." He winked at Annie, who was about to smack him on the back of the head.

"We still haven't covered London yet," Nikki pointed out.

"We'll wait to hear back from Avery to see what Eileen was able to discover. Then we'll make a plan. I'm curious about that rubbish Jerry Hardy. I wonder if he's cheeking for Marcus," Charles said.

"Cheeking?" several of the sisters asked quizzically.

Both Charles and Fergus snorted. "Sorry. Old Brit slang for someone who transports drugs between their butt cheeks."

Hysterical laughter bounced off the walls.

"He looks too skinny to even have butt cheeks," Kathryn roared. Tears of laughter were running down almost everyone's face.

Charles whistled. "All right. Everyone calm down. As of tomorrow morning, you will all be on your way to your appointed destinations, except Nikki. Be safe."

A resounding "Amen" came from the group as they rose, saluted, and began to prepare for their assignments.

CHAPTER 28

Two town cars entered the gates of Pinewood to carry the sisters to the starting points. Isabelle and Alexis were heading to Leesburg Executive Airport, where Annie kept her private jet; Myra, Annie, and Charlotte were going to Union Station. Maggie had already left to meet with Mrs. Ringwood.

Alexis managed fabulous disguises for both herself and Isabelle. One could never be too careful in their line of work. Or was it more of a hobby these days? A very intricate one, to be sure.

Alexis thought the trashy *Real Housewives* look would be a hoot while they were in transit — coming and going from airports. Alexis donned an overly padded leopard spandex jumpsuit, fake glittered one-inch fingernails, a very long black wig, lots of black eyeliner, hot pink lipstick, and so much bling that she almost toppled over in her stiletto heels. Both women were on the verge of hyperventilating with laughter.

"They'll think you're drunk!" Isabelle howled.

"And what are you going to wear?" Alexis stared at her through tinted contact lenses.

"I'm thinking blond dreadlocks."

"And?" Alexis poked her.

"And a pumped-up spandex number like yours. Mine will be black."

"Same amount of bling? I don't want to be the only one staggering."

"Yes, honeypot. And a big gold lamé belt."

"Stilettos?"

"Like I need to make my legs any longer? I'm thinking boots. With a heel. I don't want to tower over you," Isabelle said.

"We'll walk arm in arm. If we're going to be obnoxious, we might as well go all the way! It's almost too bad that we're flying by private jet. Think how much fun it would be to be flying commercial in these outfits."

Isabelle hooted.

Myra entered the room where the two women were dressing. "What is all the cackling? Sounds like the two of you are having too much fun! You better shake a leg. The cars are waiting."

"We're ready! What do you think?" Both women struck a pose.

Myra burst into laughter. "Now, that's a reality show I think I'd rather skip!"

"Very funny. Don't mock my creativity," Alexis crowed back. She knew Myra was joking, and she, too, would rather skip that show.

Annie came into the room. "You both look fantastic! I would never recognize either one of you. I arranged for the ski lodge to be ready for your arrival. No point in staying in a hotel. Yolanda will see that there is food in the fridge and fresh linens on the beds. That way, you can keep a low profile."

"Excellent!" both women declared.

Alexis and Isabelle stood in front of the full-length mirror to get one more glimpse of their over-the-top getups.

"Mission accomplished. At least this one." Isabelle grabbed an oversized hobo handbag with as much bling as she was wearing. "Let's roll, sister!"

The two women linked arms and half stumbled to the awaiting cars. Myra and Annie followed suit.

Charles and Fergus were waiting by the limos when the women exited the house. Catcalls and whistles filled the air.

"I trust that's for us," Myra cautioned him.

"Absolutely, my love." Charles gave her a

peck on the cheek and a love tap on her rear as he winked at Alexis and Isabelle. "Glorious job, Alexis. Bravo!"

Alexis popped a big piece of bubble gum in her mouth and started smacking it.

"I hope you're not planning on doing that during the flight." Isabelle looked at her sternly.

"Don't be ridiculous. I'm simply getting into character."

"You're a character, all right." Isabelle put out her hand. "Fire with fire. Where's mine?"

Alexis handed her a wad of gum as Fergus put the luggage in the trunk. The cars departed to their appointed destinations.

Isabelle and Alexis arrived at the small airport, boarded Annie's private jet, and settled into their seats. "This really is the only way to travel," Isabelle said wistfully. "Don't you just love it when we can go on a mission when Annie's jet is available?"

"You've got that right! I don't suppose we could start off with a mimosa?" Alexis said slyly.

"Let's start with our strategy first. Then we can relax. The flight is just over four hours," Isabelle responded.

The women pulled out their laptops and began to review the information they had on their subject. *Marjorie Brewster. Age sixty-five. Widowed. No children. Now residing in a nursing home. She has one sister, who lives in Boulder.* That was all they had. For now.

"I think we should visit Mrs. Brewster and see what her condition is. Last information we had was that she had slipped into a coma, but things could have changed," Alexis suggested.

Isabelle checked the file. "She was an art teacher before she got married. He had gobs of money. We can say we were students of hers."

"Perfect. Art teacher in local community college. We're here for a reunion, heard about her being ill, and want to visit."

"Sounds like a plan. We can do that this afternoon. The flight is four hours, but with the two-hour time-zone difference, we'll be there by one at the latest. We'll go to the lodge, get changed, and head over to the nursing home. Annie said we can use the Jeep in the garage," Isabelle added. "By the way, what do you have in mind for our next costume?" She rolled her eyes in anticipation.

"Let me think on that." Alexis looked at the list of outfits she had packed. "Hmmm. What would artists wear? Ah. Here we go. You get the maxi skirt, denim jacket, and a short pink pixie wig. Big black glasses, like the ones Annie sometimes wears."

"And you?" Isabelle gave her a sideways look.

"I'll be wearing denim overalls with a T-shirt and combat boots. And I'll use the wig you're wearing now."

"Speaking of which, do you think we should change into civilian clothes now?" Isabelle suggested. "I'm feeling a bit inflated in this thing!"

"I think we should wait until we get to the lodge, just in case we're caught on camera at the airport. That way, they'll never find the two big-assed, over-the-top bling chicks." Alexis chuckled.

"Good point. Too bad the flight is so long." Isabelle readjusted herself in the plush leather seat. "Once we check on Mrs. Brewster, we can head over to the hospital."

"Not before we change into something different." Alexis looked at her list again. "We'll be very corporate. I have a brown bob-cut wig for you, and I have a very short curly one for me. Remember, we're part of a scouting team doing research on skiing recuperation."

"Got it." Isabelle checked her laptop again. "I have the blueprints for the hospital administration offices. There is also a video of parts of the interior, including the floor plans. It looks like there is an office for the director of the hospital, two small offices, and an open section with workstations. I count four of them. I imagine that's where all the data from all the departments is stored. I'll check the electrical specs. That will tell me which section has the most cable connectivity, and that should indicate where the computers are located." Isabelle tapped a few strokes. "Yep. Looks like the four cubbies have the most outlets."

"Now, how do we get into their system?" Alexis looked at Isabelle. "I would imagine that information is highly guarded, no?"

"That depends. Even though HIPAA requires that a patient's privacy be maintained, that doesn't mean that the computer system itself has particularly tight security."

Alexis looked a little confused. "I'm not sure what you mean. Aren't patient records private?"

"Yes, but what that actually means is the information about a patient cannot be shared without the patient's consent. You signed those waivers anytime you went to the doctor."

"Sure. I give them the name of someone who they can call."

"Right. But as I was saying, they aren't

necessarily required to keep everything in a vault."

"Good thing. We already have three to deal with," Alexis said dryly.

"True. But what I was saying is that the hospital or doctor's office must provide a means by which to secure that information. Obviously, password-protected files, but the files could be accessed by several employees, all with their own password. And there are files that are not accessible to everyone."

"You mean the hospital may not have the tidiest means of securing the database?" Alexis seemed surprised.

"I can't tell yet. I'll have to get a look at the workstations and chat with some of the employees. Let's think on this. I can ask them to show me how their software program works. I could suggest using a file from someone who is deceased. Those are probably archived in a separate program. Or I may fake a need to use the Internet. I'll figure it out once I get the lay of the land."

Alexis sat back in her seat and crossed her arms across her fake overly voluptuous chest. "Well, I'll be darned. Abner has taught you well!" She gave her companion a wide grin.

"You ain't seen nothin' yet," Isabelle

replied. "I've been practicing. Abner gives me programs to hack. I think I've moved from 'intermediate hacker' to 'almost excellent hacker.'"

The women burst into laughter. "I'll drink to that!" Alexis pressed the button for the flight attendant. "My friend and I would like mimosas and a snack, please."

The middle-aged man, dressed in a white jacket, nodded. "Of course. What would you prefer to eat? We have smoked salmon with crème fraîche, poached chicken salad, roasted vegetable salad, or a charcuterie board."

Isabelle spoke first. "I'll have the salmon, please."

"Madame?" The attendant looked at Alexis.

"Charcuterie board, please. And sparkling water, too."

"Very well." The man nodded again, turned, and walked back to the galley.

"Now, this is the way to fly." Isabelle sighed.

"Yeah. Ain't that the truth." Alexis chuckled.

Several minutes passed, and the women moved to the other side of the jet, where there were two identical chairs and a table.

The flight attendant returned with a rolling cart and set their food on the table.

Isabelle grinned and started in on her food. Alexis did likewise.

After they finished their lunch, the women went back to the other table and scrolled through their information again, watched the video, and studied the layout of the offices. Luckily, it wasn't massive, like Bethesda or the Mayo Clinic. Aspen was famous for the celebrities during skiing season — which was why this hospital specialized in orthopedics. But the general population of Aspen was less than eight thousand people, and if there was a major medical crisis, one could go to Denver.

Thinking about that point, Isabelle asked Alexis, "Do we know if Mrs. Brewster was transferred to Denver? It doesn't look like they could accommodate someone in her condition for any length of time. It would make sense if they transferred her there." Isabelle kept sifting through pages on her screen but could not find any information about possible transfers.

"That should be on her release form, right?" Alexis asked. "Have you thought about how you are going to gain access to one of the computers? You know, the distracting people part?"

"As soon as we get there! But most likely,

I'll pretend I got an e-mail saying they — the home office — need me to look at some schematic, but the file is too big to download on my phone, and I don't have my laptop with me, and is there a computer terminal I could use for a couple of minutes? Then you are going to have to distract whoever else is hanging about."

"Sounds pretty sketchy, but it could work." Alexis considered. "You're right. We'll have to wait to see how it all plays out, how many people are on staff, in the area, et cetera."

The steward returned to the cabin. "I beg your pardon, but we are beginning our descent into the Aspen area. Please fasten your seat belts and store your electronic equipment. Please let me know if I can be of service."

The women looked up. Isabelle responded, "Thank you. I think we're fine. Alexis?"

"Yes. Thank you."

Alexis powered down her laptop, and Isabelle did the same. They stowed them in their humongous Fendi and Versace bags. Alexis pulled out another wad of gum and handed a piece to Isabelle.

"Ready for action?"

"You bet!" Isabelle gave her a high five.

The plane touched down without a bump and glided into the small area near the quaint alpine-and-stone terminal of Aspen-Pitkin County Airport. There was a commercial propeller plane nearby. Unlike at the huge metropolitan airports, with Jetways to the gate, the grounds people here had to roll portable stairs to the planes for the passengers to get on and off.

Just as they had done earlier, the women linked arms when their feet hit the ground, making a little bit of a scene. No one would recognize either one of them on any other occasion without that disguise. They were memorable, no doubt. But in the best way possible. No one would remember Isabelle or Alexis. Only the two bimbos named Chantal and Monique, whose names were on a sign being held by what appeared to be a driver.

The women waved their arms wildly. "Yoo-hoo! Here we are!" Alexis shrieked. The women wobbled toward the man, whose face was quickly turning red. "Hey! Hey! You our driver?"

With less enthusiasm than a mannequin, the young man barely mumbled, "Yes, I am, ma'am."

"Don't you be calling us ma'ams. Ya hear? We are ladies." Alexis was pouring it on thick. Isabelle gave her an elbow. "What's wrong with you?"

"Nothing, Monique, but don't you be harassing this fine young man. He's got to take us to our place." Isabelle directed her attention to the driver. "How do you do? Don't you mind her. She gets all uppity when anyone calls her ma'am. We should get a move on. We have a few bags . . . Er, what was your name again?"

"Richard," he answered reluctantly.

"Well, Richard, can you go fetch our suitcases please?" Monique/Alexis turned on the charm.

"Yes, of course." Richard pulled down the brim of his cap and retrieved their bags from the cart. "Follow me please." He couldn't walk fast enough. He practically threw the luggage into the back of the SUV, helped the women into their seats, and dived into the vehicle.

"Do you have the address?" Isabelle asked.

"Yes, ninety-three Primrose Path." Richard stepped on the accelerator as if he were stomping out a fire.

Isabelle and Alexis were trying very hard not to laugh, to the point where their bodies started shaking and then tears started rolling down their faces. When Isabelle's nose started to run, that was the final straw. They couldn't contain themselves any longer. The burst of laughter came as an explosion, causing Richard to slam on the brakes. Both women slid off their seats and ended up on the floor of the car. That brought more laughter when Isabelle's dreadlocks got tangled.

Richard pulled over to the side of the road. "Are you ladies all right?" He didn't know what to think or do.

The women straightened up, got back into their seats, and buckled up. "I guess we should have done this sooner," Isabelle said sheepishly as she clicked herself in. "Sorry, Richard. We just got in a laughing fit. Don't you pay us no mind. We're just happy to be away from our husbands. Ya know?"

Richard peered into the rearview mirror. "I suppose. I'm not married." *And I hope I'll never be . . . at least to anything like you two,* he thought to himself.

Primrose Path was just a few short blocks from the hospital, so they had the option of walking, but first, it was unpack, change, and visit Mrs. Brewster. They were hoping one of the other women would have some information on Brewster's sister in Boulder. Nikki was going to check legal records, and Maggie was checking the press.

When the vehicle stopped at the lodge,

Richard assisted the women as they got out, removed their bags from the back of the SUV, and brought them to the front door. He could not get back in the vehicle fast enough and peeled out as Monique/Alexis was waving a twenty-dollar bill.

"Wait! Richard! Your tip!"

He just kept on driving.

Alexis and Isabelle were doubled over with hilarity. "If only he knew what we really did to certain people." Isabelle could barely get the words out.

Yolanda opened the front door and stared, with her mouth agape. She knew that Isabelle and Alexis were coming. But who were these two?

"Yolanda!" Isabelle blurted. "It's us. We were practicing for a masquerade party! What do you think?"

"I think I have no idea who you are." Yolanda looked at them with suspicion. "Miss Annie said to expect Isabelle and Alexis."

Alexis was the first one to remove her wig. Isabelle followed.

"Oh, my Lord! The two of you had me going there! Come in! Come in! Your rooms are ready. Monte! Monte! Come get the girls' luggage." Yolanda led them through the foyer, then into the massive living room with vaulted ceilings.

"I forgot how magnificent this place is!" Isabelle looked out the floor-to-ceiling windows. They afforded a spectacular view of the mountains, still with snow-covered peaks.

"Yes. Stunning," Alexis said in agreement.

Monte called from the entry. "Hey, girls! Nice to see you! Where do you want me to put your stuff?"

The guest rooms were almost identical, each with a private bath, a balcony, and a view.

"Wherever. The black luggage is mine. The tan is Isabelle's," Alexis instructed. "Put hers in one room and mine in the other. Thanks!"

"Are you girls hungry? Thirsty? There's food in the fridge, wine, beer. Annie said you'd probably be staying three or four days. If you need anything, send me a text. I'll be back in the morning to make the beds and do the breakfast dishes," Yolanda informed them.

"That won't be necessary, Yolanda. Alexis and I can make our own beds and do our own dishes."

"Miss Annie said whatever you want."

"Yes, and we want you not to worry about us!" Alexis was very matter of fact. "We're here to do a little research and relax a bit."

"Okay, but I will tell Miss Annie you want to be on your own."

"No problem. We'll let her know. And we'll let *you* know if we need anything. Okay? We really do appreciate everything," Isabelle reassured her.

"All right. You can text me anytime. Enjoy your stay." With that, Yolanda left through the kitchen door.

"Looks like that cover-up was right on the money!" Isabelle slapped her friend on the back. "Time for the next costume change! Come on, master of disguise." She grabbed Alexis's hand as they marched up the stairs to the guest quarters.

Within the hour, they had unpacked their suitcases and begun the second transformation of the day. Both were happy to be rid of most of the makeup and the toe-pinching shoes and boots, but they were especially thrilled to get out of the padded bimbo outfits. It had made each of them look thirty pounds heavier.

"Remind me never to eat chocolate cake again," Isabelle muttered to herself.

The newly created "former art students" looked up directions to the nursing home and wrote them on a piece of paper. They didn't want Annie's vehicle to have any information stored on its GPS so they decided to go on foot. The nursing home was only minutes away.

It was a very small facility. Only forty beds. The women approached the receptionist's desk. A very leathery, too-much-sun middle-aged woman looked up. "How may I help you?"

"Hello. We're former students of Marjorie Brewster. We're in town for a reunion and heard she was staying here. We wanted to say hello, if that's possible," Isabelle informed the woman, who gave her a look of surprise.

"Uh, well, I don't know. Who did you say you were? Former students?"

"Yes. Is there a problem?" Alexis asked innocently.

"Uh, Mrs. Brewster has been in a coma for a while."

"You mean as in coma, coma? Like unconscious?" Isabelle played dumb.

"Yes, that is what a coma is. What did you say your names were?" Leather face, whose name was Jeanne, peered at them.

"Cherie and Mackenzie." Alexis threw the names out with practiced skill. All the sisters had a slew of aliases they could use in a flash.

"Just a minute." Jeanne turned and walked

into an adjoining office. Isabelle leaned over the counter to get a glimpse of the computer screen, but it was facing away at an angle.

"You're taller than I am," Isabelle whispered. "You try."

Alexis stretched and peeked at the screen. "I can't see it, either."

"Watch it. Here she comes." Isabelle had spotted the woman through the blinds on the window of the office. They settled back into their normal stances.

"I am going to have to call her sister to get permission. Mrs. Brewster never has visitors except for when her sister comes every couple of weeks." Jeanne picked up the phone and began dialing the number on the computer.

"Sure."

"Of course."

Marjorie Brewster's sister wouldn't know who they were, so things could go either way: she would say yes or no depending on how she felt about her sister having visitors.

"Hello? This is Jeanne from Mountain Hills Nursing Home." A pause, then, "No. Everything is fine. There are two women here who were students, and they wanted to see Marjorie." She listened for a response and looked at the women. "Yes, I explained her condition to them." Another pause.

"Oh. Okay. Yes, I will. Thank you." She hung up and repeated what she was told. "You can go in. Perhaps talk to her a bit. They say that people in comas can hear you. I don't know if that's true, but I suppose it can't do any harm. I have heard some stories myself, working here these many years. You should see some of the people who have had skiing accidents. I used to ski a lot, but now it's tennis whenever I get a chance. But working here . . . Well, the hours aren't terrible, but sometimes the shifts are not conducive to outdoor activity." Jeanne had become more animated, which made her look like a worn-out talking baseball glove.

Alexis gave Isabelle a slight kick, knowing they were both thinking the same thing. *Batter up!*

Trying to get the situation moving forward, Isabelle politely said, "Thank you very much, Jeanne. Can you direct us to her room, please?"

"Oh, of course. I tend to ramble a lot. All the way down at the end of the hall." She pointed in the direction of the room.

Isabelle and Alexis tried to maintain their composure. They took deep breaths and slowly moved toward Marjorie Brewster's room.

"This feels a little creepy," Alexis confessed. "It's like we're intruding."

"I know it feels that way, but we need to do this so we can report back to Myra and Annie."

"What about the sister? Should someone contact her?" Alexis queried.

"Once we get the info from the hospital, and depending on what we find at the end of this hallway, we'll send everything to Myra and Annie. There is a lot of information for them to evaluate, with more coming. I know they'll have a plan as soon as they have the whole picture."

"Okay. Here's her room." Alexis pointed at the name plaque next to the door.

Both women took a deep breath and squeezed each other's hand for reassurance. Despite all the missions they had gone on in the past, they always felt a sense of dread when a new one came along, since each one brought its own kind of horror, shock, and anger. And, they hoped, with the help of the sisters, justice.

A woman in her sixties lay perfectly still. Wires and tubes entered and exited various parts of her body. Beeps and blinks emanated from the machines that recorded her vital signs.

Isabelle approached the woman first. She

reached for the hand that was free of needles and whispered softly, "Hello, Marjorie. You don't really know us, but we come as friends." Isabelle flashed a look at Alexis. She thought she saw Marjorie's eyes flutter. She shrugged and continued. "We are going to try to help you come back to this side, but if we can't, we are going to go after the people responsible for this and see to it that they pay dearly for what they have done to you." She patted the woman's hand. Again, a slight flutter of the eyes.

Isabelle pointed to Marjorie's face and mouthed the words, "Look at her eyes." Alexis nodded, and then Isabelle continued. "We know you were taking special vitamins from Dr. Steinwood." Marjorie's hand started to twitch, setting off an alarm. Three nurses rushed in.

"What did you do?" one asked accusingly as the two others tended to Marjorie.

"Nothing. We were talking to her. Reminiscing about her art classes," Alexis replied.

Isabelle tried to deflect the tension with a joke. "I guess we were crummy students?"

A brutish-looking nurse did not think it was funny and cleared her throat. "This is not a laughing matter, miss. Mrs. Brewster is very fragile."

"I didn't mean any disrespect. And yes,

she looks very frail. I am so sorry if we did anything to upset her."

Alexis added, "Truly. We thought maybe hearing familiar voices might help. They say that some people do come out of comas after they have had stimulation from things in their life."

"My dear young lady. We don't need *you* to *tell* us what can and cannot happen. We are professionals and have far more experience than you do," the brute admonished them.

"Sorry. We were trying to be optimistic." Isabelle apologized and gave Alexis a hint to do the same.

"Yes, we apologize. All we wanted was to let her know what a great teacher she was and how much she inspired us." Alexis was pouring it on thick.

"If it weren't for Mrs. Brewster, we wouldn't be working artists today!" Even thicker from Isabelle.

The two other nurses had already left the room, after noting that Mrs. Brewster's vitals were stable. Brute motioned toward the door. "I think Mrs. Brewster needs to rest now. Thank you for visiting."

Isabelle and Alexis scurried through the door and walked quickly to the reception area. "Mrs. Brewster needs her rest?" Isabelle said in a loud whisper. "What do they think she's doing in there? Jumping jacks?"

"Hush." Alexis tried to calm Isabelle. "I don't want them physically throwing us out of here."

"Yeah, but did you notice that it was when I mentioned Steinwood that the ruckus started?"

"The theory may be right. They can hear what's going on." Alexis put her arm through Isabelle's as they waved at Jeanne. "Thanks very much! Bye-Bye!"

Jeanne waved back at them.

As soon as they jumped into the Jeep, Isabelle texted Myra. **Saw MB. Hand twitched when I mentioned DS. Then they threw us out. But all okay. Will call in later.**

"Wow. You're right about that twitching. Too bad we didn't have more time with her." Alexis drummed her fingers on the dashboard.

"I see those wheels turning. No, we are not going to break into this place later. We have our assignment. Besides, if we had said anything else, she might have died!" Isabelle's eyes widened.

"Huh. She's as good as dead," Alexis said bitterly.

"Hey, don't talk like that. Look what we went through, and our lives turned around."

"Yeah, but we weren't in a coma."

They drove back to the lodge in silence, each thinking back to her own personal nightmare: when Isabelle lost her job, her man, and was framed for drunk driving, and when Alexis was wrongfully imprisoned for fraud. Yes, each of them had suffered great losses, but life was still worth living, thanks to people like Myra Rutledge and Anna Ryland de Silva.

CHAPTER 29

London

Eileen found a perfect go-go outfit for the fund-raiser being held in the conservatory in Dr. Marcus's building. A red leather miniskirt, white leather boots, fake-fur vest, and a pixie wig, with a big shoulder bag on her arm. There was nothing in there that would set off security, and the devices she needed to plant in the apartment were tucked inside her bra. The contents of her bag were normal items, including a large shawl, foldable ballet flats for when her feet were tired of being tortured by high heels, a makeup case, phone charger, wallet, keys. The only thing was that the information in her wallet was fake, the phone charger was for the surveillance equipment, the shawl concealed an extra outfit, and the makeup was for the purpose of changing her look. The slippers were just for what they were meant to do and more. They gave her feet a break but were also made of special material that left no prints.

She approached the security desk in the lobby, then offered her purse to the guard, who simply nodded in her direction and let her pass through the small acrylic gate. She gave him a wink. He tipped his hat. *Yes, they will remember the cute chick in the sixties outfit. They will not remember the plain and simple, mousy-looking girl.*

Eileen made her way through the guests, had a few hors d'oeuvres, and snatched a glass of champagne from a waiter passing by with a trayful. Pretending to take a sip, Eileen looked around for the ladies' room. It was in the far corner, next to an exit. When Eileen had studied the blueprints, she had etched the exact location of the stairs into her memory.

She smiled and nodded to several people as she approached the bathroom. There was a woman washing her hands as Eileen entered. "Good evenings" were exchanged, and Eileen went into one of the stalls. She quickly removed her wig, boots, skirt, and vest and replaced them with a long prairie-style skirt, tan blouse, brown hair in a bun, and granny glasses. And the flat shoes. She stepped on the toilet to see if there was anyone else in the room. It was empty.

She turned her bag inside out, and it now looked like an old satchel. She took a quick look in the mirror. *Yes.* She'd blend right into the woodwork.

Slowly opening the door, she peered out to see if anyone was looking in her direction. There were a few people engaged in conversation nearby, so she avoided making eye contact with any of them. With catlike moves, she was in the stairwell. She waited. Listened. Nothing.

She looked around for security cameras, just in case they had changed the layout since the building opened. Everything appeared to be in the locations indicated on the plans. She knew where the cameras were and how to dodge them. She had already made her way to Marcus's floor when she saw the NO REENTRY sign on the door. *Damn.* That information had been omitted. She made her way to the floor below Marcus's and was able to enter the corridor. She would have to take the lift up, but she had to avoid the camera. Or change her disguise again. Thinking quickly, she pulled out the scarf, wrapped it around her head like a hijab, untucked her blouse, and made her way to the lift. The lift dinged when it reached Marcus's floor. Carefully looking in each direction, she proceeded to Marcus's flat. The hallway was very quiet except for the sound of soft classical music coming from one of the apartments. When she reached the door to Marcus's flat, she rang the buzzer. If anyone answered, she would use the "I'm lost or wrong number" excuse.

A second attempt. Nothing. After picking the lock, she slipped in. Listening for any sounds, she moved quickly, placing listening devices in key locations. She entered the master bedroom suite and placed a bug on the back of the headboard. The door to the walk-in closet/dressing area was ajar, so she peeked in and spotted the jewelry safe. She snapped a few photos and tried to decide if she should open it. With a little patience and the right technology, any lock could be picked. She tapped her watch to access the listening equipment she had assigned to Marcus's office. She could hear the two women chatting at the front desk.

"What do you suppose is going on with the doc?" one asked.

"What cha mean?" asked the other.

"You know. Him running in and out, that creepy kid who keeps coming around. And his moods. One minute he's a snarky old bear, and the next he's dancing on his tiptoes."

"Well, you know that wife of 'is drives him

crazy with all the money she spends!"

"Do tell!"

As much as Eileen wanted the dirty gossip, she needed to find out if he was still in his office. Then she heard the response.

"She's out drinking bottles and bottles of champagne, buying diamonds like they're candy, clothes, shoes. She's really something. I overheard him say she was going to send him to the poorhouse!"

"Get out! Really?"

"Aye. She keeps Harrods in business! And I know she's out spendin' again today. He was talkin' to her earlier. He told her he was going to the pub."

That was all Eileen had to hear. She hoped the information was right and she had some time. With great speed, she pulled out her pick tool. Next to the number pad was a small plastic piece that covered a keyhole. The keyhole was a backup in case the safe's battery ran out. Most people didn't know this tidbit. She pried off the plastic cover and inserted her pick tool. One full turn to the right, and it opened.

She snapped photos of the contents. Lots of diamonds and gold. Lots. She immediately sent the photos to Avery, who would relay them to Charles.

After setting everything back into place,

she slithered her way out the door and down the hall to the stairwell. The doors opened out, as required by law. Avoiding the cameras, she removed her latest disguise, down to her leotard and tights. She wrapped the shawl around her waist, making it look as if she were on her way to a yoga class.

CHAPTER 30

New York City

The three women exited the Acela train that had brought them from Washington to Penn Station. Annie could not help but comment on the difference between Union Station in D.C. and what she called "this poor excuse for a transportation hub."

"It's disgraceful. The original building was demolished in nineteen sixty-three, causing a big controversy with historical preservationists in New York."

"It is rather shabby," Myra commented. "And I know they have problems every day. But let's not dwell on this hot mess. Let's get to our hotel and lunch!"

Annie looked for a redcap to help with their luggage. She finally spotted what seemed to be the only one in sight and flagged him over. "Hello. Would you be so kind as to assist us with our luggage?"

The man beamed and pulled the dolly

over to where they were standing. The train conductors had helped them off with their belongings. "I would be happy to. Are all these yours?" He pointed to the assortment of bags and suitcases.

"We like to travel light." Everyone cackled at Annie's remark.

"You plan on staying awhile?" the redcap asked.

"Just a few days," Myra answered, not offering any other information.

They proceeded to the elevator, which seemed to be in New Jersey. After a long walk, they finally squeezed themselves and the luggage into the elevator car. When they reached the main level, the redcap delivered them to the sidewalk, and Annie gave him a twenty-dollar bill.

He tipped his hat. "Thank you very much. You enjoy your stay."

Annie looked for the car that was supposed to be waiting for them. She knew the three of them and all their luggage would not fit into a regular taxi. Through the bustle of cars, cabs, and vans, she spotted the vehicle with her preassigned number in the window.

"There he is!" She waved in his direction.

The problem was getting their luggage across the four lanes of traffic. It was a free-for-all. Horns beeping, people yelling, police blowing whistles. Myra thought Charlotte might just faint.

"Are you okay?" She took Charlotte by the elbow.

"Yes. I'm just, well, a little overwhelmed, I guess you'd say." Charlotte took a deep breath.

"No doubt. You've been through a lot, and now we sucked you into this," Annie said while trying to stop traffic. "No! *You* get out of the way!" she shouted at a cabdriver.

Charlotte cringed and pulled Myra closer to her. Myra chuckled softly. "Don't worry, dear. She won't get us killed. Arrested? Maybe." That made Charlotte giggle as they moved closer to the waiting car.

The driver got out and stowed their bags in the trunk of the town car. "Ritz-Carlton?" he asked.

"Yes," they said in unison, causing the driver to look in his rearview mirror. They looked like three women who were on a crazy road trip. Little did he know that he wasn't far from wrong.

The traffic was like traffic any day in New York. Slow. Jammed. Loud. A fire truck came screaming up Eighth Avenue, alerting cars to pull over. The problem was there was no room to go anywhere, but somehow the sea of cars opened, allowing for New York's Bravest to get through. When it came to a crisis, New Yorkers always stepped up. Overall, New Yorkers were very friendly and helpful. They simply needed to be approached the right way. Despite that, the city could be intimidating to visitors.

The car made a right turn from Eighth Avenue onto Central Park South and pulled in front of the hotel. The driver popped the trunk, and what seemed like an army of bellmen stormed the car. One of them recognized Annie right away.

"Countess! So nice to see you again!" He pecked the back of Annie's hand. "And Mrs. Rutledge! Hello!" Another peck. "I see you brought a friend." He nodded toward Charlotte.

"Jean-Luc! Lovely to see you, too. This is our friend Charlotte. She is a children's book author! Charlotte, this is Jean-Luc, chief concierge," Myra said.

Charlotte looked puzzled for a moment, remembering the description Charles had given her of Franny O'Rourke. Then she giggled. Myra and Annie looked at her and realized what must have been going through her head and laughed.

"My, you ladies are in a fine mood." Jean-Luc smiled as he led them through the doors of the elegant hotel. "How long will you be staying with us?"

"We're not sure yet. You know me. It could be a few days. A few weeks. We'll take each day as it comes!"

"Ah, one of the many things I appreciate about you, Countess, your joie de vivre! After you, ladies," he instructed his guests. "One moment." Jean-Luc walked over to his desk and retrieved three envelopes. He returned and handed them to Annie. "You are all checked in. Your rooms await."

Charlotte noticed that in the short time between getting out of the car and being handed their envelopes, their luggage had been swiftly shuttled to their rooms. It was as if guests didn't have to think about anything.

"Shall we?" Annie prodded. The women linked arms and walked to the elevators, where a security guard welcomed them.

"Good afternoon, Countess. Mrs. Rutledge. Mrs. Hansen."

Charlotte gave Annie a questioning look. Annie whispered, "They make it a habit of knowing who comes and goes here."

"I see. But won't that . . . I mean, what about?" Charlotte was thinking about their undercover operation, as she liked to call it.

Annie gave her a quiet "Shh . . ." and winked.

Charlotte vacillated from anxious to excited. She thought a glass of sherry might help. She certainly didn't want to take any more pills. Even if they were prescribed by a real doctor.

Two bellmen showed the women to their rooms. Exactly as Annie had specified. A suite with adjoining rooms. With spectacular views of Central Park.

"Oh my!" Charlotte said in awe. "This is beautiful!" She approached the other two women and embraced them. "You are too good to me. I cannot thank you enough."

"True, but please stop!" Annie laughed. "We are on a mission, my friend. And other people will benefit from your bravery."

"Brave?" Charlotte was skeptical. "Me? How?"

"You came to us with a very serious problem. Many people would never have had the courage to admit they were having problems. Not only did you tell me, but you are also doing something to change it," Myra reassured her.

"Thank you. I mean, never mind!" Charlotte joked.

"Let's unpack and freshen up. We have a lunch date!" Annie directed them. "Let's regroup in a half hour. Is that enough time for everyone to get ready?"

"What shall I wear?" Charlotte asked.

"That lovely white suit," Myra called out. "I'll be in navy, and I know Annie will be wearing something red with her boots! We'll look very patriotic together!"

Within thirty minutes, the women were ready and on their way to the restaurant. They walked along the south side of Central Park in the direction of Columbus Circle, admiring the budding trees.

"I remember when Central Park had a terrible reputation," commented Charlotte. "Purse snatching, muggings. That poor girl who was murdered by that preppy kid, then the jogger."

"But look at it now," Annie exclaimed. "When Giuliani took office, he kicked a lot of ass cleaning up the city. Then Bloomberg stepped in and continued much of the progress. Although I don't particularly agree with everything they did, they did turn the city around."

"They could have turned it around quicker if they had had us on their team," Myra said wryly.

They entered the luxurious restaurant and were greeted as old friends. "Countess. Mrs. Rutledge. And whom do I have the pleasure?" The maître d' took Charlotte's extended hand.

"This is our dear friend Charlotte Hansen," Myra explained. "She is a children's book author."

"Lovely to meet you. Celine will show you to your table."

The women followed the tall, exotic model type to a table, where Victor was waiting. Lots of "Darlings!" "Hello, Gorgeous!" and "Fabulous!" were bandied about among kisses on both cheeks.

"Tell me, what brings you to our fair city?" Victor asked. "Shopping for a new something? Anything?"

"Perhaps. But, most of all, we are shopping for information." Annie got right to the point. "Are you familiar with a Dr. Raymond Corbett? He has a practice on Long Island, though he lives in the city."

"Oh, darling, I do know this Dr. Corbett." Victor batted his eyes at her.

Annie leaned into the middle of the table. Victor obliged. "We need to know if Dr. Corbett has been in contact with Christie's, and if so, what for?"

Victor leaned in closer. "Yes. Arrangements have been made for him to acquire a Chagall that is in private hands. The change of ownership is being handled by us at the request of the owner. It is one of the recovered pieces the Nazis stole."

"But shouldn't that go back to the country of origin?" Myra asked.

"That's been an ongoing issue for years," Victor explained. "France, Germany, the Netherlands, and several other countries are battling with the survivors of families who originally owned the art before it was taken from them."

"I recall reading an article in the *New York Times* about several Rembrandts that are in question," Annie said.

"Yes, it's a sticky situation. However, the piece we have is being sold by the person who found it, in an attic, of all places. Such luck, eh? And it's a private sale, not an auction."

"Tell us more about Corbett and this painting," Myra pushed.

"Corbett has already set up an account. He apparently reached an agreement with the owner, who wishes to remain anonymous, to purchase it for one million dollars. Then he came to us and asked that we broker the transaction. We, of course, were happy to do so. Commissions are always welcome, you know."

"Interesting. Some might say it's worth twenty million," Myra commented.

"And that is what makes the art world so mysterious. Whatever the bidder is willing to pay. But in this case, it's not an auction we're talking about." Victor clapped his hands. "Ta-da!"

"When is this sale taking place?" Annie asked anxiously.

"Sometime next week. It will be conducted over the phone." Victor sighed.

Myra and Annie looked at each other and grinned. Perfect timing.

"Then what happens, as far as taking possession?" Myra asked.

"The successful bidder, or buyer in this case, makes arrangements for security and transportation."

"What if the person is not ready to take possession? What do you do with it?" Myra asked slyly.

"In this case, we do not actually have the painting on the premises. It's at a holding facility, awaiting international clearance, customs, and all."

The wheels were spinning in the women's heads. They could barely get through the rest of their lunch. Lots more idle chatter ensued, but Annie's knee was bobbing up and down under the table. *These boots were made for walkin' . . . ,* she said to herself, chuckling.

"Victor darling, this was a wonderful treat to see you."

"For you, anything." Victor embraced Annie, then Myra, and gave a hug to Charlotte.

Victor headed downtown as the women made their way east to their hotel. Annie was practically jogging and was dodging oncoming pedestrians, dogs, and bicycles. Charlotte could hardly keep up.

"Ladies! Please! Slow down!"

Myra looked over her shoulder at Charlotte and said, "You should see her drive!" She slowed down so Charlotte could catch up. "Let her scamper off. She has to stop at the crosswalk. I don't think she'd take the chance on jaywalking! Not with all this traffic."

Myra and Charlotte caught up to Annie, who was waiting for the signal of an outline of a person to turn from red to white. Myra pointed. "They have a countdown so you know how many seconds you have before you get hit by a bus!"

The three women crossed the busy street, entered the hotel, and made a beeline to the elevator bank. As soon as they caught their breath, they burst into laughter. Annie put her hand up, and they all high-fived!

Annie was the first to whip open her

tablet. "Looks like Charles has some information. Apparently, Avery and his team are going to extreme lengths to get deep."

"As he should, after the fiasco during the Forrester mission." Myra stroked her pearls.

"Remember, Myra, that really wasn't his fault. Charles and Fergus gave him the instructions," Annie recalled.

"Yes, I know, and they paid dearly." Myra started to laugh; Annie followed. They had been infuriated with Charles and Fergus for changing up the plan. Luckily, everything had turned out fine. More than fine.

They pulled out their phones and dialed in to conference with everyone.

Charles started. "I trust you are enjoying your holiday?"

Murmurs of "Uh-huh," "Yes, we are," and "Indeed" flowed through the lines.

"Splendid. London, office and flat are bugged. Vault in office contains cartons of green bottles numerically labeled. Photos match those from Charlotte. Casoro jewelry safe in apartment. Operative was able to get a look inside. Lots of diamonds. Women's jewelry. Sending photos to you. Dr. Marcus has been visited by that drug-delivery bloke, Jerry Hardy, twice. Marcus seen traveling crosstown to a jewelry store. Items bought or sold not yet confirmed."

Annie was opening the photos as Charles continued. "I also suspect that given the amount of jewelry in the safe, his visit to a jeweler's across town is not a coincidence."

Myra leaned over Annie's shoulder to look at the photos. "Impressive," Annie remarked.

"Was able to get Marcus's bank records. His wife likes to spend a lot of money, which is evident from that cache. He's barely making it from one month to the next."

Myra was taking notes. Charlotte was mesmerized.

Charles went on. "On to Aspen. Trust-fund baby. Likes expensive cars. Waiting on inventory analysis. Avery got footage of contents of vault. Same, probably identical packaging. Green bottles. Hundreds. He's in Vegas for car show. Avery will stay in Aspen to get vehicle inventory. Isabelle and Alexis visited Marjorie Brewster in the nursing home. She is still in a coma, but when Isabelle mentioned Steinwood's name, Mrs. Brewster started twitching, which set off alarms. Practically got the girls tossed out."

"That's incredible. A physical reaction to a name." Myra contemplated. "I suppose it was best the girls left. They could have done more damage."

Charles moved on. "They'll be visiting the hospital tomorrow to check the medical records, especially her admission forms. They should be on their way back day after tomorrow."

"There's nothing we can do about Mrs. Brewster's condition, but there is something we can do to help pay for her care. Now that we know Steinwood's soft spot." Myra fiddled with her pearls again. "Do you have info on Dr. Corbett? Because *we* certainly do!"

"Please. Share." Charles could imagine Myra beaming and brimming.

"Annie's friend Victor told us Corbett has arranged to buy a Chagall that was allegedly found in an attic in the German countryside. Stolen by the Nazis. It's a private sale, to be handled by Christie's. Victor also thinks that Corbett will lend it to MoMA once it gets the publicity he is seeking."

"That does not seem to explain the Christie's catalog," Charles noted, "since there is no auction involved, but perhaps he just got interested in what Christie's had available. I don't suppose it matters. Just our luck to have learned of the Christie's connection and to have found out what he was doing."

"As I was saying, we now know Steinwood's and Corbett's weaknesses. Marcus's is the remaining question," Myra said.

"I think it might be drugs." Charlotte surprised everyone with her comment.

"Do tell." Annie smiled conspiratorially.

"The few times I went to see him, I thought — I know this may sound a little mean — for a doctor he sure sweats a lot. Profusely at times. Sometimes his hands would tremble. Once he asked the nurse to give me that shot. He said it was a pinched nerve."

"We need to find out what is going on with the jeweler. Why would he go so far out of his way?" Myra added.

"And does that fit in with his wife's diamond mine? And if so, how?" Annie mused. "I think we need to hop over the pond, as they say."

"This works out perfectly," Myra added. "Steinwood asked Maryann to try to talk Charlotte into returning to London. I suggested she keep the option open, and here we are."

"As soon as Isabelle and Alexis are back from Aspen, we'll take my jet to London. I don't think we need to stop in Sag Harbor. I think we have all the information we need on Corbett. Victor will let me know when Corbett gets the Chagall." Annie punched some notes into her tablet.

"And what about that property in Michigan? What is Kathryn and Yoko's ETA, Charles?" Annie asked.

"Tomorrow. As soon as Kathryn is done with her run, they'll check out the property," Charles replied.

"Tell Avery they're doing a superb job!" Myra wanted to be sure there were still no hard feelings.

Annie looked up from her tablet. "As of now, we still need to uncover Marcus's passion and what is on the property in Michigan. My guess? A pill mill. That's probably where they're getting their supplies from."

Myra snapped her fingers. "I bet you're right! I can't wait to hear what Yoko and Kathryn find out."

Charles spoke again. "Logistically speaking, the plane will be available day after tomorrow. Do you think you can keep yourselves amused until then?" he teased.

"We'll do our best." Annie turned to Charlotte and said, "Charlotte will call her daughter and arrange for the three of us to see Dr. Marcus. We're her referrals."

Annie checked her tablet again. "Maggie spent the afternoon with Mrs. Ringwood, Lorraine Thompson's daughter. She showed Maggie a folder containing paperwork —

copies of the nondisclosure form and a nonliability agreement and disclaimer. She told Maggie that she was not happy about her mother going to 'that place' and 'that doctor,' as she put it. She said it wasn't just about the money. It wasn't helping her mother. She was disoriented one day and manic the next. The daughter had suspected either dementia or schizophrenia. Lorraine was in the program less than three months before she died. The daughter blames the doctor, even if it was self inflicted. She believes her mother would never have taken her own life, but she can't do anything about it legally."

"Ha. But we can," Myra said. The women high-fived each other.

Annie added, "Thompson's daughter gave Maggie copies of the paperwork. She is going to have Nikki comb through it to see if there is any way around it. Nikki will probably consult with Lizzie to see if she has any suggestions about getting around the agreement."

Lizzie Fox was one of the sharpest lawyers in the world, and if anyone could bring home the bacon on this matter, it was she.

Charles added a few more comments. "Everyone knows what their next steps should be, but let me ask something. What else will you be doing in London besides meeting Marcus?"

"Oh, maybe a little B&E and safecracking." Annie winked at Charlotte and Myra.

Charlotte shrugged her shoulders and whispered, "What's B&E?"

With a devilish grin, Myra whispered, "Breaking and entering."

Charlotte caught her breath. "Oh my!" Then she giggled.

CHAPTER 31

Rural Michigan

"I don't know how you do this," Yoko whined as she adjusted herself for the umpteenth time. "It's not that this fine seat isn't comfortable, but sitting for such a long time and dealing with all these distracted drivers . . . I swear, I think I'd ram them off the road. You have the patience of a saint when you're driving, that's for sure!"

"Put a lid on it, would you?" Kathryn joked. "I'm immune to it. After all these years hauling cross-country, you get to know the roads, for sure. Surprisingly, you get to know a lot of people, too. There are thousands of drivers like me. Well, not exactly like *me.*" She laughed. "We have a network and keep each other apprised of any situations. As soon as I hit the road, I call in to anyone who is on the same route. We look out for each other . . ." Her voice trailed off. "Except for that one time."

"I really admire your grit. I don't know if I could ever get back behind a wheel after what happened to you," Yoko said with compassion.

"It somehow, in some weird way, keeps me connected to Alan." Kathryn sighed, remembering her husband, who had died, and trying not to remember how she was brutally raped as he was forced to watch from his wheelchair.

Noticing the expression turning dark on Kathryn's face, Yoko asked, "So you never wanted to go back into engineering?"

Kathryn slapped the dashboard of the eighteen-wheeler. "This is all the engine I need!"

Both laughed. The mood was lifted. They were on a mission.

Yoko pulled out the road atlas. They did not want any electronic trail on the GPS. "According to this, the property is about thirty miles northeast of where you make your delivery."

"We should be arriving at the drop-off in about half an hour. I'm leaving the rig at the truck stop and borrowing a car. This big thing may be too obvious. We'll stop for lunch, then head in that direction." Kathryn shifted gears and pulled into the passing lane on the interstate. "I swear, drivers get worse every year," she mumbled as she cranked up Donna Summer's "She Works Hard for the Money" on the radio. They both sang along at the top of their lungs.

When the song was over, they burst into laughter. "I can't remember the last time I did that," Yoko exclaimed. "That felt really good!"

"Another reason I like hitting the road." Kathryn moved back into the right lane. "I can sing whatever I want, as loud as I want, and there's nobody around to tell me to shut up!"

"You must get some crazy looks," Yoko replied.

"That ain't all!" Kathryn howled.

A squawk came from her CB radio. "That you, K? Screaming your lungs out again?"

"Hey, Josh! How'd you know it was me?" Kathryn replied.

"Ain't nobody else sounds that bad. You're scaring away the cows!"

"Where the heck are you, Mr. Funny Man?" Kathryn called out.

"About two miles behind. Where you headed?"

"Have one stop and then taking my friend for a ride through the countryside." Kathryn turned on her directional signal, indicating she was exiting the interstate.

"Now, that's almost as funny as your singing! Ain't no countryside to see no more."

"Such a comedian. Be careful out there. Over and out!" Kathryn clicked off the CB. "There's an app for my phone, but this is still easier to manage, and it doesn't use up my data allotment," she explained to Yoko.

"You live in a different world, for sure."

"Oh, and yours is so normal." Kathryn elbowed her. "Wait here. I'll go tell the manager to open the loading dock."

A few minutes later, Kathryn returned and pulled the rig to the back of the auto-parts distribution center.

"All this time, I forgot to ask what you are hauling," Yoko said.

"Tires. Glamorous, huh?" Kathryn smiled. "I know a lot of people in the car-dealership, auto-replacement biz. That's how I ended up coming out to Detroit so often. But not so much anymore." She jumped from the rig and handed a clipboard to one of the dockworkers.

"Hey!" and "How ya doin'?" came from the workers.

Kathryn exchanged the same pleasantries. "Where do you want me to leave the trailer?" The arrangements usually called for her to unhitch the trailer and pick up another one to take goods back East, but this time she would deadhead home with just the cab of the truck. She knew that once they got a look at the property, she would need speed and flexibility on the return trip.

As soon as they freed the cab from the trailer, Kathryn took the clipboard back and jumped into the truck. Lots of waves and hollers followed.

"Nice people. Salt of the earth. Too bad many of them lost their jobs in the auto industry. But at least they're still gainfully employed, I suppose," she told Yoko. She maneuvered the cab onto the highway and headed to the truck stop. "Hungry?"

"Yes!"

"Excellent. You're in for some good eats," Kathryn shouted over the noise of the grinding gears and rolled up her window. Within a few minutes, they pulled into the truck stop.

"Rosie's Diner? For real?" Yoko said with surprise.

"Wait until you meet her!" Kathryn chuckled. "C'mon. Home fries are waiting!"

They walked into what looked like something that had been frozen in time. The time was circa 1957.

"Wow. Look at this place. They even have jukeboxes in the booths." Yoko was in awe.

"They're just for show. Pretty cool,

though." Kathryn waved her arms at another throwback. This time it was Rosie, granddaughter of the original, decked out in a pink-striped uniform with a white collar and trim, a white apron, and a peaked cap, complete with the ugliest white shoes.

"Kathryn! Babe! How the heck are you?" Rosie sauntered over and gave Kathryn a bear hug. "Who is this pretty thing?" She pointed at Yoko.

"A good friend. Yoko, meet Rosie."

Rosie's hands were as large as Kathryn's, and she almost crushed Yoko's fine fingers with her grip. Yoko tried to hide a wince. "Nice to meet you. Kathryn tells me you have the best food in Michigan."

"She's got that right. Come sit over here, away from the cigarette smoke."

"Isn't that illegal?" Yoko asked innocently. Kathryn kicked her in the foot.

"Nobody cares around these here parts. I only let my regulars do it. There's only a couple of 'em left," Rosie explained. "We ain't that far from Flint. Now *there's* a problem that needs fixin'." She handed them plastic-coated menus that had seen better days. "Meat loaf is fresh this morning. Take a few minutes. Coffee? Tea? Soda?"

Thinking about the water problem in Flint, Yoko opted for something that came in a bottle. "Coke? Pepsi?"

"Pepsi, dollface. Kath? You?"

"Coffee. Thanks."

Rosie waddled across the room, weaving in and out of the square Formica tables, which had also seen better days.

"It's kind of depressing, isn't it?" Yoko whispered.

"I prefer to think it's quaint. But you're right. Business has fallen off a cliff. It's amazing she's still here. But she owns the building, so that's one bill she doesn't have to pay." Kathryn scanned the room. "I'm going for the meat loaf. Mashed potatoes. Gravy."

Yoko looked at the menu. Not exactly what she was used to, especially when she was at Pinewood, with Charles's fine cooking. Kathryn sensed Yoko's apprehension.

"Bacon and eggs. Always a safe bet."

"Nah. I'll have what you're having." Yoko smiled when Rosie returned to the table with their beverages and took their order.

When the food arrived, it looked exactly like the picture on the menu. "Rosie's specialty." Rosie pointed to the food. "Enjoy!"

The women dived into the comfort food, which, Yoko noted, was really, really good.

"See! I told ya," Kathryn boomed. "Let's

hit the ladies' room and get going."

Kathryn motioned for the check, pulled out her cash, and left a hundred-dollar bill under the saltshaker. "Come on. I don't want Rosie yelling at me. She hates it when I overtip!" They made a beeline for the bathroom, washed up, and bolted.

Before they had left Virginia, Kathryn had arranged for a friend to leave a car at the diner. They would use it for the few hours needed to check out the property. Kathryn pulled out a license plate from the back of the cab. After looking around to see that no one was watching, she swapped the "extra" plate with the one on her friend's car.

"Grab the road atlas," she directed Yoko. "I'll get my gear." Her gear consisted of binoculars, several cameras, and a drone/camera kit. Fergus had showed her how to assemble the Wi-Fi-enabled drone/camera kit. The camera was equipped to send the photos to Kathryn's tablet and to Charles. It was a backup in case they couldn't get onto the property. Aerial photos would be perfect, provided they didn't get caught and someone didn't shoot the drone down.

Yoko opened the road atlas and began giving Kathryn directions. It took about thirty minutes before they came upon a chain-link fence topped with barbed wire and a sign that said BEWARE. NO TRESPASSING.

Yoko said somberly, "This looks nasty. And scary."

"Let's drive around and see how far this fence goes." Kathryn drove for almost a mile before they came to the end of the fence at an intersection. "With all the brush and overgrowth, I can barely make out a building in the distance." She dragged binoculars from her gear bag. "Hard to tell what it is. Except it's a big building."

Yoko took the binoculars from Kathryn and looked. "Some kind of factory? Warehouse?"

"But which is it?" Kathryn looked at the photo from Google Earth. "I guess we need to launch our little friend." She patted the box sitting between them. "Finally, my engineering degree will come in handy." She opened the trunk to give herself some room to assemble the drone without it being in plain sight. She checked for security cameras. None this close to the road, but she suspected there would be several along the perimeter of the building.

In a few short minutes, she had the device ready for takeoff. "We'll drive around a bit more to see if there is a better vantage point." Kathryn shut the trunk and jumped back into the driver's seat. They turned the corner and followed the fence for another mile. "This is like a compound." They came upon a gate with the same warning: BEWARE. NO TRESPASSING.

Next to the gate was a camera and a single phone, protected in a box. "I guess they don't get a lot of visitors. Let's get away from any prying eyes," Kathryn said.

She drove the car another mile, to what seemed to be the rear part of the property, assuming the gate was at the front. The car rolled slowly onto the gravel shoulder opposite the property, where they waited for a few minutes to get a sense of the traffic flow. There seemed to be none. The women got out and switched seats so Kathryn could launch the drone without being seen from the road. The real-time transmission and wide angle were in working order. She directed Yoko to ping Charles so he could upload the feed and observe as the drone flew over the fence.

Despite her big hands, Kathryn maneuvered the drone's control box with the skill and agility of a surgeon. The drone moved up and over the overgrown fence, putting it out of their sight. The only view they had came from the camera mounted on the drone. Using the panoramic lens, Kathryn scanned the side of the building. There were several security cameras, alarms, blacked-out windows, and a dozen steel overhead doors. Nothing gave away the contents of the building. Except they didn't want visitors.

"Wow. What is this place?" Kathryn asked.

Yoko was about to look over Kathryn's shoulder when the alert signal went off on both of their phones. The sound meant "Abort!" It came from Charles. Within seconds, a round of gunshots went off.

The women dashed back into the car. As Kathryn peeled away, kicking up gravel and dust in their wake, Yoko kept a steady watch out the rear window. So far, no one was following them. Still, Kathryn kept the pedal to the metal and soared down the country road at eighty miles per hour.

Charles pinged them: **Two men dressed in orange coveralls with hoods.** He had been able to see them as they ran out of the building with their weapons. Seconds later, the transmission from the drone went dead.

Yoko turned to look at Kathryn. "There must be something very serious going on in that place."

"You got that right. But what? And how do we find out? Wait. I have an idea. I'm willing to bet that whoever works there goes out for a beer after his shift. Maybe with some coworkers. Let's check out some local bars tonight."

Yoko looked stunned at the suggestion. "What are we supposed to do? Walk up to them and ask, 'Hey, do you work at that secret place where they shoot drones?' "

"Nooo . . . but we could be two people passin' through, stopping for something to drink," Kathryn offered.

"Still, what do we say to them?" Yoko pressed.

"We smile and say hello. Start a little conversation. I don't expect them to spill their guts, but you know how men like to brag. Especially if it's something they're *not* supposed to talk about. After a few beers, they may say certain things. Who knows? Maybe the place is hiring! I think it's worth a shot."

"We need to clear this with Annie and Myra," Yoko reminded her. "We don't deviate without consulting the others unless lives are at stake."

"You're right. See if Charles can reach them. Meanwhile, we'll head back to the diner. I need a piece of pie." Kathryn sighed.

By the time they pulled into the parking lot, Charles had got back to them on their idea of staking out a bar. "Just one bar. One night. Keep the radio on."

Rosie welcomed them again. "Hey, girls. Back so soon? I bet you remembered you didn't have pie! Am I right?"

"You're a regular psychic," Kathryn teased.

"No mumbo jumbo about my cherry pie. You never left before without having some or taking a slice with you," Rosie reminded her.

"Some memory, you have." Kathryn smirked.

"I know my customers." Rosie gave them a wink. "Coming right up!"

It dawned on Kathryn that maybe Rosie had some info on the mysterious property. She leaned in and whispered to Yoko, "We should see if Rosie has the lowdown or some info on that place."

"Good idea. I'll start the conversation."

Rosie lumbered across the room, carrying a pot of coffee in one hand and two slices of juicy cherry pie in the other. "You girls spending some time in our lovely county?" She was half joking.

"Kinda," Yoko answered. "We were talking about what a beautiful state Michigan is and how it gets a bad rep because of Flint and the ups and downs of Detroit. So she wanted to show me some of the country-side." Kathryn rolled her eyes as Yoko continued. "It's sad to see abandoned property and buildings."

Rosie stood with the coffeepot and sighed. "Yep. Way too many of them around here."

"I noticed one place that had BEWARE signs. Beware of what?" Yoko asked innocently. "Are there dangerous animals around here or something?"

"Or do most people put signs like that up?" Kathryn asked.

"You mean the place about thirty minutes from here? With all the barbed wire?" Rosie asked.

"Sounds about right," Kathryn said.

"Not sure. They say it's some kind of secret government location. Hardly nobody goes out that way."

"Do you ever meet people who work there?" Kathryn asked. "But I guess if it's top secret, they can't tell you!"

The three women laughed at the idea.

"You're right about that." Rosie leaned in closer to the women's faces. "But I did hear two guys talkin' one day about 'pill man,' but they shut up as soon as I got closer to the table. Ain't been back since."

"Do you think they worked there?" Yoko asked casually.

"Hard to say. But that's all the secret talk I ever heard personally. Everyone else in here is bitchin' and complainin' about work, no work, kids, and what team lost in sports." Rosie noticed two more patrons entering the diner. "Better get back to work."

"Pill man?" Kathryn's eyes sparkled. She pulled out a twenty-dollar bill and put it on the table.

Back in the parking lot, Kathryn replaced the license plate on the car and left an envelope beneath the visor with the spare key and five hundred dollars. She locked the car, knowing her friend had her own key. Kathryn had a few friends around the country who had keys to each other's cars, apartments, houses, boats, and so on. Just in case. Like now.

Since they already had the information they might have gotten by staking out a bar, they decided to stay in a motel before heading back to Pinewood and reporting everything back to Charles. The pieces were definitely fitting together.

CHAPTER 32

Pinewood

Charles and Fergus sat in front of the monitors, viewing the latest information. While the brief flight of the drone did not yield any solid evidence, the compound itself was suspect. Charles watched the short footage again. Solar panels and generators. That kept the electric bill from becoming too high, which would draw suspicion. Many drug busts occurred simply because of enormous electric bills for property that didn't seem to warrant it. *So obvious. So stupid,* Charles thought to himself.

He looked over at Fergus, who was reviewing surveillance footage from the offices. "Besides greed, the common denominator appears to be the pills. The property in Michigan is most likely their pill mill. Learning that droplet of information about 'pill man' from Rosie was nothing short of serendipitous."

"Should we bring in Jay Sparrow?" Fergus asked, referring to their contact with the FBI, who at one time happened to be the Bureau's director. "This could be one of the biggest drug busts in history if they play it well."

"True. But timing is everything. I don't imagine they will close their operation in Michigan anytime soon. At least not for a few weeks." Charles grinned. "I know Annie and Myra want everything to go down at the same time."

"I'm sure you're correct, old chap. Do we know yet when they'll leave for London?"

"Tomorrow. As soon as Isabelle and Alexis get back from Aspen."

Preparing for their tour at Aspen Valley Hospital, Isabelle and Alexis donned their normal-looking business suits and short wigs. They pinned on the phony SKIING ATHLETICA name tags Fergus had made for them. Yep. They certainly looked official.

When they arrived at the front desk, they were greeted by a bouncy, blond, pigtailed volunteer. "Hey! I'm Brandy! I will be your personal tour guide for today!" She giggled.

"Nice to meet you, Brandy! We are very excited to see your facility. As you know, we conduct research on orthopedic facilities for the Olympic teams," Alexis said.

"Oh wow! You guys are in the Olympics?" Brandy bounced some more.

Isabelle gave Alexis the "This is going to be too easy" look. "No. We aren't, but we kinda work for them, ya know?" Isabelle was dumbing down her speech pattern for Bouncing Brandy.

"So, like, what do you do for them?" Brandy was still confused. Obviously, she didn't know that there was more to the Olympics than the athletes.

Taking Isabelle's cue, Alexis explained. "We're, like, kinda behind the scenes, ya know? We help them get stuff set up and all."

"Wow. That is *way* cool. So, like, what are you setting up here?"

"We're not setting anything up at the hospital. We're gathering information about hospitals that do a lot of orthopedic procedures. You know, for when an athlete gets hurt and stuff."

"Oh . . ." Brandy seemed to understand from her millennial point of view. "Okay. Where do you want to start?"

"How about admissions?" Isabelle urged.

"But they don't operate in there." Brandy was still confused.

Isabelle and Alexis tried to stifle a laugh.

"That is correct. We would like to see the process. You know, like, when a patient is brought in. How that gets processed. Then what happens to the patient," Alexis said.

"Well, okay. Sounds kinda boring. Follow me." Brandy turned on her heel and bounced her way to the admissions-office area. "Hi, everyone. This is . . ." Her voice trailed off when she realized she had not gotten their names. Nor had she noticed their badges. Maybe they should have taken a selfie and shown it to her.

"Hi. I'm Georgina." Isabelle extended her hand and pointed to her name tag. "This is Stephanie." She pointed to Alexis and her name tag.

A tall, thin man stood. "Dennis. This is Mabel," he said, introducing his coworker. Brandy was right. Dennis and Mabel could have blended into the beige walls, floors, and desks. They said that people and their pets started to look alike. In this case, everything looked alike.

"You're here to take a tour and do what again?" Mabel asked in a tone that displayed slight annoyance.

"They're on the Olympics," Brandy burst out.

Isabelle held her breath for a second. "We do research for the teams. Orthopedics in particular."

"What do you want to know?" Dennis asked, folding his arms across his chest.

"How you process patients who come here for emergency orthopedic care." Alexis was starting to think it was going to take all day just to explain why they were there. The pretending part, that is.

"Oh." Mabel did not sound the least bit interested.

"Where do you want to start?" Dennis asked.

Isabelle thought she was going to smack the three of them. "Let's start with processing. We can skip the ambulance emergency arrival."

"You mean 'intake'?" Dennis offered.

"Exactly." Alexis was trying to move this laborious process along.

"Someone sits at the desk and takes the information. The ER people figure out which doctor will see the patient. If they need emergency surgery, they go to the surgical unit. If not, they get assigned to a room." Dennis seemed exasperated. "Not very complicated."

Alexis casually put her hand into her jacket pocket and secretly buzzed Isabelle. **Time to get that e-mail you can't open.**

"Excuse me." Isabelle reached for her

phone and then looked up at Dennis. "My apologies. I've been waiting for some information from our office, and I can't download the e-mail. Do you have a terminal I could use to access the Internet? I'll just be a minute. I am so sorry, but it's very important."

Dennis shrugged. "Yeah, sure. You can sit in that cubicle back there. Click on the Google Chrome icon."

"Thank you *so* much." Isabelle nodded at Alexis to keep the others occupied and made a beeline for the desk.

Isabelle pulled out a flash drive and inserted it into the computer. She typed in several numbers and gained access to the mainframe. She looked feverishly for anything that resembled patient information. Click. *No.* Click. *No.* Click. *No.* Click. *No.* She typed in a few more numbers and letters that Abner had taught her. Click. Double Click. *Patient archive.* Another click. *Bingo.* Scrolling through as quickly as she could, she found the following: *Marjorie Brewster. Admitted 03 March to ER. EMT answered call. Suffered convulsions. Unconscious upon arrival. Irregular heartbeat. Given carbamazepine. Lapsed into coma. CT scan showed signs of brain function, but no response from patient.* Isabelle skipped the rest of the details involving the day-to-day records and moved to the day Marjorie Brewster was released six weeks later. *Patient released into care and custody of Mountain Hills.*

Alexis had run out of small talk and gave a wave to Isabelle.

"My apologies. There always seems to be a fire drill at the home office." Isabelle gave them a sheepish grin. "I'm sure you folks go through that all the time with the higher-ups, eh?"

Dennis and Mabel finally showed signs of being humans rather than androids. "You got that right," Mabel said, taking the opportunity to complain. "Speaking of fires, they keep firing people and making the rest of us take on more responsibility."

"Oh boy, do we know what that's like, right, Steph?" Isabelle elbowed Alexis. "Listen, we don't want to take up any more of your time. Maybe Brandy can give us a quick tour, and we'll be out of your way."

"Fer sure," Brandy insisted. "C'mon!"

They shook hands with the admissions people and followed Bouncing Brandy.

CHAPTER 33

The war room

Charles and Fergus read the latest information to Myra and Annie who are in their suite at the Ritz-Carlton in Manhattan.

"Brewster was admitted to the hospital after suffering from convulsions and was given carbamazepine. If she had taken too much phenobarbital from her green bottles, the carbamazepine would have certainly put her in a coma if it didn't kill her." Charles's voice was even. "The good news is that her CT scan found brain activity, but she was unresponsive."

"Maybe there is some hope for her," Myra said softly as she clutched at her pearls. "She obviously had a reaction to Steinwood's name. Once we finish this mission, we'll send in our own team of doctors to Mountain Hills Nursing Home."

"Splendid idea. We'll arrange to get permission from her sister," Charles added.

"We have news from Kathryn and Yoko. The property is highly secured, with fences and security. They shot down Kathryn's drone," Fergus said.

"What? Is Kathryn okay? Yoko?" Myra was about to panic.

"They're both okay and on their way back," Charles said. "It seems the drone was caught on the building's security camera, and two men in orange jumpsuits ran out of the building and shot it down. I noticed that they use generators and solar panels to keep their electric bill from being too high. Unfortunately, that was all we could get from the property itself. But Kathryn and Yoko gleaned an interesting bit of information over a piece of cherry pie."

"Charles, please get to the point! What does pie have to do with anything?" Myra was getting impatient. She was motioning to Annie to hurry and power up her tablet.

Charles chuckled softly. "I love it when you get your dander up, old girl!"

"Charles, *please*!"

"Rosie, of the eponymous Rosie's Diner, told them that she overheard two men talking one day and that one used the words 'pill man.' I think that's a critical link to how these people are getting the drugs they are administering to their patients."

Annie added her thoughts. "Connect the dots. These doctors are not really practicing medicine — they are not even licensed where they are — so they have to get the pills from somewhere. The property deed lists the owner as LLL Ltd., which is a trade name for Live-Life-Long Limited Partnership. I wonder if Dr. Corbett has the only copy of the deed."

"From what we've pulled together, Dr. Marcus doesn't seem organized enough, and Dr. Steinwood is a bit aloof. Corbett appears to be the most aggressive. He is the marketing guy, after all," Myra said, expressing her assessment of the men. "And Corbett is in the process of acquiring a Chagall. Wants to show it off to his friends. At least that's what Annie pried out of Victor."

"We also believe that Marcus may have some extracurricular drug dealings. A mangy drug-delivery boy has been seen entering and leaving Marcus's office, and in one of the photos Eileen sent, it looks like there is a residue of white powder on his desk. He also has some dealings with a jeweler. There is a Casoro jewelry safe in his apartment. Eileen was able to get in and took photos." Charles clicked on the photos, so Myra and Annie could see them.

Annie let out a whistle. "That's one

boatload of diamonds." She was already dreaming about cracking the safe. Even though Eileen had done so already, Annie needed to dig deeper, so to speak. At least that was what she told herself. Safecracking was always exhilarating, even when it was as easy as cracking this safe would be.

"According to the surveillance from Avery's group, Marcus seems to be having some financial woes. Fergus was able to get a look at his bank records. Whatever goes in leaves immediately. Apparently, Mrs. Marcus likes to shop, drink, and show off," Charles conveyed.

"I must say, Avery's people have done a wonderful job." Myra wanted Charles to be sure she had forgiven them for pulling Avery off a previous mission. A little reminder wouldn't hurt.

"Eileen is going to continue to tail Marcus until she can find out what business he's conducting with the jeweler all the way across town," Fergus said.

"Excellent. Maybe she'll have an answer by the time we arrive in London," Annie added.

"Isabelle and Yoko should be getting back later. We'll send the jet to Teterboro and give you an ETA. Is Charlotte ready for this?" Fergus asked.

Annie looked over at Charlotte, who was gazing at the spectacular view of Central Park from the living-room area of the suite. "She is *so* ready. Quite the team player!" She waved at Charlotte across the room.

"I don't think she has felt this good in a long time." Myra smiled at her friend.

Charlotte nodded and gave her the thumbs-up sign.

"Any other news from Maggie?" Charles asked Annie.

"She's giving the paperwork to Nikki, for her and Lizzie to vet. Maybe there is a way out of the situation, particularly if they are doing something illegal. Which they are."

"Which we are going to fix!" Myra said emphatically.

"Avery's next step is to find out precisely what's in the garage. We should have that news very soon. We know it's high-end cars. How many and how much they are worth is what he needs to uncover." Charles was looking down the list of sisters and assignments. "That brings everyone up to date." He cleared his throat. "Fergus and I were discussing bringing the FBI in on the Michigan property. That way, law enforcement can look into what is going on there." Charles waited for Myra's and Annie's response.

After a moment of silence, Myra announced, "Yes, but it all needs to happen at the same time. We want this despicable bunch to go up in a blaze."

"You are formulating the endgame, my love." Charles made it a statement rather than a question.

"We are indeed. The humiliation and retribution will be epic," Myra said wryly.

The serious conversation was broken by Annie's wild "Woo-hoo! Game on!"

They said their fond "Ciaos," "Byes," "See yas," and "Love yas" and disconnected their electronic devices.

CHAPTER 34

New York to London

The three women were standing in front of the Ritz-Carlton, tipping and saying their farewells to the staff, when the limo arrived to take them to the private airport in New Jersey. The ride should take under an hour.

The jet was ready when they arrived. Their luggage was stowed, and they relaxed in the lounge area of the jet, where they would remain until their pilot had clearance from the tower. At that point, they would take their seats and buckle in. Once they were at the proper altitude, they could move back to the sofa in the lounge area. The jet's interior was the size of a studio apartment. Maybe larger.

Myra took Charlotte's hand. "I'm pretty sure I know the answer to this, but are you ready for this?"

"Myra, this is the most excitement I have ever had in my life!" Charlotte's eyes filled with tears. "Your friendship, your loyalty, your integrity and generosity are unparalleled." She turned to Annie. "I do mean both of you." Myra offered her a handkerchief. "And look. Look at this." Charlotte motioned to the luxurious interior of the plane. "It's a little overwhelming. Not that I'm complaining!" Charlotte burst into laughter. "As long as I'm with both of you, I know that everything is going to be fine. Exciting. And tons of fun to boot!" She raised her hand for the three of them to slap a high five.

The pilot's voice came over the plane's sound system. "Good afternoon, Countess, Mrs. Rutledge, and Mrs. Hansen. Please move to the forward-facing seats and buckle your seat belts. We will be moving shortly."

"I'm all atwitter!" Charlotte giggled. "It's going to be a very interesting encounter with Dr. Marcus now that I know what he's been up to. Of course, I'm going to have to control myself and keep from knocking the living you-know-what out of him."

"You can say 'shit,' " Annie teased.

"When it's appropriate," Myra retorted.

All three broke into hysterics. The howling caught the ear of Patrice, the flight attendant, who peeked behind the privacy door. "Everything okay back there?"

"Couldn't be better!" Annie hooted.

Once they reached cruising altitude, the captain turned off the seat-belt sign to indicate that they could go back to the plane's lounge area.

"It's going to be about seven hours. Do you want to watch a flick?" Annie turned on the sixty-inch-screen TV. "Pretty much anything you want." She handed the remote to Charlotte.

Annie went on. "When we land, it will be around ten P.M. London time. Patrice will fix dinner for us. What do you think you'll be in the mood for?"

"I could use something right now. Maybe a snack?" Charlotte asked sheepishly. "Whatever you have for dinner, I will also."

"Meat, fish, poultry? You decide." Annie called over to Patrice, "Could you fix us a little something to munch on?"

"Shrimp cocktails and crabmeat salads?" Patrice suggested.

"Sounds divine," Myra answered. She then whispered, "I must admit, no matter where I go, the food can't compare to Charles's. I'm really spoiled."

"Boo-hoo," Annie joked.

"Ha!" Myra returned fire. "You and Fergus get to share most of it, Countess!"

Annie turned to Charlotte. "And this is

303

why we're friends." She paused. "Charles's cooking!"

Patrice rolled over a cart that looked like it belonged in a fine restaurant rather than in an airplane. It held a platter of colossal shrimp, chunks of crabmeat, and seviche. A crisp Sancerre wine was in a silver bucket.

"This looks divine," Annie said with glee. Myra and Charlotte agreed, and they all indulged in the luscious seafood.

As they were finishing their repast, Myra turned to Charlotte. "Maryann must be thrilled that you're coming back to London."

"She was very surprised, to say the least. Especially when I told her you and Annie were coming with me."

"And she's okay with you staying at my brownstone?" Annie asked.

"Yes. She said she understood wanting to have 'girl time,' as she put it. And I think it's less pressure for her. Their flat is rather small. I told her we would plan a nice lunch for all of us once we get settled," Charlotte replied. "She made the appointments for the three of us to meet with Marcus tomorrow."

"Oh, he must be wetting his pants in anticipation of the money he thinks he's going to squeeze out of us!" Annie smirked.

The other two laughed at the remark. "We need to manipulate him into inviting us to his flat. Maybe the conservatory. I have to get into his place and check the safe."

Myra offered a suggestion. "He knows you are a countess. We know his wife is a social climber. I am willing to bet she would be over the moon to show you off to her friends."

Annie snapped her fingers. "How about this? I'll throw a cocktail party at the Plimsoll Building, in their conservatory. It will be a fund-raiser for the kennel club, and I'll invite the Marcuses and pretend that it's a marvelous coincidence that they live there. That will make Mrs. Marcus pee in *her* pants!" The women howled with laughter. "I'll tell him that she can invite her friends, and that any donation is welcome."

"Yes! We'll get a small doghouse, and people can put their donations in it," Myra added.

"Perfecto," Annie said with glee.

"Wow. You women never cease to amaze me!" Charlotte was enthralled.

"I'll get my people on it right now." Annie got up from the sofa and moved to a table, where she pulled out her tablet. She feverishly typed for a few minutes, then turned to the others. "Done! And done! Now all we need is for him to take the bait."

Myra stroked her pearls. "I don't think that will be a problem."

The rest of the journey was smooth, and the women dozed, watched *Under the Tuscan Sun,* regrouped for dinner, then freshened up. They would be landing in an hour. With the time change and the jet lag, they were ready for a good night's sleep at Annie's brownstone. Days before, she had phoned ahead to be sure all the linens were fresh, the kitchen was stocked, and the house was well staffed. She didn't know how long they would be there, but the staff was accustomed to Annie's wild ways and always looked forward to her visits. She kept the brownstone for friends and family, and for those "other" times. Just in case.

When they arrived at the brownstone, they were greeted by the butler and housekeeper.

Annie introduced Byron and Jessica to Charlotte. They knew Myra well. "Charlotte, Byron has been with the family for over twenty years. Then he married Jessica and dragged her into service."

Jessica made a slight curtsy. "Pleased to meet you, ma'am." She nodded at Myra. "Lovely to see you, Mrs. Rutledge."

Byron followed suit without the curtsy, making a short bow instead.

Charlotte took in the antique wood and the art. "This is beautiful, Annie. Thank you so much for your hospitality."

"It's a pleasure." Annie winked. "Come. Let's get you unpacked."

Back in Aspen, Avery discovered the system Steinwood used for his security cameras outside his garage. Disabling it was a lot easier than Avery had expected. From the bucket to the utility truck, he was able to register the frequency, then clone the control panel that operated the cameras. With a few strokes, he jammed the frequency so whatever image the cameras were focused on would freeze. He figured he would only have a few minutes to get down from the bucket, enter the garage from the rear, take photos, and get the heck out. He shifted gears, and the bucket descended. He jumped out as soon as it hit the ground.

After skirting the perimeter of the garage, he found the rear entrance. The doors had two major security locks. All of Avery's people carried pick tools, but he also had a neodymium magnet in a long sock, just in case. The problem with the magnet was its strength. That was the reason for the sock. It was the only way one could pull the magnet off from whatever it was stuck to.

He hoped he didn't have to use it. He also hoped there wasn't a dead bolt on the other side. He inserted the tool in one lock, and it opened easily. The second went just as smoothly. He gripped the handles and took a deep breath as he pulled on the steel doors. They slid open, revealing four gleaming, beautiful sports cars.

There was an empty area where Avery figured Steinwood kept his Jaguar. He noticed another empty space toward the front. By the looks of it, Steinwood was expecting another addition to his collection. The Maserati. He snapped as many photos as he could in less than a minute and uploaded them to Charles. After checking that he hadn't tracked in any dirt or left any footprints, he pulled the doors shut and reset the locks. He jogged back to the utility truck, reactivated the security cameras, and beat it out of there.

In London the women unpacked, changed into comfortable clothes, and convened by the cozy fireplace.

"Byron always knows what to do and when." Annie made a sweeping gesture toward the fireplace and the three glasses of brandy sitting on a silver tray.

They sat in a circle on the floor, waiting

for the call from Charles and Fergus. Charlotte looked completely relaxed; Annie and Myra were ready to pounce. The ding of the tablet made the three of them jump.

"Hello, love!" Charles's face appeared on the tablet, with Fergus looking over his shoulder. "Did you have a good flight?"

"Lovely, darling," Myra answered.

"Yes, lovely," Charlotte echoed. Then Annie.

"Don't keep us in suspense. What is the latest from Avery?" Annie pleaded.

"Steinwood has a pristine collection of fine sports cars. Seems like he's adding something to his mix," Fergus informed them. "That would make six altogether."

"Excellent. We can get Kathryn on that part of the mission. She knows every car hauler on the road," Myra said.

"What do you have in mind?" Charles inquired.

"Annie and I have been discussing how to make this an unmitigated disaster for them."

"Do tell," Charles implored.

"Yes! Please!" and a variety of pleading voices came from the background.

Annie and Myra chimed in together, "Hello, Sisters! Everyone okay?"

Lots of chatter came from the other side.

"We want everything to happen on the

same day. If we do it piecemeal, it won't have the same humiliating effect," Myra answered.

"Agreed," they chorused.

Kathryn shared the information she had obtained from Rosie. "According to Rosie, most people think it's some sort of 'secret government facility.' Then she said she overheard two local-looking guys mention 'the pill man.' It all adds up, if you ask me."

Fergus once again suggested they reach out to Jay. "It shouldn't take him more than one or two phone calls to find out whether or not it's a government facility. And if it is, the question becomes, What do Corbett and his cronies have to do with it? It seems like a rather odd relationship, unless they are leasing the property to the government. But given what we've discovered about the so-called supplements, I am virtually certain that Dr. Corbett is running a pill mill. The FBI should be able to determine whether or not it's drug related."

"I think Fergus has a good point." This time it was Nikki speaking.

Annie took the lead. "Then let's contact him. What does everyone else think?"

Sounds of approval came through the air. Annie nodded to Myra and Charlotte. "Fergus, would you get in touch with him?

See if the FBI knows anything about that piece of property."

"Will do."

Myra went down the list of what they knew. "Corbett is buying a Chagall, Steinwood has a car collection, and Marcus might be involved in drugs other than the ones he's pushing." Then she recited what they needed to find out. "What is in the safe? What does Marcus have to do with a drug runner and a jeweler?"

"I'll have Avery send Eileen to the jewelry store, where she'll pretend she is picking up something for Marcus. She'll record the conversation," Charles said.

"During the flight, we devised a plan. We have an appointment with Marcus tomorrow. We are going to be Charlotte's referrals for the doc. I booked the conservatory at the Plimsoll Building for an impromptu cocktail party fundraiser for the kennel club," Annie said with delight. "We'll bring it up during our appointment. I'll mention I'm busy with a fund-raiser at the Plimsoll Building. It will go something like, 'What a coincidence. *You* live in the Plimsoll Building?' And then I'll invite him."

"Brilliant!" Fergus said proudly of Annie.

Another disembodied voice came over the phone. It was Isabelle this time. "Do you think he'll go for it?"

"I am certain that Mrs. Marcus would be thrilled to show off her new friend, Countess Anna Ryland de Silva, to her group of dilettantes," Myra said confidently.

"Myra and Charlotte can distract them while I go to their apartment and pick that safe," Annie exclaimed with gusto.

Hoots and laughter bellowed through the phones. "If anyone can do this, we certainly can!" Myra said.

"Do we have our endgame planned yet?" Nikki asked.

"We need to find out what Marcus is up to and what's on that property. We're working on our plot for Corbett, and with the information from Avery about Steinwood, I'm formulating an idea," Myra said.

"That's my cheeky girl! If we can gather the missing pieces, we should be able to accomplish this very soon," Charles interjected. "Should we alert Pearl?"

"We still have a few more loose ends, but yes, we can let her know we will be needing her help." Myra continued, "Kathryn? Can you let her know?"

Kathryn groaned. "Sure. Okay." She still had a thing with Pearl, and it was not necessarily a good thing. Myra kept assigning

Kathryn to Pearl, hoping they could mend fences.

Charles wrapped up the conference call, informing them they would reconnect the following evening, after Myra, Annie, and Charlotte had met with Marcus. Perhaps Eileen would have more info by then, as well.

The next morning Byron served up a typical English breakfast for the women. "I didn't know your schedule and wanted to be sure you were well nourished before you left."

"Do all English gentlemen have a knack for food? I never thought of the British as being culinary experts," Charlotte remarked.

"They. Are. Not. It doesn't take a lot of expertise to fry up bacon, mash potatoes, and spoon out jam." Annie laughed. "Take it from me. That's the only wizardry Fergus can conjure in a kitchen."

They helped themselves to the buffet and chatted about the day ahead.

Charlotte was getting giddy again. "What if I blow it? I might burst out laughing at some point."

"We'll blame it on the drugs!" Annie smiled devilishly.

"You can do this." Myra placed her hand on Charlotte's. "You don't really have to say anything. Just remember to turn on the recording device on your phone. Obviously, without Dr. Marcus seeing you."

"What about the shot?" Charlotte asked. "I don't know what it was, and I absolutely do not want to get another one."

"Just simply tell him you want to skip it," Myra suggested.

"I don't think he'll go for that. He'll want his five thousand dollars," Charlotte said, dismayed.

"Not if he thinks he's going to make triple that from enrolling us in his protocol," Annie said smugly. "We'll support you. Don't worry. Another idea is to ask him if you can take it with you. Jessica is a registered nurse. You can tell him she'll administer the shot."

"That might work. I think the most important thing to him is the money. Remember, we'll be right there. If he tries to bully you, which I doubt, or pressure you, we'll step in," Myra said reassuringly.

Charlotte gave a sigh of relief.

Byron entered the dining room and asked if there was anything else they wanted or needed. All said, "No, thank you." He bowed and retreated into the kitchen.

The women stood and formed a small

circle, holding hands.

"We can do this." Annie spoke softly.

Charlotte and Myra responded, "Amen!"

Then came the high fives!

A chime from the doorbell indicated their car was waiting. They were on their way to see the Live-Life-Long practitioner and edge their way into his circle of dupes.

Dr. Julian Marcus was beside himself with delight. *The* Countess Anna de Silva was coming to his office! And she was bringing her friend, another well-heeled, monied sixty-something-year-old woman. He thought perhaps his luck was finally changing for the better. He was almost giddy. He checked his watch for the zillionth time. Only thirty minutes to go! He could barely contain his excitement.

A half hour later, when the buzzer sounded, he almost jumped out of his skin. *They're here!* He pulled out a small hand-held mirror and checked his balding head one more time. *Good. No sweating.* He patted it with his handkerchief just in case. He cleared his throat and, trying to sound nonchalant, said, "Yes, Gloria?" A slight pause, then, "Please show them in."

Gloria rapped softly on the door. Even that tiny sound made Marcus jump. A great deal was at stake. Regaining Charlotte Hansen and adding the countess *and* Mrs. Rutledge? His hands began to sweat. He wiped them on his trousers as discreetly as possible.

"Charlotte! I am delighted you've returned. So good of you to bring your friends," he said. If nothing else, his tone of voice was suitable. He extended his hand to her and quickly moved toward Annie. "Oh, and Countess. This is a wonderful honor to meet you. And Mrs. Rutledge. I've heard marvelous stories of your philanthropy. Please do sit down." He motioned to the comfortable seating area across from his desk.

Addressing his audience, Marcus began, "Has Charlotte told you much about our program?"

"Nothing in great detail, except that she feels so much better every time she leaves your office." Myra faked it well. "That's one of the reasons why we're here."

Annie broke in. "I will be staying in London for . . . Well, I'm really not sure. They are redecorating my place here. Charlotte spoke so highly of you that we decided to make it a girls' trip and drag Charlotte back!"

Marcus started beaming. "I am very

happy to hear this. Let's begin, shall we?" He looked down at the brochures on his desk. "We will discuss what areas are your primary concerns. Is it memory? Fatigue? Balance? Concentration? And so forth. Once we identify the target areas, we formulate a program for you to follow. That includes taking supplements specifically compounded for you —"

Myra interrupted. "You are saying that the supplements are individually compounded according to my body's needs?"

"Precisely." Dr. Marcus leaned back and laced his fingers across his chest, but then he thought better of his body language and sat up straight. "We do a blood workup, urine sample, and saliva. It's all done right here, so you don't have to go to a clinic." He sat up even taller. "And we also supply you with the supplements, so you don't have to go to a pharmacy." He was giving that "See what a great deal this is?" look.

"Why, that's marvelous," Myra cooed. "You make the treatments sound so easy. I much prefer not to have my personal business spread all over town." She was pouring it on thick. "I also like your office. It is well designed and comfortable."

"Well, thank you very much. My partners and I put a lot of thought into it." Marcus beamed.

"I can only imagine," Annie said with a perfectly straight face.

"Indeed," Myra echoed. She looked over at Charlotte to make sure she wasn't going to faint. Or laugh.

"So, what's the next step?" Annie asked coyly.

"If you have time today, we can begin the tests. Our lab will have the results back in twenty-four hours, so you'll be able to begin as soon as two days from now."

"You can compound supplements in twenty-four hours?" Myra acted surprised.

"Yes. That is another great service we offer. Almost immediate delivery. The lab works twenty-four hours a day. We have three shifts." Marcus was trying to recover from his close encounter with a misstep. "It's up in Yorkshire. Small shop." He realized he should simply shut it and move on.

"And what are the fees?" Myra asked.

"It averages around twenty-five thousand dollars a month." Marcus held his breath, waiting for a response.

"Well, if it works, then it's for me!" Annie gushed.

"If it's good enough for Annie, who am I to say no?" Myra chimed in.

"Marvelous!" Marcus thought he was going to explode with relief, relief at getting out of the financial hole he had allowed Norma to dig. And the trench he had dug for himself with his cocaine habit and Franny O'Rourke? Well, he would deal with that after he swapped all his wife's diamonds for cubic zirconia. Even if he had the cash for Franny, he was tired of her pissing away all his money. This would be insurance. Insurance in case Live-Life-Long was not going to be around much longer. Maybe even a divorce. That could happen. His luck was definitely changing. Things were looking up.

"Let's have Gloria set you ladies up in our patient suites." He pressed the intercom. "Gloria, please escort the countess and Mrs. Rutledge to suites and ask Cynthia to start the usual round of tests. I'd like to speak with Charlotte. And then we can have her sit in the atrium area."

"Of course, Doctor," Gloria chirped back.

A few moments later, she entered the office and escorted Annie and Myra to two separate suites. Charlotte gave Annie and Myra a frightened look. They subtly gestured that everything would be okay.

Once the two women had left the room,

Charlotte secretly clicked RECORD on her phone.

Marcus spoke first. "Charlotte, I cannot express how happy I am to see you again. I was concerned you had abandoned hope in our program."

"Oh no, Dr. Marcus. I think I was feeling a bit overwhelmed with the traveling and such." She leaned in, as if to share a secret. "You see, my daughter and son-in-law's flat is tight enough without having a houseguest. I felt as if we were tripping all over each other. And raising a little boy is exhausting." She took a deep breath, laying it on thick. "I felt as if I was getting in the way." She let out a big sigh. "But when I visited Myra and Annie and discovered they were coming to London for an extended stay, and Annie offered her guest room, I was thrilled to accept the invitation."

Marcus leaned back in his chair again and interlocked his fingers across his chest. He was feeling a little too relaxed. "Splendid. Do you have any indication how long the countess will be in town?"

Charlotte could not believe her ears. "I know she's quite busy with the renovation and an impromptu cocktail-party fundraiser at the Plimsoll Building day after tomorrow."

"The Plimsoll Building?" Marcus almost catapulted from his seat. "That's where we live!" He lowered his voice. "You don't suppose we could get invited? My wife would over the moon flip to meet her."

"I can certainly mention it. Perhaps say something like, 'Annie, did you know Dr. Marcus and his wife live at the Plimsoll?' Then maybe she'll ask you to join us." She was pulling him into her confidence.

"Marvelous!" Julian Marcus was all atwitter. "Now let's get on with your shot. It's been two weeks."

"If you don't mind, Dr. Marcus, I prefer not to have it today. I've been feeling quite good with just the supplements." Charlotte was getting more confident in her fabrications. "Annie's housekeeper was a nurse for an elderly gentleman for several years. If you want to give me the vial, I can ask her to administer the shot in a few days."

Marcus made an odd face and thought for a moment. That could cause problems if the nurse-turned-housekeeper mucked it up. On the other hand, he would still charge Charlotte the five thousand dollars. "It's a little, let's just say, out of the ordinary." He pretended to ponder the request before saying, "But with the resources the countess has, I am certain she wouldn't have someone working under her roof who did not have impeccable credentials." Decision made. "It is a supplement. Therefore, I would not be asking someone to administer drugs. If the nurse has no problem with it, then neither do I." He knew he was lying, of course, but that was standard operating procedure in their racket. He couldn't remember the last time he had told a patient the truth.

"Thank you, Doctor. Of course, I'll ask Annie, I mean the countess, for her approval." Charlotte was relishing her new role as supersleuth.

"By all means." Marcus had taken on a whole new attitude. He was convinced his luck had changed. He pressed a button on his phone. "Gloria, would you package up Mrs. Hansen's vial and syringe? She will be taking them with her."

"Righto," came the reply.

Gloria returned to the doctor's office with a black bag containing the mysterious liquid-filled vial. Charlotte was beside herself with excitement, anticipating how proud Myra and Annie would be of her little coup.

Marcus escorted Charlotte to the small atrium area, where she waited for Myra and Annie to finish up their tests. He practically skipped back to his office and sent a text to Jerry. **Coffee. Six sugars. Five o'clock.** He knew he was doubling his normal order, but he was feeling quite upbeat. A quarter of an ounce of cocaine should get him through the week and possibly the weekend. As soon as the women were finished with their tests, he would go to the jewelry exchange and pick up both the real diamond bracelet and the fake one. He knew he had to be careful not to mix them up. He could get killed if he mistakenly gave Franny the fake one.

An hour later, the women went to the atrium area to meet up with Charlotte, who was having trouble hiding her glee.

Marcus joined the group. "We should have the results by late tomorrow. Do you want to arrange to come in the day after?"

"Let me check my calendar." Annie pulled out one of her phones. "I have a meeting with a caterer and a fund-raiser."

Charlotte took the opportunity to interject her contribution to the con. "Annie, you are not going to believe this, but Dr. and Mrs. Marcus live at the Plimsoll!"

"You don't say?" Annie put on a most dumbfounded expression. "Now, *that* is quite a coincidence."

"Indeed it is." Marcus was shuffling his feet the way the creepy kid Jerry did.

323

After a short silence, Annie added, "If you and your wife are free, please join us. I'm expecting about forty or so people. It's what I call an impromptu fund-raiser for the kennel club. No set price. Sort of a 'come as you are' party and bring your checkbook!" Annie laughed. Charlotte was almost giddy.

Marcus was atwitter with anticipation. "We would be honored. I'll let Norma know."

"If she wants to invite any of her friends, that would be fine, too." Annie grinned. "As long as they make a donation!"

"We wouldn't want to intrude," Marcus said thoughtfully.

"Not at all. The more money, the better! Half past seven. Day after tomorrow. We'll make our appointment to come back the following day."

"Fantastic!" Marcus wasn't sure what he was more excited about. The cocktail party, the cocaine, or the money. Probably all three. Unbeknownst to Marcus, of course, all of them were part of one big bomb that was about to blow up in his face.

Gloria set up the appointments for them to return in three days. The next appointment after that would be in two weeks. Obviously, none of them would be keeping either one.

Marcus hustled across town to the jeweler. Eileen was not far behind. He was in and out of the shop quickly. A few minutes later, Eileen entered the shop and walked over to the jeweler.

"Good afternoon. I am here to pick up a package for Dr. Julian Marcus."

The jeweler looked confused. "I beg your pardon?"

"Dr. Marcus? Julian Marcus? He sent me here to pick up an order for him," Eileen said with complete confidence.

"But he just left."

"Now, that's odd. He specifically told me to pick up a package. Can you tell me what it was that you gave him? Perhaps he meant something else."

The jeweler hesitated for a moment. The woman looked quite businesslike. And who but Marcus would send her? Perhaps it was a simple misunderstanding. "It was a reproduction of a gold bracelet with diamonds, and the original."

Eileen gave him a knowing look. "Reproductions seem to be the trend these days. Hard to tell them apart from the real thing, especially if you are good at it, which I am sure you are." The flattery was working. The jeweler became chatty.

"Yes, he's having his wife's jewelry replicated so she can wear what she wants without worrying about losing items."

"Huh. I thought that was what insurance was for!" Eileen laughed.

"Indeed, but as you said, it's a trend." The jeweler shrugged.

"What do you suppose he was expecting me to get from you?"

"He just dropped off a diamond tennis bracelet, but I told him that would take a day or so."

"Probably just a lack of communication. Sorry to have bothered you." Eileen smiled, made a quick turn, and headed out the door.

"No trouble. Ta," the jeweler replied and gave a wave.

As soon as she was far enough from the shop and away from the crowd, she tapped her phone to send a text to Avery. **Marcus is replacing wife's jewels with fakes. So far one gold bangle with diamonds and waiting for diamond tennis bracelet.** Avery sent the information to Charles.

Marcus was back in the office, awaiting the arrival of Jerry. Only a few minutes to go. Marcus was unusually calm. He was already high on the prospects of his future.

Annie, Charlotte, and Myra returned to the brownstone — everyone had a load of information to share. The three of them gathered in front of the large computer screen Annie had stowed in a private office. At Pinewood, the sisters, Charles, and Fergus sat in the war room, monitors glowing. Everyone could see everyone else's faces. Technology at its finest. Annie, Myra, and Charlotte saluted Lady Justice from afar before the conference began.

Annie started by reiterating and expanding upon the information she had received from Victor. Corbett had arranged for Christie's to broker a private purchase from the seller. Corbett was planning a private showing at his yacht club in Sag Harbor, but the painting was still awaiting customs clearance.

Charles added Avery's information about the inventory of Steinwood's garage — a showroom holding five high-end sports cars — and revealed that Marcus was swapping his wife's jewelry for replicas. Most likely without her consent. During their conference call, Avery sent Charles another message. He had more info coming in from the audio and video feed in Marcus's office. Jerry, the drug messenger, was there. Marcus gave him a gold bracelet; Jerry gave him a bag with small white rocks the size of marbles.

There it was. Marcus had a cocaine problem and was swapping the jewelry to pay off his drug dealer, although this method of payment seemed to be fairly new. Perhaps he hadn't replaced all the jewelry yet. There was only one way to find out. Annie asked Charles to enlarge the photos Eileen had taken of the safe's contents. Annie recognized many of the pieces: several David Yurman rings, which would fetch around five thousand dollars each; a Cartier trinity necklace, approximate value seven thousand dollars; a diamond firefly pendant from Tiffany; an assortment of diamond stud earrings ranging from four to five carats; and, literally, diamonds by the yard.

The plan for Marcus was forming. Annie would forward the photos to her jeweler and have him replicate the contents of the safe. But it would have to be quick. She needed the replicas in less than twenty-four hours if she was going to replace the originals during the cocktail party.

Lots of chatter came from the sisters as they refined the overall plan.

When it came to Corbett, Annie would ask Victor who was the best and fastest artist who could make a copy of the Chagall.

Charles and Fergus would find the exact location where the artwork was being held and would reach out to their US Customs connection.

As for Steinwood, Kathryn would get in touch with some of her road travelers, particularly the less than honest types who hauled stolen cars to send overseas.

Jay had reported that there was no secret government installation on the property in Michigan owned by Live-Life-Long. Avery's people were tailing the people who had shot down the drone in Michigan. Charles had been able to run facial recognition software on the partial photos of the men taken before the drone was blown out of the sky. Both were ex-convicts who were trying to live off the grid when they weren't reporting to their parole officers. All indications were that it was as they had suspected. A pill mill.

Jay would wait for a signal from Charles before the FBI took any action.

Kathryn told the group that Pearl was on call, but Marcus would require a different disposal plan.

Annie suggested that this might not be necessary. Franny O'Rourke might become their accomplice, whether he knew it or not. A roar of laughter came from both sides of the Atlantic Ocean. The sisters had a very good idea what could happen to a man who tried to screw his drug dealer.

CHAPTER 35

The Plimsoll Building

The conservatory was buzzing with florists, maintenance people, bartenders, waitstaff, and caterers. A small jazz trio was setting up in the corner, and a local carpenter was carrying a small doghouse into the room. It was three feet high and five feet deep, with a sign painted over the door: A FOREVER HOME. There was a slot at the peak of the roof for people to make their donations. The little door was locked, just in case anyone would dare put their hand in to swipe any of the donations.

Annie was pacing, waiting for the person who would deliver the replica jewelry she was planning to swap for the real goods. An elegantly dressed man who appeared to be in his late sixties approached her.

"Lincoln! Good to see you. Aren't you looking like the dog's dinner!" She meant that in more ways than one. She chuckled.

"Dog's dinner" was a compliment about how one was dressed, and the evening was for the dogs.

Lincoln Gladwell was among the world's foremost gemologists and jewelry designers. If anyone could replicate a piece, it was Lincoln. She took his arm and escorted him to a small private room off the main area.

He spoke with the most elegant British accent. "My dear Annie. If it were not for you, my life would be a complete bore. You really made me shake a leg this time."

"It's all for a good cause, my friend." Annie pecked him on the cheek. "I hope you can stay for some refreshments and conversation?"

"I would be delighted." He handed her several bags. Annie was wearing a flowing silk kimono with a wide obi sash, allowing her to stash the velvet bags around her waist. "And I am certainly not going to ask you what in the bloody blazes you are doing." He tried to stifle a guffaw. He knew Annie could be up to almost anything.

"Excellent idea. The less you know . . . as the saying goes." She tied the sash in the traditional way, wrapping it from front to back and around the front again, then fastening it securely with a knot. Confident she had the faux jewels well hidden, she and

Lincoln returned to the main room. She gave him a pat on the bum and sent him off to the mingling crowd. "We'll catch up in a bit."

Annie motioned for Charlotte and Myra to join her across the room. They huddled in a corner, fleshing out their plan. Annie would greet Dr. and Mrs. Marcus, with Myra and Charlotte in tow. After several minutes of idle conversation, Annie would excuse herself, and then Myra and Charlotte would keep the Marcuses distracted by having them introduce their friends. They knew that Norma Marcus would be eager to show off for the countess, but if she were to get antsy and look for Annie, Myra would sidetrack her. Annie had less than ten minutes to complete the exchange of the jewelry before people would be wondering where she was. Lincoln could be a good backup if necessary.

"We can do this. We *will* do this," Myra and Annie said in unison, and then Charlotte echoed their determination. They grabbed each other's hands, said a silent prayer, and finished with a whispered "Amen."

They expected Julian and Norma Marcus to be the first to arrive. And they were. Norma Marcus was wearing a bright puffy pink thing that served as her dress, with black patent stiletto shoes. But it was the garish red lipstick that made Myra flinch.

Annie did a once-over, checking for which baubles Mrs. Marcus was wearing. She was surprised that there wasn't much. Large chandelier earrings and her seven-carat diamond engagement ring. Maybe she figured she could not outdo Annie, so she hadn't bothered to try. Lucky break. But that dress. It was a tutu on steroids.

Annie let Norma prattle on about nothing of interest. She wanted to exhaust her requisite hostess time with the bawdy bimbo and extend as little hospitality as possible. Myra, Annie, and Charlotte tried to avoid making eye contact with each other in fear of bursting out laughing. Women like Norma Marcus gave women a bad name, and that name was bimbo. The only thing that was missing was the bubble gum. That was when Charlotte remembered how Isabelle and Alexis were dressed when they had left for Aspen. Her body started shaking as she ferociously tried to keep from laughing. She cracked. Myra followed. Then Annie. The three of them were howling as their guests stared in shock.

Surprised and perplexed expressions ran across Julian's and Norma's faces. Annie was the first to gain her composure.

"I am so sorry. My apologies. It's a silly private joke we used to share when we were kids." She took Norma's hand. "So tell me a little about yourself." She guided Norma through the growing crowd. "I plan on staying in London for a brief time. I always welcome new donors to my animal charities." Norma seemed a little unsteady on the spiked heels. Perhaps the word *charity* was a curse word to Norma.

After a half hour of "How do you dos" with Norma's friends, Annie politely excused herself. "I must attend to my other guests. We'll catch up some more later."

Eyeing Myra and Charlotte, Annie signaled that she was on the move. Charlotte and Myra were to keep their eyes on the Marcuses. Annie slipped through the crowd, kissing cheeks. When it appeared no one was looking in her direction, she slipped out the door to the side stairwell. Debating whether she should slide down the handrails, she realized there wouldn't be a pile of pillows at the bottom or Charles and Fergus to bounce off. That was something that would have to wait until she got back to Myra's. She moved swiftly down the stairs, remembering that she had to go one flight below the apartment and then take the lift up. That could eat up several minutes. Lifts did not always arrive on your schedule. Especially when you were in a hurry.

She was careful to avoid the security cameras but was thrown off when the doors to the lift opened and several of her party invitees were inside.

"Annie!" said some of the guests.

"Countess!" other surprised guests blurted.

"Darlings! Good of you to come! You did bring your checkbook, I trust!" Annie was going to get ahead of them before anyone could ask what she was doing in the lift. "Private talk with the doorman."

"Yes, but this is going up."

"And so it is. Silly me. So much going on!" She pushed the button for the Marcuses' floor. "I'll pop out and grab the next one going down. Be back in a flash!"

She blew kisses as the doors slid shut. She scurried to the Marcuses' door and picked the lock. She had the floor plan memorized and headed straight to the bedroom closet that housed the stash. She flipped the plastic cover off the emergency lock, inserted her pick tool, jiggled it to the right, left, right, left. The whirring sound of the cylinders falling into place was music to her ears. She took a quick photo of the contents to be sure she placed the replicas in the same positions. After untying her sash, she laid it on the floor and unfolded it, then emptied the contents of the velvet bags. One by one, she withdrew each piece and replaced it with the fake. She had about three more minutes before she would be discovered to be MIA.

As she was closing the safe and resetting the lock, she heard a voice. The shrill of Norma was crystal clear. *Hide. Where?* And what was Norma doing back in her flat? She realized that Norma was on her cell phone, yammering at someone. Annie dodged behind the bedroom door, hoping the pointed dazzle of her cowgirl boots wouldn't stick out.

"Yeah. I got to meet 'er. We chatted a bit." Annie could hear footsteps approaching and Norma's voice getting louder. "I forgot to wear the Cartier pendant, so I'm back at my flat. Yeah. I noticed she is wearing a Cartier diamond love ring. I want to show her I can also afford Cartier. I know it's silly, but I don't want her to think I'm pikey."

Annie plastered herself behind the bedroom door and held her breath. *Pikey is right,* she thought to herself. *Back home we call it trailer trash with fake bling. And fake it*

337

is. Annie started to lose the feeling of wanting to choke the twit. She would get her just desserts soon enough.

Norma kept babbling on her cell as she opened the safe and withdrew the fake pendant. She put the phone down as she fastened the necklace around her neck, not giving it a second glance. She practically stumbled as she picked up her phone and scampered out. "I've gotta go. Julian is probably looking for me, and I have to corner the countess one more time. I want to show her off to the club. Ta."

As soon as Annie heard the click of the front door, she carefully moved in that direction. She put her ear up against the door to listen for any movement in the hallway. She heard the ding of the lift bell. That was probably Norma going back up to the conservatory. Annie slowly opened the door and peered in each direction. No one. She decided to take the steps to avoid any other possible encounters with partygoers.

When she reached the conservatory floor, she adjusted the sash and cautiously opened the door. She spotted Myra, who was clutching her pearls. Not necessarily a good sign.

Annie frantically gestured to get Myra's attention. Finally. Eye contact. The relief on

Myra's face could be seen across the room. She was standing with Dr. Marcus as Norma edged her way in.

"There you are!" Norma exclaimed, as she saw Annie walking toward them. Dr. Marcus was beaming. Myra was not. She softly closed her eyes and slightly shook her head. Annie was good at scaring the wits out of Myra. Not intentionally. It was Annie's wild nature. One of the many things Myra loved about her dear friend.

"Sorry. I've been pulled in all sorts of directions," Annie replied, recovering from the edge of hyperventilating. She had gotten herself out of a lot of jams in the past. Had Norma discovered Annie in her bedroom, that would have been one hell of a calamity. "My, what a stunning necklace!" Annie pointed to the Cartier. "Sorry I didn't mention it earlier."

Norma didn't flinch. "No worries. You were busy being the perfect hostess."

Annie smiled her most charming smile, all the while thinking, *Rubbish, you moron.* She leaned into Myra, knowing they were both thinking the same thing.

"Where's Charlotte?" Annie asked.

Myra had a twinkle in her eye. "She has been spending some time conversing with Lincoln." She nodded in their direction.

Charlotte was giggling like a schoolgirl. Myra was elated to see her friend laughing and what could be construed as flirting!

"Bravo!" Annie replied. "Lincoln is a wonderful man. Widower for about five years. He said it's hard to meet someone at this point in his life. I'm happy to see him enjoying himself."

"Would you excuse us a moment?" Annie said to the Marcuses. "Myra and I have a little matter we need to resolve before the evening ends. Nothing major, but you know how caterers can be." She took Myra by the elbow and shuffled her through the guests.

Myra started. "You gave me such a fright! What took you so long?"

"You had such a fright? You were supposed to keep an eye on them!" Annie was trying to keep her volume to a whisper. "Norma went back to the flat to get that necklace. I hid behind the bedroom door and held my breath."

"It happened so fast, I couldn't stop her. At first, I thought she was going to the ladies' room, and she melted into the crowd. I didn't realize what had happened until she came back with that necklace on! Thank goodness you weren't caught." She and Annie hugged.

"At least we accomplished what we came

here to do! And clearly, she is none the wiser." Myra touched her pearls again. This time in relief. "Will you look at those two?" She nudged Annie in Charlotte and Lincoln's direction. "I think Charlotte has a new friend."

"Sometimes the universe does wonderful and magical things. I'm not going to order the wedding invitations yet, though." They laughed. "But it would be nice for Charlotte to have a friend when she visits her daughter."

Another hour and a half passed before Annie went over to the doghouse to see how much money they had raised and took the microphone. "Dear friends. I am delighted you could turn out for this impromptu gathering. You know how near and dear animals are to me and Myra. Tonight we raised over nineteen thousand pounds!"

Cheers, hoots, and hollers filled the room. "Do you think we can make it an even twenty?" Annie said.

Lincoln raised his hand. "I'm good for another five hundred."

Annie stared straight at Norma.

"Oh, me! We'll kick in another five, also!" Norma was waving her arms wildly, but Annie could see the color leave Julian's face.

"And for you few Yanks, that's twenty-four

thousand US — at least last time I checked."
A rumble of chuckles came from the guests.
"Again, thank you for coming. I hope to see
you again soon!" Annie put down the mic.

The guests gave a huge round of applause
and bellowed, "Hip, hip, hooray! Hip, hip,
hooray! Hip, hip, hooray!"

The crowd began to thin, with more
alternating cheek kisses, hugs, and hand-
shakes. Lincoln was the last guest to leave.
Annie and Myra scooted to the other side
of the room so Charlotte and Lincoln could
say good night. Lincoln handed Charlotte
his card and kissed the back of her hand.
Charlotte was glowing. Most likely blush-
ing.

Annie was quite pleased with the entire
evening. It had been a bit dodgy, but it had
all worked out, and then some. Time to
head back to the brownstone and report in.

Myra and Annie purposely sat Charlotte
between them in the limo. "So?" they
demanded in unison. Charlotte was blush-
ing.

"He is very nice. He told me he was
familiar with my books. He read them to
his grandchildren! Imagine that!" Charlotte
had a dreamy look on her face.

"Okay, girlfriend. When are you seeing
him again?" Annie pushed.

"I didn't make any plans." She qualified her answer. "Yet. Not until our mission is complete."

"Spoken like a true sister." Myra squeezed Charlotte's arm affectionately. "So what did you tell him?"

"I said I would very much like to see him again and would be in touch once I got my bearings and checked with everyone else's schedule."

"You're a quick study!" Annie remarked.

"I've been trained by the best!" Charlotte reminded them.

The car pulled in front of the brownstone, and the women piled out. Before they settled in for the conference call, they got into comfortable clothes. Annie and Myra were accustomed to sitting on the floor and snuggling with the dogs when they got home, but here they had to settle for each other's company.

An hour after arriving at the brownstone, they entered the drawing room. Byron and Jessica were in their own quarters on the other side of the building, and Annie had bolted the door in the hallway that led to the annex. They had complete privacy.

After powering up their tablets and laptops, they signed into their private network. Annie updated the others on the jewelry exchange and told the story of Norma putting on the necklace and not noticing that it was a fake, once again mentioning Lincoln's superb craftsmanship. She looked at Charlotte and gave her a wink.

Annie had sent the vial from Marcus's office to a lab. It was a combination of vitamin B_{12} and niacin. Innocent enough. It was probably what kept the women's red blood cell count even. It was the rest of those supplements that were so deadly.

Charles informed them that Sasha, Avery's operative in Sag Harbor, had confirmed that the private showing of the Chagall was to be held in three days.

Myra fingered her pearls. "Do we have enough time to pull all this together?"

"Whatever it takes!" was the cheer that came from all the sisters on the conference call.

Charles gave Myra the rundown on Dr. Steinwood. He would be invited to Oscar Davis's world-renowned sports car museum in New Jersey for a private tour. It was the largest of its kind and contained some of the most valuable cars in the world. Davis had made the *New York Times* when he bought a rare Ferrari for $14.3 million at an auction. Steinwood wouldn't be able to resist that offer. Fergus would make the arrangements with Oscar's family and would send the ticket and invitation to Steinwood. While Steinwood was at the museum, Kathryn's crew of behind-the-scenes art haulers would swap Steinwood's collection for stolen cars. They would need Avery to jam the cameras one more time.

Regarding Dr. Corbett, they would swap the original Chagall with the reproduction at the customs neutral zone. They had plans for the original. But Corbett would be showing off the forgery. Charles and Fergus had contacted Interpol. They, too, would unwittingly be part of the mission.

As far as Dr. Marcus, it would be a very short matter of time before Franny O'Rourke was handed paste instead of diamonds. The sisters chattered about what Franny would do to Marcus. They would allow Franny to finish the job for them. He probably wouldn't kill Marcus, but the good doctor would wish he was dead after the beating he would be getting. All part of the Sisterhood credo.

But the timing had to be perfect.

The action was to take place in three days. Everyone was at the ready. Kathryn would meet up with her road buddies in Ohio. Avery was on call to disable the cameras while Steinwood was en route to New Jersey.

Their work in London was done. Myra and Annie had to get back to Pinewood for the grand finale. They encouraged Charlotte to stay on in London, at Annie's place. No need for her to witness the details of the final act of this play. Charlotte was undecided. She wanted to see it through. But Annie and Myra knew there were some things that should not be shared and convinced her to stay.

Annie called her pilot to have him get the jet ready for the return trip to the States.

"Tell Maryann we are sorry we missed her this trip, but something came up with Fergus and some business deal, and I have to get back." That was always a convincing excuse.

On the flight back, Myra and Annie discussed their plan for Corbett and Steinwood. Fergus would keep tabs on Marcus. If Franny didn't put him in the hospital, they would go to plan B, but they were certain Franny would handle it as well as they could. He had a reputation for showing little mercy. But after meeting Norma Marcus, Annie and Myra were almost convinced that she was torture enough.

■ ■ ■ ■

The morning after the fund-raiser, Marcus was flying high. His obtaining two new patients, Myra Rutledge and none other than Countess Anna Ryland de Silva, plus the return of Charlotte Hansen, had Marcus on cloud nine. And with the new arrangement he had with Franny, he was feeling just fine. Fine enough to order a month's worth of cocaine. That would save a lot of dealing with that rotter Jerry Hardy. Before he left for the office, he went to the jewelry safe. There were at least five tennis bracelets. Norma wouldn't miss one of them. He pinched one that had been appraised for twenty thousand dollars. Franny would give him credit for half of it. That was fine with Marcus. It was a win-win for him. He would get cocaine for diamonds and gold. The only costs were for making the fake replacements. Something Norma would never figure out.

CHAPTER 36

Pinewood

When Myra and Annie returned to Pinewood, Charles had a platter of empanadas waiting for them. "Just a little something to tide you over." He set the tray down and wrapped Myra in his arms. "Good to have you back, old girl."

Lady and her pups were yelping and yapping. Myra and Annie squatted to hug and snuggle the pooches. "I missed you so much." Myra draped her arms over as many dogs as she could.

Charles clasped Annie's shoulders. "You managed to stay out of trouble, I see," he said jokingly.

"I do the best I can!" She pecked him on the cheek. "Where's Fergus?"

"In the war room. Dealing with Interpol."

"Goody. Is he optimistic about their cooperation?" Annie asked.

"Anything Nazi related is fair game. The

girls will be arriving in about an hour to go over the rest of the details. I'll bring your bags up, and you can get comfortable. I'll let Fergus know you're here, Annie." Charles buzzed Fergus on his phone and let him know Annie and Myra were back. Then he carried Myra's luggage to the master suite, with Myra and the dogs following behind.

An hour later, the sisters began arriving. High fives to Annie for the jewelry heist; high fives to Kathryn and Yoko for discovering the pill mill; high fives to Isabelle and Alexis for the Brewster info; more slapping for Maggie's work on Lorraine Thompson's apparent suicide and for Charles's and Fergus's intel. Nikki, with assistance from Lizzie Fox in Las Vegas, had made a contribution to the mission, also. She and Lizzie had compiled a list of all previous patient victims of Live-Life-Long and were going to file a class-action suit against the individual men. But that would have to wait until they were arrested. A lawsuit could tip them off and send them running. As of now, none of them had any idea about what was coming.

After the hugging, kissing, and hand slapping, Nikki spoke up. "Where's Charlotte?"

Multiple questions flew out of the sisters'

mouths at the same time.

"Easy." Myra gestured for them to calm down. "Two things. Even though Charlotte played an enormous role in this, we felt that leaving her out of certain things would suit her preferences more than involving her. While she seemed to relish the process of gathering the ingredients, I doubt she would want to be present for the making of the sausages."

Taking the opportunity for a pun, Annie blurted, "Speaking of suits and suitors, there is Lincoln Gladwell, my personal jeweler. He and Charlotte hit it off swim-mingly."

Oohs and aahs came from the group.

"Do tell!" Alexis begged.

"Nothing to tell yet," Myra said evenly. "They met. They chatted. They plan to get together soon." She couldn't hide her joy over the new friendship. "It was sweet. Let's just leave it at that and say some prayers for Charlotte's happiness."

"Hells bells, girls! Happiness for all!" Kathryn bellowed.

Charles motioned for everyone to go to the war room to finalize their plans. After the ritual salute to Lady Justice, everyone took their seat. Charles powered up all the monitors and ran down everything they had accomplished, accumulated, and planned. Everyone knew how imperative the timing was. Once the mission began, the final challenge would be the snatch.

The FBI in the US and Scotland Yard in London had to raid the doctors' offices as well as the property in Michigan. Simultaneously, the FBI would arrest Steinwood for grand theft larceny and Corbett for multiple felonies, and in addition, Interpol would take Corbett in for international art theft. Marcus would be on the run from Franny O'Rourke, assuming that Franny hadn't found him already. It was anyone's guess how that would turn out.

Annie and Maggie would alert all their contacts to make sure the media was on standby to break the stories across the country and the free world. Live-Life-Long was going down.

CHAPTER 37

Pinewood

Three days later, the sisters gathered around the kitchen table for morning coffee, fruits, muffins, scones, and other baked goods. Myra checked the big clock in the entry. It was almost time.

"Ladies, I think we should head downstairs and watch some television," Myra announced.

The excitement among the women and the men was palpable. This was act one. Act two would follow shortly.

Sag Harbor — The big night

Raymond Corbett took another look at himself. *Perfection.* He drove himself to the yacht club, where he would greet his guests, including a representative of the Museum of Modern Art. He had made sure there would be plenty of press coverage in the Hamptons as well as New York City. When he arrived at the yacht club, he noticed several men in dark suits, with earpieces. *Must be the security team I hired.* He nodded at the men and tossed his car keys to the valet. He straightened his shirt cuffs to reveal his expensive cuff links, adjusted his ascot, and sauntered up the steps.

The big question was, Where was he going to stand? On the veranda? Next to the screen that hid the painting from view? No. There were two security guards, one on each side of the screen. He knew that he would stand out between the stark guards, but not enough to suit him. He picked the veranda. This way, everyone would spot him immediately. Some of the men in the dark suits spoke into small microphones clipped to their lapels; some spoke into the band on their wrists.

The guests started to arrive, and Corbett was elated. He had not had so much attention from the local society people since the party he had given to celebrate his admission to the yacht club about a month ago. There had to be over a hundred of the most socially influential people at this gala to unveil the Chagall he had purchased. It was going to be a very big night for him.

Within the hour, the room was alive with chatter, and the time had arrived for Corbett to mingle with his elite guests. He searched the room for the representative from MoMA, a curator at the museum, and spotted her standing next to the screen that shielded the painting. Corbett strolled over to her with his chest puffed out like a rooster's.

"Good evening, Mrs. Spencer. So glad you could join us this evening."

"I thought it would be a good opportunity for publicity for you, the painting, and the museum. May I look before you unveil it?" Mrs. Spencer asked in a quiet, gentle voice.

Corbett was smiling like the Cheshire cat. "Of course," he replied and escorted her to the area behind the screen, where the Chagall awaited its unveiling.

She looked closely at the piece of art and frowned. "Dr. Corbett, I think there may be a problem." Corbett could not imagine what sort of problem she could be having until she spoke her next words. "The signature seems to be slightly off."

"What do you mean, slightly off?" Corbett retorted a tiny bit belligerently.

"The signature, Dr. Corbett. It looks slightly askew. I am going to have to take a closer look."

"Can't that wait?" Corbett was becoming irritated. This woman was not going to ruin

354

his evening, because she thought something was "slightly off."

While this conversation was taking place, there was a commotion on the other side of the screen, a commotion that kept getting louder and louder. Corbett peeked around and saw a dozen men walking toward him.

"Dr. Raymond Corbett?" A man pulled out a badge. FBI. "You are under arrest for manufacturing and distributing a controlled substance."

A second man pulled out his badge. Interpol. He slid the screen to one side to reveal the painting. "You are also under arrest for possession of stolen property. This painting is owned by France, and the country is claiming all rights to it."

At that point, Mrs. Spencer intervened, saying, "But this painting is a forgery. I very much doubt that France or any other country owns it or even wants to own it." That comment stopped everyone in their tracks.

Corbett whirled around and stared at her. "Don't be ridiculous." Then he turned to the men who were placing him under arrest. "And you . . . What do you mean, I'm under arrest?"

"You need to come with us, Dr. Corbett," the FBI agent said.

The men he thought were part of his

security detail were actually federal agents! When they tried to pull his arms behind his back, he went ballistic.

"You have no right to come here! Unhand me!"

The resulting scuffle got everyone's attention, including members of the press, who had been given a tip that something big was going to happen. At first, the reporters had thought it was the usual celebrity sighting, until the FBI agents had leaped from the vans. Add art forgery to the mix, and it was a melee of shocked guests and reporters.

Yes, reporters were everywhere, just as Corbett had wanted. But his being arrested was not what he had intended or had expected them to write about. He was squirming and thrashing as the FBI agents led him out the door. Camera flashes were going off from different directions.

Someone from one of the city's news networks shoved a microphone in his face. "Dr. Corbett, did you know you bought a fake?"

He was screaming, "This is bullshit," when the agent from Interpol approached him again.

"Where is the original painting, Dr. Corbett? You can save yourself a lot of trouble if you tell us where it is immediately."

"I don't know what you are talking about!" Corbett was still squealing as the FBI agents escorted him toward one of the dark vans.

Reporters were shoving microphones in his face.

"What about the drugs?" shouted one.

"Is that how you paid for the artwork?" shouted another.

He could still hear the reporters yammering as the agents placed him in the rear seat of the van.

"What about the raid on your property in Michigan?"

"Is it true you were supplying Adderall to a prep school?"

The radio in the van was broadcasting, too. Live-Life-Long offices had been raided, as had the Michigan property. A student at a very prestigious prep school who had ties to Corbett had also been arrested in New York City for distribution of drugs. Owing to his age, his identity was being withheld.

Newark, New Jersey
Harold Steinwood almost had an erection when he saw the collection of cars in Oscar Davis's museum. From a 1937 BMW 328 Roadster to the 1964 Ferrari Davis had bought for $14.3 million, and everything in

357

between. It was an auto-orgasmic experience. He could barely breathe from the beauty of the sleek lines, the highly polished chrome, the leather interiors. They were truly works of art.

After the tour, they were about to leave for dinner when several black vehicles swarmed into the parking lot. At least a dozen FBI agents sprang from the vans. The one who looked to be the agent in charge announced, "Harold Steinwood. You are under arrest!"

Steinwood was stunned. "I'm *what*? What is going on here? What are you charging me with?" He tried resisting as one of the agents spun him around and slapped handcuffs on his wrists.

"Grand theft larceny," one of the FBI agents replied.

"Manufacturing and distributing a controlled substance, schedule two, three, and four," added another.

"Grand theft? This must be a mistake. What are you talking about? What am I supposed to have stolen? And drugs?" Steinwood was almost shrieking. He could not believe they had been exposed. It was not possible. They had been painfully careful. That was when he noticed television cameras, reporters, and microphones all around them. To one side, he recognized several reporters from Fox News, CNN, MSNBC, CBS, NBC, ABC. It was a media circus.

"We are at the Oscar Davis museum in New Jersey. Harold Steinwood, one of the founders of Live-Life-Long, has been arrested by the FBI for grand theft larceny and manufacturing and distributing schedule two, three, and four substances." The reporter paused for a moment. "We also have footage of his office in Aspen being raided by the FBI."

Aspen

The national networks switched to the local channels in Aspen to report the breaking news as cameras tracked men in SWAT uniforms storming the office of Live-Life-Long while the receptionist and nurse shrieked in terror. Then the television station showed what was happening at Steinwood's garage.

The local newscaster chimed in, saying, "Yes, Anthony, we are now in front of Harold Steinwood's home, where the FBI has surrounded the garage and is removing five stolen high-end sports cars."

London

Every radio station and TV channel interrupted its regular programming for a bulletin. "This just in. The offices of Live-Life-Long here and in the United States have been raided by the FBI in the US and Scotland Yard here. Dr. Julian Marcus, who operated the office in London, was found severely beaten in an alley and was taken to a hospital. Police are trying to ascertain if the doctor's beating and the drug raid are connected. His partners in the US, Dr. Harold Steinwood of Aspen and Dr. Raymond Corbett of New York, have been taken into custody, and all Live-Life-Long property has been seized, including a large parcel of land in the state of Michigan, where, it appears, there is a manufacturing plant for the drugs the doctors allegedly prescribed to their patients. More on that later."

Michigan

"This is Greg Langley from FOX Two Detroit. We're here in a rural area outside Detroit, where, as you can see, FBI helicopters are overhead and SWAT teams are on the ground.

"This remote area houses a seemingly abandoned warehouse, which appears not to be abandoned at all. Sources say that the building was being used as a pill mill to manufacture drugs for the Live-Life-Long organization. Other sources have reported that the three offices of Live-Life-Long have also been raided, and two of the alleged perpetrators, Harold Steinwood of Aspen and Raymond Corbett of New York, have been taken into custody. Julian Marcus of London has been found severely beaten and was taken to a hospital. We'll be following this story tonight on our nightly news."

Pinewood

Screams and howls of laughter echoed off the walls in the war room, and there were fist pumps, high fives, hugs, and some tears.

Myra stood with her arm around Annie. "That was quite a spectacle. Everyone and everything getting busted across televisions everywhere."

"It's all in the timing." Annie chuckled. "Almost every newspaper in the country is going to run the headline BITTER PILL. But we now have to put the second phase into action."

"Yes, we do," Charles added. "We are getting the information from all law enforcement agencies as to where and when they are going to transfer the prisoners."

"Let's not forget Interpol," Fergus reminded them. "When the original painting is returned to France, there will be a reward.

Do we have a plan for that, and who will get the money?"

Myra looked at Annie, who in turn looked at Fergus. "When *don't* we have a plan?"

More laughter ensued.

"We have a plan for everything!"

Nikki spoke up. "As I mentioned a few days ago, Lizzie and I were able to find most of the Live-Life-Long patients, and we are about to launch a class-action suit against the individual men and their assets."

"But they were seized, right?" Yoko asked.

Charles spoke next. "We, as in us, and our contacts can unfreeze them, but we want to wait until the snatch is complete."

"I must confess, I have what one could call contraband." Annie plunked several velvet bags on the conference table. It was the real jewelry from Norma's safe. "I think if we pool all the resources, we should have a nice sum to divide up among the families. There will be the reward from the motorcars and the reward from the painting."

"How do we determine who gets the reward money?" Kathryn asked.

"We gave the name of Marjorie Brewster's sister to the FBI for blowing the whistle on Steinwood's garage," Charles explained. "She'll get that reward money for the recovery of the stolen cars from the various insurance companies. Steinwood's real cars will be auctioned by Christie's, and the money will go into the kitty."

"And Victor will get commissions on those." Annie folded her arms and nodded.

Charles added, "There is also a reward for blowing the whistle on the Michigan property. That, too, will be added to the fund."

"What do we do about the painting?" one of the sisters asked.

"Maggie is going to call Lorraine Thompson's daughter and instruct her to go to the local flea market in Huntington on Saturday. She is to look for booth one-twenty-nine, where she will ask for Rudy. Rudy will sell her the Chagall for twenty-five dollars. She'll take the painting home, and Mrs. Spencer from MoMA will pay her a visit. Mrs. Spencer will authenticate the painting and arrange for it to be returned to France. France will give Lorraine's daughter the reward money."

"Whatever is left, such as the doctors' homes and personal property, will be part of the class-action suit against each individual. It is a civil suit, so we don't have to wait for convictions," Nikki added. "We just need to prove harm and ask for damages. Their attorneys will represent them at the hearing. That is, if their attorneys will work pro bono!"

"I'm not too sure about Marcus. I think we are holding the only assets he had. The wife was like a sponge, soaking up his earnings, and the drugs took care of the rest." Annie patted the bags. "But we have this. Speaking of Marcus, any word on him?"

Fergus tapped a few keys on his laptop. "Seems like he's going to be in traction for several months. Several major bones were broken. If he ever recovers, he'll have a serious limp. And all his teeth were knocked out."

"I don't think we could have done a better job," Annie exclaimed. "Maybe we should keep Franny on retainer," she said jokingly.

"Okay, ladies." Myra reeled everyone in. "We need to move to the next stage. Charles? Fergus? Are the arrangements made?"

"Yes. The transfers are day after tomorrow. The rooms are ready," Charles replied.

The next morning, the whole gang met for breakfast. This time it was a big fry-up. Everyone fixed a plate and took a seat at the long kitchen table. Myra asked Nikki to open her laptop and Skype Charlotte. The singsong theme played as Charlotte's face came into view. She was howling with laughter as everyone waved at the screen.

Maggie held her overloaded plate up to the camera. "Sorry you're missing this. So I'll eat for both of us!"

Everyone laughed, and the dogs barked their opinion of the whole matter.

Charlotte started. "I am at a loss for words. Imagine. A writer. No words. That could put me permanently out of business! How on earth? What in the world?" Charlotte was referring to the breaking news, which in the UK was already old news, about Live-Life-Long.

The sisters doubled over with laughter. Maggie almost spit out her eggs. The hilarity lasted a couple of minutes, as half of them wiped tears from their face. Maggie wiped her chin.

Myra was the first one to speak. "My dear friend Charlotte. Do you realize what a hero you are?"

"Me? But you people did everything!" Charlotte protested.

"Think about it," Myra said. "You came to me with a very personal problem. Something that was embarrassing, humiliating, and very costly. Because you had the courage to speak up, we were able to take down three despicable men who preyed on vulnerable women and to bust a pill mill that was also supplying drugs to teenagers."

Charlotte blushed. "Since you put it that way. Tell me, what is going to happen to the doctors now?"

They all looked at each other, then back at the camera, and shrugged.

"Let's just say karma is a bitch. Especially when you mess with our friends."

Charles leaned in. "Please rest assured. They won't be harming anyone ever again."

A robust "Amen!" came from the group.

Nikki spoke up next. "Charlotte, we are going to start a class-action suit against their holdings. It's a civil suit. As long as we can show damages, the judge will most likely rule in our favor. It might take a while, but I don't think any of the doctors will object."

Fergus eyed Charles. Nope. They certainly wouldn't be around to object. And lawyers wanted to get paid, which they wouldn't. And since it would be a civil action lawsuit, there would be no court-appointed attorney or public defender. "According to our calculations, their entire net worth is around thirty million."

Charlotte gasped. "Thirty million? That much?"

"Yes. We have been able to find a hundred

and sixty-seven of their previous patients. Victims. That sum would probably be enough for everyone to be reimbursed," Nikki added.

"The insurance company is going to pay Marjorie Brewster's family a reward for the return of the stolen cars. It's around four hundred thousand dollars. That should help her recovery. Speaking of which, she has turned a corner and is able to smile and acknowledge people in the room. They're hopeful she will continue to improve," Myra said.

"My head is spinning." Charlotte chuckled. "What about the diamonds?"

"We're throwing those into the overall fund," Annie said. "The other piece of good news is that Norma Marcus's check for the kennel club cleared before they froze the account!"

Everyone applauded, and the pups howled their approval.

After a bit more conversation, they signed off, but not before promising to speak again in a few days.

Chapter 38

During the arrests, none of the officers in any of the raids spoke except to give the prisoners instructions. "Sit down." "Shut up." The officers remained indifferent, despite the demands and screams of those they had arrested. For two days, Corbett and Steinwood were kept in isolation. Steinwood had been arrested in New Jersey and Corbett in New York, and both were taken to an undisclosed location. Each was incarcerated in a solid concrete cell. Each cell was soundproof. Neither of them knew of the other's whereabouts or what was to come next. Steinwood demanded his one phone call but was told it would have to wait. Corbett received a similar denial. Neither could get anyone to talk to him, creating panic and fear in both men. Marcus lay in a semicomatose state in a hospital in London. He was probably better off than the other two.

Food was brought to them in plastic pails. They had to eat in a six-foot-by-nine-foot space they shared with a bucket of their excrement. They had not showered, either. The smell alone was enough to make someone vomit.

Demanding shrieks bounced off the walls of Corbett's soundproof cell, but only he could hear his rage. Steinwood remained silent. He was convinced it was all a bad dream, and he would wake up at any minute. Marcus, on the other hand, had recurring nightmares while he went in and out of a state of semiconsciousness. All in all, the three men had been cut off, in one way or another, from civilization.

Near the end of the second full day of incarceration, the clanking of keys drew Steinwood out of his trance. Locks clicked, and the door opened, and what appeared to be a camera flash went off in his face. A large figure stood over him.

"Turn around," the figure demanded.

Steinwood obeyed the order while fearing the worst. The man pulled Steinwood's arms behind his back and secured them with a zip tie that Houdini himself would have had trouble slipping out of. The man shackled Steinwood's ankles together, put duct tape over his mouth, and placed a burlap bag over his head. Steinwood could not stop himself from urinating in his pants.

The large man looked down. "Too bad the Laundromat is closed," he said. "Now walk."

Steinwood tried to mumble something.

The large man said, "Shuffle," and gave him a nudge. "Move! Don't worry. I won't let you fall down a manhole."

Steinwood moved slowly as his urine-soaked pants stuck to his legs.

Corbett ranted almost the entire time he was awake. He thought he might go mad.

Did he hear keys, or was he beginning to hallucinate? A bolt turned, and a bright light filled the cell. It almost blinded him. Someone took his photo. He could not figure out how long he had been sitting in the corner, trying to avoid the stench of his own excrement. He rubbed his face and felt what he thought might be two full days of stubble.

A large man filled the doorway. "Stand up," he commanded. "Turn around."

Corbett was about to start shouting at the man but thought better of it. He had heard enough horror stories about prison. For the first time in several days, Corbett remained silent. As he had done with Steinwood, the large man secured Corbett's wrists with a zip tie, shackled his ankles, covered his mouth with duct tape, and put a burlap bag over his head.

"Make one sound, and I'll stuff you like an Idaho potato," the man warned.

Marcus kept fading in and out of semiconsciousness. Lights. Lots of them. In his mental haze, he saw what looked like snowmen and circus tents floating around him. He could not feel anything except the cold fluid that was being pushed into the back of his hand. The last thing he remembered was Franny O'Rourke standing over him with a cinder block. He wasn't sure if he was dead and had gone to hell. Someone appeared in his peripheral vision and shined what seemed like a laser into his left eye. Then the right. There was gibberish he could not understand. He tried to speak, but his lips were swollen shut. He was convinced he *was* in hell when he heard the shrill voice of Norma as she flew into the room in a rage.

"What in the blazes have you done, you arsehole? Where is my jewelry?" She was almost on top of him before someone was able to pull her away from the ICU bed. "You'd better get it back, or I'll unplug all these machines!"

The nurse dragged her out into the hallway. "We're sorry, miss, but this man is in very bad shape. It's best he doesn't have visitors."

Norma kept yelling that she had rights, and that they couldn't keep her away from her husband, but the constable who guarded Marcus's door informed her otherwise. If Marcus were able, he would have laughed at Norma's expulsion from his room. If he could speak, he would have also told her to cheese off.

Steinwood and Corbett were kept separated, but they were both on their way to the same facility, where they would once again be held in isolation in secluded quarters. But *quarters* wasn't quite an accurate description of the place where they would be incarcerated. The cells they had previously occupied would seem like the Waldorf-Astoria compared to their new ones.

The men were guided into two different vans, and their shackles were cuffed to a bolt on the floor. Corbett started moaning. No one said anything. In the other vehicle, Steinwood listened for any clues as to where they were or where they might be going. None of what was happening to him seemed real.

Corbett started planning his revenge in his head. As soon as he had the opportunity, the shit would hit the fan. He had essentially been abducted by the FBI agents, taken to an undisclosed location, not given access to a lawyer, and treated inhumanely. He would sue every branch of the government. Cruel and unusual punishment. What he didn't know was that all his property was frozen, and the Live-Life-Long company was virtually out of existence.

The drive took about four hours, during which there was no sound of any sort coming from anyone. No cell phones ringing, no radio noise. The moaning had stopped. It was a long, dark journey to parts unknown.

When the vans pulled up to Myra's farmhouse, everything was eerily quiet except for the sound of the gravel beneath the tires. The men unloaded the vans one at a time to assure that neither prisoner knew the other was there. Corbett was removed first. His warders uncuffed the shackles from the bolt, pulled him out of his seat, and steered him to the back door of the kitchen, the same kitchen where Charles prepared the luscious food he cooked. But Corbett would not be a dinner guest. Not ever, and probably not anywhere else ever again. Myra nodded at the guards, Avery Snowden's more muscular employees, indicating they could leave. Kathryn grabbed Corbett's arm and walked him down the stone steps.

On the other side of the basement, where the underground tunnels were hidden, there were two rooms. Dungeons would be a better description. Each had one bare light-bulb, a thin mattress, and a bucket for urinating and defecating. The setup was much the same as the men's previous accommodations, except a little smaller. Kathryn put Corbett in one of the closet-sized spaces, told him to sit down, and informed him that someone would be back shortly.

Once the first van pulled away, the second one delivered Steinwood. Avery's men released the shackles from the bolt and pulled him out. Myra and Annie watched as Kathryn yanked him down the same set of stone steps and saw him to his own private accommodations.

The sisters gathered in the kitchen. A late dinner would soon be served. They hooted when Charles let them know that Steinwood and Corbett were indisposed and would not be joining them. He had prepared a special stew for them.

Annie pulled out a few bottles of Dom Pérignon champagne. "We aren't finished yet, but we are in the home-stretch. We accomplished a heck of a lot in a very short time. I think a toast to the final act is appropriate." Maggie gave her a high five, and the rest followed suit. She popped the corks and poured the contents of the bottles into coffee mugs. Myra smiled. She loved to do things in a proper manner, but Annie was spontaneous, and the mugs were the closest things to the fridge. "Here's to us! The best bunch of sisters anyone could have!"

Cheers and whoops came from the group, setting off Lady and her pups, who yapped in agreement.

The sisters were hanging about the kitchen when Maggie asked Charles, "So, what kind of stew?"

"The expression 'a taste of their own medicine' would fit here, since that medicine is, indeed, a part of the recipe," he said with a twinkle in his eye, causing the sisters to cackle with glee. "Tonight will be the Adderall cuisine." He pointed to the mortar and pestle sitting in the butler pantry. "A little more than a pinch should do." More hooting and laughing came from the girls. "And tomorrow phenobarbital will be the plat du jour."

Myra explained they were going to put Steinwood and Corbett on the same roller-coaster ride they had inflicted on their trusting patients.

Annie chimed in with the entertainment part of the program. "Isabelle and Nikki created a video loop they'll be forced to watch twenty-four/seven as they take their mind-bending rides. Fergus and Charles installed sixty-inch TV screens on all four walls of each cell. It will be bigger than life. Our version of an IMAX theater." She couldn't help but giggle. "We'll show you the video after dinner."

"Speaking of dinner, the coq au vin is ready." Charles took a short bow and motioned to the buffet. The chicken had been prepared to perfection, along with the egg noodles, mashed potatoes, and biscuits. A side of crumbled bacon was there for anyone who wanted to use it to garnish the chicken.

As the sisters filled their plates, they chatted about their day, significant others, hobbies, and the news. From the upbeat mood of the room, no one would suspect they were holding two despicable men several feet below. But not unexpectedly for the sisters, that was exactly the mood they would be in knowing that they had put an end to terrible wrong-doings and that justice would be served — literally.

An hour later, the kitchen was spick and

span. Not a crumb in sight. This time it took less than twelve minutes. The women scrambled to the war room to watch the video Isabelle and Nikki had produced, and saluted Lady Justice as they entered.

Once everyone was seated, Charles fired up all the monitors. The first shot was the front page of the *Post,* with the headline BITTER PILL! There was an accompanying photo montage of Corbett, taken after he had spent two nights in his cell. He looked exactly like someone who had slept in a box with a bucket of human waste. To say he resembled a derelict would be an insult to the derelicts of the world. There was no sign of a cashmere blazer or ascot, gold cuff links, or Italian leather. Steinwood had a similar look but with much more fear in his eyes. The only footage they had of Marcus was the police photo taken at the scene where he was found. He looked like a smashed pumpkin, only white.

The video continued with images of the arrests and the raids on the offices, including shots of the FBI helicopters circling the warehouse in Michigan. The audio was snippets of newscasters from all over the country and headlines: LIVE-LIFE-WRONG! PILL MILL BUST! DR. DRUGS! FRAUD IN THE HAMPTONS! Every major network and its local affiliates were covering the story. You couldn't turn on the television without seeing the raids on the various locations and the arrests. In the case of Marcus, the press covered the ambulance ride from the scene of his beating to the hospital. There was still no word on who was responsible.

The video was almost five minutes of police raids, helicopters, newscasters, and medical correspondents, interspersed with the recent third-day grunge photos of Steinwood and Corbett, interspersed with the mangled Marcus. They would be forced to watch the same five minutes of their undoing over and over while their bodies were being pumped with their homemade "supplements." The sisters would keep them on this regimen until the men wished they were dead. They were less concerned about Marcus's fate. He would have to avoid Franny O'Rourke, even with a constable outside his door. Franny had a lot of contacts. Almost as many as Annie, but not quite, and certainly not in the same circles.

The sisters watched the video several times, while Charles and Fergus went back to the kitchen to fetch the special stew Charles had prepared. A huge round of applause and fist pumps filled the room.

"Woo-hoo!" Kathryn bellowed. "Do you

think we can enter this in a film festival?"

Everyone hooted.

Myra was the first to speak. "I would like to be the one who pulls the duct tape off Corbett's face."

"And I want Steinwood," Annie chirped.

"And we want to watch," Maggie said with glee.

"Me toos" from all around the table.

Charles stood. "Shall we begin?" He handed Myra the remote control that would start the video loop in the cells. There was also a closed-circuit camera in each cell that would record Corbett and Steinwood; and anyone could get a live look at any time.

The women marched past Lady Justice and saluted. One by one they walked to the first cell. Corbett squirmed at the jangle of keys and the sound of the door opening. It sounded like several people had entered the tight space.

Myra pulled the bag off his head. He had a blank expression on his face.

"Good evening, Dr. Corbett. I call you *Dr. Corbett*, but since you have never been licensed to practice medicine, are you really and truly a doctor? Nor is what you practiced on your patients really medicine. So perhaps I should just call you Mr. Corbett. But whatever I call you, you are not an honest or decent human being. You embody at least four of the seven deadly sins, greed being number one on the list. Not only did you cheat hundreds of women out of millions of dollars, but you were also cheating your criminal partners. I'm talking about that little side business you had. You were the supplier to a very elite prep school in New York City, fostering drug addiction among teenagers. Yes, the young man confessed. Clearly, you don't discriminate, since you have no regard for anyone, of any age. As long as your dupes had enough money, you were happy to provide them with your wares.

"We are going to remove the zip tie, but don't try anything stupid. If you think you've had a rough few days, let me assure you that fighting back will only make things worse. Nod if you understand."

Corbett vigorously nodded. He had no fight left in him. He would have to regroup somehow, find a way out, or convince his captors to show some mercy.

Myra held her breath as she got close to his face. "Think of it like a Band-Aid. Best to be removed with one quick pull." The blank expression turned to horror as she reached for the tape and ripped it off his face. A low growl of agony came from his throat. "See? All better."

Kathryn pulled him off the floor and held him tightly as Fergus cut the zip tie.

Myra stepped back and pressed the button on the remote. "And now for your dining pleasure. Enjoy."

Charles handed him the bowl of his special stew. "Eat up, champ."

Before Corbett could utter a word, everyone retreated from the space and the door was slammed shut and locked.

Corbett sat in horror as he watched his life crumble before him. How had this happened?

Who had betrayed them, and why? Everyone had been making plenty of money. They had had a tight group. He started to wail like a baby. *Why? Why? Why? Where am I? Who are these people?*

A short time later, he realized he had cried himself to sleep. He didn't know how long ago he had nodded off. What he did know was that he needed to take a piss. He reached for the bucket in the corner and relieved himself for the first time in over twelve hours as more tears ran down his face. He sat on the thin mattress and reached for the bowl of stew. The food was at room temperature. And that damned video was still running. Corbett forced himself to eat the unidentifiable concoction. It had a very bitter taste, but it was food. He couldn't remember the last time he had eaten anything. He had no idea what day it was or what time it was. All he knew was that he was in the worst place in his life.

While Corbett sobbed himself to sleep, the sisters marched to the other end of the hallway to deal with Steinwood.

He didn't stir when they opened the door. Not a peep. Not a move. He was literally scared stiff, except for pooping in his pants.

"Whoa!" Kathryn roared. "Need a diaper? Jeez, I'd be passed out, too, if I had to spend one more minute in here." She kicked his foot to see if he was conscious. "Hey! You!" Steinwood curled into a ball, and Kathryn poked Annie. "Make it quick. The stench is burning my nostrils."

Annie leaned over the crumpled man. "Dr. Steinwood. You are here because you are a despicable human being. You and your partners preyed on vulnerable women, taking advantage of their trust. You cheated and lied. You put their health at risk. One of them died, and another is in a semiconscious state. Yes, we know everything about you, Corbett, and Marcus. You and your high-end sports cars."

Steinwood started shaking his head and

tried to speak.

"It appears that you want to say something?" Annie said.

He nodded vigorously.

"We are going to remove the bag, but you need to sit still. Shake your head 'yes' if you understand."

He whimpered and complied. Annie removed the bag. Everyone saw the terror in his eyes as he blinked uncontrollably from the bright light. Annie was about to pat him on the head but thought better of it. She wasn't about to ruin a good pair of slacks from wiping whatever grime was in his hair. He flinched away.

"I am going to remove the tape now." Annie leaned over and pulled the duct tape off his face in one swoop. The sounds coming from his throat were a mix of coughing and gagging. He tried to speak.

"I . . . I . . . didn't mean to hurt anyone." It came out in a rasp.

"Well, whatever you meant to do, you did hurt people." Annie crossed her arms over her chest. "And you are going to pay for it." She nodded to Myra to start the video loop. "Enjoy the show."

Kathryn reached behind him and cut the zip tie, handed him the stew, and backed out of the very small space. The rest of the women retreated to the hallway before Annie slammed the steel door shut. The sound of the keys made him shudder. The fact that his pants were still wet was not helping.

384

CHAPTER 39

London

Marcus's legs twitched as his vision went from darkness to fog. He couldn't focus. He tried to speak, but nothing but spittle and slurred speech came from his mouth. He felt a small tube in his hand. It was the call button for the nurse. He pressed it several times. Within minutes, two very imposing nurses stood before him. One was a very large black man who looked like he spent most of his free hours in a gym. His arms were solid muscle. At least that was what they looked like to Marcus. The other looked like Nurse Ratched from *One Flew Over the Cuckoo's Nest* — mean, cold, heartless.

"What is it, Dr. Marcus?" she growled.

He had questions, but he couldn't form words.

"Dr. Marcus, we can't have you pushing that button all willy-nilly. What do you want?" she demanded.

The large black nurse was a bit kinder. "Dr. Marcus, do you know where you are?"

Marcus tried to find a body part that was functioning besides the thumb that seemed to be stuck to the call button. He squinted through his swollen eyes. His lids were the size of golf balls.

"Dr. Marcus, you are in the Royal London Hospital. You were found by a delivery chap in an alley outside your office. You've suffered very severe injuries. You have a broken leg. Shattered, actually, as is your left elbow. Your jaw and both eye sockets are fractured. You have a collapsed lung, a concussion, and a number of hematomas." Marcus closed his eyes as the large black nurse rattled off more medical conditions. "You are a very lucky man, Dr. Marcus. Try to get some rest."

Lucky? Marcus thought to himself. By the sound of what he had been told, he thought he would probably never walk again. Maybe not even talk. The upside was maybe he wouldn't see Norma again. Now, *that* would be lucky. Through the slits in his eyes, he could barely make out the figure of the constable sitting outside his door. He didn't know if that was a good thing or a bad thing as he drifted off into the other place in which he had been spending the past few days. La-la land.

Franny O'Rourke was pacing his office. He was perturbed that he had been unable to finish off Marcus. Damn delivery boy. Good thing he had spotted the lad before he was seen smashing Marcus's face. One final blow would have done it, but now Marcus was in hospital, being guarded by the police. Franny pounded his fist on the table. He was going to get even with Marcus one way or another.

He picked up the phone and called a buddy of his in the police force. Bribery knew no boundaries. It was as prevalent in England as anywhere else.

A chipper young voice answered. "And what can I do for you today? Need someone to look the other way?" Franny O'Rourke's inside man had a burner phone that Franny would replace every couple of days by leaving one in a locker at the bus station.

Franny replied, "Nope. Need to find out where they're holding Julian Marcus. Which hospital?"

The voice at the other end of the phone remained silent.

"Didn't you hear me?" Franny was losing his patience.

"Er . . . that's under a lid. Only the top brass know." The cheerful voice had become somber. He knew the reaction he was about to get.

"You bloody well better find out!" Franny shouted and threw his phone across the room. He was going to finish off Marcus if it was the last thing he ever did. *No one screws with me. No one.*

About an hour later, his mangled phone rang. He walked over to it and gingerly picked it up. He was glad it still worked. *These flip phones are a lot sturdier than the expensive smartphones. What's so smart about them, anyway? You need an encyclopedia to figure them out.* "Ye better 'ave some news for me," Franny snapped.

"The Royal London Hospital." Then the phone went dead.

Franny grabbed his cap and a slicker and headed out the door.

It had taken Eileen several days to get Franny's location. She had followed the slimy kid around until he was able to lead her to Franny O'Rourke. Now Franny was on the move. She sent a signal to Avery, who forwarded it to Charles. There had been a BOLO, "be on the lookout," on Franny O'Rourke for over a year. He was wanted for a number of crimes, but he was slick and always seemed to slip through the cracks. Whispers and rumors had been bandied about that he had someone on the inside of the police department, but there had been no chatter as to who it could be. Eileen tried to keep up without being spotted. Franny entered the Underground and boarded a train. Eileen was not far behind. Several stops later, Franny exited the Underground and walked toward the Royal London Hospital. Eileen signaled Avery again.

Through Charles's and Fergus's connections, they had been able to determine Marcus's whereabouts long before Franny had. The relay of information had gone through the ranks. Eileen to Avery. Avery to Charles. Charles to whomever. No one was ever quite sure.

As he turned the corner by the entrance of the hospital, Franny pulled his cap down to the bridge of his nose, put on the pair of glasses he kept in his jacket pocket, and unfolded the collapsible cane he had tucked in his belt. He couldn't risk being recognized. He also couldn't risk letting Marcus breathe another day.

Eileen was moving quickly. If no one else showed up, she would have to tackle Franny before he could get to Marcus. She whipped out her fake security badge and swept past the gate, but she couldn't get to the lift in time. She was frantically checking for the stairs when the door to another lift opened. She pushed her way forward, getting a lashing of remarks as to her rudeness. "Sah-ree, sah-ree, sah-ree," she kept saying in her favorite Brooklyn accent.

One stiff-necked gent looked over at another and mouthed the word "American."

Earlier, Avery had given Eileen the number of the floor on which Marcus was being held. He was in the room being guarded by a constable, who was sitting outside. When the elevator doors opened, Eileen rushed through the crowd and spotted Franny within a few feet of Marcus's room. *How is he going to get past the guard at the door?* she wondered. But then she realized the cop was there to keep Marcus from getting out. There was no reason to try to keep people from going in, unless it was his unhinged wife.

"Franny O'Rourke?" The constable stood. "We've been expecting you."

"What all?" Franny said with total surprise. He turned to run, but over a half dozen men in various uniforms surrounded him.

"Yer coming with us." The mix of London

law enforcement officers cuffed him and marched him to the bank of lifts, where an empty car waited.

And thus a Sisterhood operation, one that began with putting three doctors who preyed upon rich widows out of commission, brought about the arrest of one of the most notorious criminals in the UK.

Marcus watched in horror from his bed. He couldn't tell if he was awake or having another nightmare. Or was this simply one continuous nightmare? The appearance of Nurse Ratched confirmed it for him. It was one terrifying moment after another.

Eileen pinged Avery. "All clear."

"Roger that," was the reply.

Marcus strained to hear what people were saying in the hallway. The buzz in his head subsided. He wasn't dreaming.

"Sorry about the commotion, Dr. Marcus. Evidently, you're not allowed certain visitors." The cranky nurse snickered and walked out of the room.

Franny O'Rourke had been apprehended. But that left Marcus with another problem. If he was ever getting out of this hospital, he would be going to jail. It was all coming back to him. When the officers began to raid the office, he had bolted out the back door into the alley. The alley where Franny

O'Rourke had been waiting with a cinder block. He started forming real thoughts. *If I go to jail, Franny will surely finish me off, even if he doesn't do it himself.* Marcus concluded that he had to get out of the hospital without being seen. *How?* He was a hot mess. He had to think. First thing he would do was stop the pain meds. As much as he liked the high, staying alive had to be his priority. He rang for the nurse. He hoped it was the kinder of the two.

This time a young woman wearing a bright pink uniform stood in the doorway. "Yes, Mr. Marcus?"

He wasn't able to form full words yet, so he motioned to the IV drip with his head.

"You want me to do something with this?" she asked.

He got off a weak nod.

"Do you want more?"

His swollen eyes almost bulged out of his head as he tried to shake it to say no.

"No?" the young woman asked quizzically.

He shut his eyes and nodded, as if to say yes.

The woman was confused. "Do you want more? Or less?"

Marcus was getting frustrated, but that was a good sign. That meant he was getting his wits back. He moved his hand sideways in a motion to cut off the supply.

"Oh, no more?" The pink lady smiled. He gave it his best shot. "Are you sure?" she prodded.

Marcus was feeling weary. It shouldn't be this hard. He dropped the plunger that was in his hand. Maybe she would get the message.

"Ah. Would you like me to adjust your bed?"

Marcus tried to blink a message.

"You just let me know when to stop." She approached the bed and pushed a few buttons to elevate him. Now he could get a clear look down the hallway. If someone was coming after him, he was a sitting duck. He had to get some mobility. He looked at one arm in a cast and a leg in traction. Impossible. He couldn't imagine what his face looked like.

Marcus strained to stay focused and paid close attention to his surroundings. The next few days could be a matter of life or death.

CHAPTER 40

Pinewood

After breakfast the next morning, Kathryn spoke up. "I know this sounds like I'm getting soft, but do you think we should get those slimeballs clean jumpsuits? It really stinks down there. I think it's coming through the walls." There was a loud burst of laughter. "I mean, who even wants to open the scuttle door to throw the food at them?" Everyone turned their head away. "Just as I thought."

Charles stood. "You are right. We don't want to create a hazardous situation. The bacteria alone could be lethal." Mumblings of agreement came from the ladies. "I say this is a job for Fergus!" More laughs emerged.

Fergus had a disgusted look on his face. "Why me?"

Charles chuckled. "Don't worry, mate. I'll be right behind you!"

"As long as we wear hazmat suits," Fergus snapped.

"Absolutely!"

Myra had the next question. "When do you think we should get Pearl here?"

Kathryn sank down in her chair.

"I think two to three more days of the pharmacological spin, dip, and whirl should be enough to knock them on their asses," Charles offered. "I amped up the doses. They should be on a doozy of a ride by now."

"Bravo!" Myra clapped. "Do we have any information about Marcus?"

Fergus stepped up. "He's still in hospital. They don't know when they will release him into police custody. Although that may not be good for him."

"What do you mean?" Annie asked.

"I am sure getting arrested was not part of Franny O'Rourke's plan, and in all likelihood, it infuriated him even further. If Marcus goes to jail, Franny will most certainly finish the job."

A hush fell across the room. It was never the sisters' intention to kill anyone or have someone killed.

Myra cleared her throat. "We have to try to prevent that from happening."

"Does Pearl have contacts in the UK?"

Kathryn asked.

"I don't know for sure, but you can find out," Myra instructed a reluctant Kathryn, who slouched farther down in her seat.

Fergus and Charles fitted themselves with sanitized coverall jumpsuits, complete with hoods, shoe covers, respirator masks, polyethylene aprons, and protective gloves. They carried biohazard disposable bags and fresh jumpsuits for each of their "guests." When they went from the laundry area into the kitchen, Myra and Annie broke out in full-throated guffaws.

"You two look like you're about to disarm a nuclear bomb!" Myra said.

"It sure smells like some kind of bomb went off down there!" Annie pinched her nose to emphasize the point.

"Ready, mate?" Charles asked Fergus.

"I suppose as ready as I'll ever be," he grunted.

"Come on, old boy. You've been in worse situations than this," Charles reminded the former Scotland Yard official.

"I'm trying not to remember. Let's get this over with."

The men marched down the steps as Annie and Myra waved.

The first door they opened was to Corbett's cell. The effects of the phenobarbital were obvious. He was loopy and was slurring his words. "Where am I? Who are you people?"

Fergus and Charles ignored his questions. "Take off your clothes and put them in this bag. Here's a fresh suit for you. Sorry, not Canali or Ralph Lauren." Charles tossed the items at Corbett and unshackled his legs. Corbett looked confused.

"Now don't be modest," Fergus chided him. "Move it!" Corbett began to unbutton the putrid-smelling clothes as he staggered around in the small cell. "Maybe a hose down?" Fergus looked at Charles.

Charles shrugged. "I don't think that's included in his accommodations package."

Both men chuckled. Corbett gingerly removed the cruddy suit and put on the clean one.

"That's a good boy. We'll be back with lunch shortly." Charles slammed and locked the steel door.

They proceeded to Steinwood's cell. He was sitting in a comatose state on the floor. Fergus kicked his foot. Steinwood moaned. They went through the same routine with him, but Steinwood was out of it. He barely understood what they were saying.

"Listen, you slime weasel, stand up and

change your clothes," Fergus said and kicked him again. Steinwood slowly got up and peeled his urine- and fecal-crusted layers off. Charles and Fergus were happy they were wearing masks.

Once Steinwood had fumbled his way through their instructions, Fergus and Charles exited as quickly as possible. They took turns stripping down and quickly showering in the basement's bathroom, and then they dumped the bags of rancid clothing in a biohazard-waste container. The proper experts would retrieve the mess later.

When they climbed back up and entered the kitchen, Annie was waiting with two bowls of scrambled eggs à la Adderall. "Breakfast for our guests." She handed the bowls to Fergus.

Fergus brought them downstairs and inserted the bowls through the small sliding steel box at the bottom of the cell doors. "Room service!" Fergus announced.

Marcus opened his eyes to see the large black nurse standing over him. "Good morning, Dr. Marcus." He showed a big bright smile. "We're going on a journey." The nurse took Marcus's chart, laid it at the foot of his bed, and began to wheel him into the hallway. He nodded at the constable, who nodded in return.

Fear tore through Marcus's beaten body. He tried to twist and form words, but it was as if he had a mouthful of cotton. "Wha wah we gowha?"

"Easy there, Dr. Marcus. You're going on a long ride." The nurse moved the gurney slowly and methodically, bobbing his head with "Good mornings" to his associates, as he wheeled Marcus down the hall and into the lift. He pushed the button that said LOWER LEVEL, the level where the morgue was located.

Marcus's mind was a flurry of nightmarish thoughts. His worst fear was about to come true. Franny O'Rourke was going to do him in.

"By the way, Dr. Marcus, your wife filed for divorce. Once she realized all your accounts were frozen, she had the papers drawn up," the nurse explained in a matter-of-fact way.

Marcus's neurons were firing rapidly. Even though he was relieved that he would be rid of her, he asked himself, *How does the nurse know about that?* As they moved farther down the hall, Marcus noticed several gurneys on which lay bodies covered in sheets. His heart started racing when the nurse stopped. The nurse checked the chart of one of the corpses and swapped it with Marcus's.

"That ought to do it." The nurse smiled down at him and pulled a large black body bag from a shelf. He disconnected the traction and lowered Marcus's leg. He slipped the bag under Marcus's body and pulled it up until it was over his shoulders. Marcus was in a panic. The nurse wrapped the top of the bag around Marcus's head, reached for the zipper, and zipped him in like a mummy. "Don't you move or say a word. Or you're a dead man," the nurse whispered through the bag.

Marcus held his breath, waiting for the next blow. The nurse proceeded to push Marcus along until they came to the large doors at the end of the hall. A black van that looked like a hearse was waiting.

He felt the gurney being raised and slid into the back of the parked van. Once the van was far enough from the hospital car park, a voice from the front seat addressed him. "Good morning, Dr. Marcus. We are here to inform you that you are a dead man." Marcus almost pissed. "Officially, that is." The woman's voice was clear. She reached around the seat and pulled the zipper down, uncovering his head and face. "You are being transported to a nursing home, where you will recover under the name James Sherman. Once you are able to walk and function, you will remain at said nursing home as a member of the custodial staff for the rest of Mr. Sherman's life. You will never venture more than a hundred feet from the facility. To make sure you do not, you will be monitored. Do I make myself clear? Grunt once for yes, two for no."

One grunt. Marcus was hearing the words, but they made no sense. There would be no trial, but he would be under house arrest forever. The more he thought about it, the more confused he got.

"Franny O'Rourke will no longer be a threat to you, and you will no longer be a threat to the rest of the world," the woman continued. "You suffered a severe beating, lost all your material possessions, and now you will spend the rest of your life helping people.

"As soon as your wife filed the divorce papers, she left town. The press was all over her. Last we heard, she had moved to Belgium and is working as a cocktail waitress."

Marcus wished he could ask questions. Maybe try to talk again? Then he remembered the warning about making no sound.

"Dr. Marcus, grunt once if you are understanding this."

Two grunts.

"Then let me go through it again." The woman painstakingly repeated what she had told him, pausing between sentences. She had to recite some of it several times before Marcus was down to only one grunt.

The vehicle drove for several hours before it arrived at its final destination. It was the nursing home the woman had spoken of.

"Remember, Dr. Marcus is dead. You are James Sherman. Make up whatever story you want about your past, as long as it does not contain any part of the truth. Understood?"

One grunt.

CHAPTER 41

It was the fifth day of Corbett's and Steinwood's unpleasant stay at Chateau Justice. Kathryn reluctantly made contact with Pearl. The last part of the final phase was approaching. Out of respect for Pearl's facilitators, the sisters agreed to let the two scum buckets shower and put on clean orange jumpsuits. They didn't want any of their associates to have to suffer the stench of the men's unwashed bodies.

Charles escorted Corbett to the shower, with Fergus watching closely. The two men would go one at a time, still not knowing the whereabouts of the other. Steinwood and Corbett could barely stand, let alone walk. Neither was a threat. They were deflated, humiliated, and destroyed. Even with a shower and clean hair, Corbett looked grizzly. Steinwood looked like a schlump. Corbett opened his mouth to speak, but Charles gave him a look that said,

"Don't you dare."

Charles pulled Corbett's arms behind his back and zip-tied his wrists together. Corbett started to yell, but Fergus shoved a sock in his mouth. "Keep your piehole shut," Charles barked and reapplied duct tape to the man's mouth. He marched Corbett up the steps, as the sisters lined up and watched him do the walk of shame. Then a burlap bag went over his head and he was passed on to Pearl and her crew, who would relocate Corbett to some unknown place, a place so remote, he would never be found.

Once the van carrying Corbett was off the property, it was Steinwood's turn to do the walk of shame as the sisters looked on and to be transferred to the tender mercies of Pearl's people. He would be relocated to a different place than Corbett. There was no chance that the two would ever again meet. The official word was that they had escaped during a transfer and were now on the FBI's and Interpol's most wanted lists.

The entire departure took about an hour. The Sisterhood wanted to have enough "checkout" time for their guests. Neither man had ever known what was happening to the other, and at no time had either of them asked. Selfish bastards.

As the last car disappeared through the

gate, the sisters high-fived, fist pumped, hooted, and hopped around.

"Woo-hoo!"

"Yeehaw!"

"Hootie toot-toot!"

They backslapped one another and doubled over in fits of laughter; the pups howled and wagged their tails in unison.

Annie wrapped her arm around Myra's neck. "We have an exceptional crew working with us and for us. Seems like we just keep getting better and better."

EPILOGUE

Myra, Charles, Annie, and Fergus were lounging about in the atrium. Charles was sorting through papers. What conversation there was, was about what was on the dinner menu. The dinner was to celebrate another mission accomplished.

The original choice was between having a clambake or a roast. They eventually voted for the roast — the same as the first dinner they had shared with Charlotte. Maggie had already put her order in for "extra everything." It didn't matter to her as long as the food was plentiful.

The sisters started to arrive about an hour before dinner was to be served. Yoko brought a magnificent centerpiece of red peonies for the table and several other luscious arrangements for the rest of the house. Kathryn helped her carry them in. Once everyone was there, they began their methodical dance of setting the table. Myra suggested the same crystal and china, the Hermès Mosaique and the Waterford.

Myra stood in the doorway and stared at the beautiful table setting. She sighed. Charles came up from behind. "What is it, dear?"

Myra fidgeted with her pearls. "I wish Charlotte were here."

"I know. But remember, it's also the adrenaline rush of the mission, then the slide down to the humdrum of everyday life."

"Oh, Charles, life with you would never, *could* never, be humdrum. But I suppose you're right. This is what it must be like for entertainers. You're on a high in anticipation of the show, and then you do the show, and then the show is over."

"Listen, old girl, the show will never, ever be over." Charles put his hands on her waist and kissed the back of her neck. Myra reached for his hand and brushed it with her lips. "Oh, now, don't you be naughty! We have guests!"

Myra giggled like a schoolgirl and began to blush. "Charles, you have made my life very rich, exciting, and rewarding."

"Ditto, my darling. Now let's get busy." Charles took her hand and led her back to the kitchen. "I need help opening the champagne."

"Did I hear someone say 'champagne'?" Annie chirped.

"You did, indeed." Fergus was ahead of them, popping the first cork.

The sisters each took a glass and seated themselves at the table. Charles pulled a large TV screen into the dining room.

"Charles? What is this?" Myra was stunned at the electronic intrusion.

"One moment, my dear." Charles grabbed the remote and pointed at the TV.

The screen lit up, and Charlotte's face appeared. "Darlings!"

"Hot damn!" Maggie yelled.

"How cool!" Yoko cooed.

"This is great!" Kathryn bellowed as more sounds of delight came from the others.

Myra touched her pearls as tears filled her eyes. "Charlotte! We miss you!"

"Thank you for the invite!" The camera on Charlotte's side pulled back, revealing the same roast and accompaniments on her table, including fuchsia peonies.

Myra looked a bit puzzled, until she realized that Charles and Fergus had planned for Charlotte to be a dinner guest via satellite! Since Charlotte was staying at Annie's flat in London, it had been easy to plan with

Annie's London staff. The camera panned the room. Sitting to one side of Charlotte was Lincoln Gladwell, the gemologist! Myra gasped a sound of delight. "Hello, Lincoln! Nice of you to join us!" Then she heard the sound of a dog barking. The camera panned to the other side of the table. A big golden Lab sat up and gave a soft "Woof!"

"Who is that I hear?" Myra smiled.

"This is Jewel!" Charlotte beamed. "Lincoln's dog! Annie said it would be okay for her to visit."

"Annie, were you in on this?" Myra pretended to challenge her.

Annie couldn't help but laugh. "Gotcha!"

The evening lasted for several hours, with everyone conversing as if they were all in the same room. At one point Charlotte indicated that she had been wondering about the real Chagall. Had it ever been recovered?

So Annie explained that it had. "Mrs. Spencer from Christie's was able to locate the original. It was such a coincidence." She gave Myra a wink. "Lorraine Thompson's daughter Genevieve Ringwood was at a flea market the Saturday after everything went down and bought it for twenty-five dollars. When a friend suggested she have someone look at it, she phoned the local art gallery, who referred her to Mrs. Spencer. The French government sent her a check for one hundred fifty thousand dollars. It didn't bring her mother back, but now she has some financial breathing room to help raise her daughter."

Once Charlotte's curiosity about the painting was satisfied, everyone went back to eating. It was a delightful dinner, with many toasts and hugs. Charlotte and Lincoln signed off with help from Jewel, and there was a response from Lady and her pups. Dishes were cleared, cleaned, and the kitchen was made spick and span. Another spectacular meal celebrating "mission accomplished."

Later that evening, when Charles and Myra were getting ready for bed, Charles pulled a sheet of paper from his trouser pocket.

"What's that?" Myra asked.

Charles unfolded the paper. "It's a bill."

"From where?"

"NYPD. We owe them for the vans they had to ditch after letting Avery's people use them to deliver Steinwood and Corbett to us. No evidence, love." He gave her a wicked smile.

"How much is it?" Myra asked.

"Two hundred fifty thousand," Charles

said, not batting an eye.

"It was worth it," Myra commented casually.

"It always is." Charles kissed her on the cheek.

"And justice can be a bitter pill to swallow." Myra beamed.

ABOUT THE AUTHOR

Fern Michaels is the *USA Today* and *New York Times* bestselling author of the Sisterhood, Men of the Sisterhood, the Godmothers series, and dozens of other novels and novellas. There are more than ninety-five million copies of her books in print. Fern Michaels has built and funded several large day-care centers in her hometown and is a passionate animal lover who has outfitted police dogs across the country with special bulletproof vests. She shares her home in South Carolina with her four dogs and a resident ghost named Mary Margaret. Visit her website at FernMichaels.com.

The employees of Thorndike Press hope you have enjoyed this Large Print book. All our Thorndike, Wheeler, and Kennebec Large Print titles are designed for easy reading, and all our books are made to last. Other Thorndike Press Large Print books are available at your library, through selected bookstores, or directly from us.

For information about titles, please call:
  (800) 223-1244

or visit our website at:
  gale.com/thorndike

To share your comments, please write:
  Publisher
  Thorndike Press
  10 Water St., Suite 310
  Waterville, ME 04901